Praise for

Ariella Papa

"Glossy and light, and filled with glamorous parties,
exciting hookups, and cocktails,
Papa's hip romance is right on target
for twentysomethings."
—*Booklist* on *On the Verge*

"Filled with witty lines and hilariously detailed
events, Ariella Papa's debut novel is a winner."
—*Romantic Times* on *On the Verge*

"A delightfully wry take on the aftermath
of being 27 and downsized."
—*Albuquerque Journal* on *Up & Out*

"Papa's entertaining second novel is ideal reading
for women in their twenties and thirties who are still
struggling to find their niches in life."
—*Booklist* on *Up & Out*

Ariella Papa

Bundle of Joy?

RED
DRESS
INK
TM

First edition February 2005

BUNDLE OF JOY?

A Red Dress Ink novel

ISBN 0-373-89510-0

www.RedDressInk.com

Printed in U.S.A.

For Michael William Greaney,
plate maker extraordinaire.

Big thanks to Ellie for teaching me a lot and having such a funny mommy. Special thanks to Isabella, who has given me a new appreciation for fondue and whose mother always answered my questions. Thanks to Jack and Maeve for picking moms who shared gross stories with me. And thanks to Ryan Michael, our founding baby.

Thanks also to Mrs. Orlando Bloom for a night with taxicab comedians; Mrs. McCann for breakable pacts; and Mrs. Dolvie Hackett for children's anecdotes.

More thanks to Zoe Ragouzeos for listening and translating; Laura Corby for stop, drop and rolling; Kurt Roth, Esq., for deciphering real estate; and Farrin Jacobs, a fabulous editor who likes melty cheese.

Swimming Upstream

1

I was procrastinating when it happened. I should have been doing a lot of things. I should have been calling various executives at the airline whose in-flight magazine I was writing an article for, but I wasn't sure I could work up the enthusiasm to discuss statistics. I should have been paying some bills or following up with the magazines that didn't realize that freelance didn't mean free—they actually had to pay me in a timely fashion. But, I was procrastinating. It was a common occurrence.

So, I did what usually brought me the most happiness, the thing that pulled me out of my voluntary solitary existence—I called my best friend, Jamie.

"Jamie Jacobs-Sarakanti," she answered on the second ring. Her voice gave no indication of the bomb she was about to drop.

"It's me. Are you busy?"

"Oh, hey. Not really. What's up?"

"Well, I wanted to see what you were up to tonight."

"Procrastinating, are we?"

"Yep, and I'm in the awful empty time between Netflix. The next DVD probably won't arrive until tomorrow."

"The horror," she said.

"So I thought I would check to see if you wanted to go out for just one beer." That was our code for a night out. Whenever we said we were meeting for "just one beer," it turned into many beers and a long night of psychoanalyzing everyone in our families and social circle. We would have the same conversation as many times as necessary to nail down the exact reasons for my mother's psychosis or why her sister always went for women who were high maintenance.

"Actually I can't tonight."

"Re-he-heally, do you and Raj have a night planned? I thought your date nights were Wednesday." It never ceased to amaze me that my formerly wild best friend, who had once been given to spontaneous encounters with men she met on the subway, was now settled enough to have an established date night with her super-busy television producer husband.

"I wish." Her voice sounded funny.

"So what's up?"

"Well…"

And in that pause I had no warning that I was about to hear two of the grossest words in the English language.

"We're trying."

"What?" I was innocent then. I didn't believe my normally, well, *normal* best friend would ever say something along the lines of "making love" or any of those other expressions that gave me the heebie-jeebies, like calling your boyfriend "lover." So, I had no idea what she and Raj were *trying* to do.

"You know," she said, then dropped her voice lower. "Trying…to have a—" there it was, barely a breath "—baby."

"What?" I screamed. I worried that my roommate Armando would wake up, even though it was well after noon.

There was a pause (pregnant?).

"Yeah," she said. "I was going to tell you last week, but you cancelled."

Damn the breakup of Hollywood's most overexposed couple! I had to cancel our dinner plans to do some quick coverage for *Who?*, a weekly gossip rag.

"Since when?"

"Unofficially for about six months now. I don't think we really wanted to admit to ourselves that we were ready. We kept having accidents—you know 'forgetting' to use something. We were kind of just going to see what happens, but…I don't know, I'm anxious."

Anxious? "This, uh, is kind of big."

"I know. That's why I wanted to tell you last week."

My work was always getting in the way at the worst times. "Sorry I had to cancel, but—I think this is a definite reason for just one beer."

"It definitely is, but I can't. Tonight's the night."

"Huh?" It was all so unknown, then.

"I'm ovulating."

"How do you know?" And that was the first time I ever heard the laugh. The *"how could you be so ignorant about every aspect leading up to the miracle of life?"* laugh. It would not be the last.

"I took my temperature."

"Now, how does that work?" I imagined her with a thermometer lodged under her tongue.

"I have a vaginal thermometer."

"You stuck a thermometer up your hoo-hah?"

"Yeah, every morning, to help me find the right days."

I was happy she couldn't see my contorted face.

"Welcome to the world of fertility."

"Well, so what—today is like the magic day?" I asked.

"I'm pretty sure. It's all a bit overwhelming."

I'll say.

"So if you want to do it tonight, don't you think you should maybe have a drink to loosen up?"

"I might want to scale back on the drinking, too. It's not going to be just me in my body anymore."

"Hmm. Well, when does this time end, this magic fertilization time?" Maybe that came out a little too cynical. I could tell by the way she waited a minute before speaking.

"Sperm can last a few days, but you never know. I keep

thinking I'm calculating all wrong. We should probably do it for the next couple of days."

"Like rabbits."

"Voula, I know you're going to be supportive and not the typical isolationist, nihilist, pessimist that I know and love." She didn't sound convinced.

"Call me Aunt Voula. I'm ready. Really." Lies all lies. It was the beginning of the time of lies. "Do you want to meet for coffee tomorrow at Murray's? You can fill me in on the dirty blessed deed."

"Well, I'll skip the coffee and grab a bagel."

This was a woman who lived on caffeine. The coffee cup was just an extension of her hand. I couldn't believe the changes were starting so quickly.

"Cool," I lied, but at least I hadn't heard the laugh again. "I'll see you tomorrow at nine at Murray's."

"Okay, Aunt Voula— I have another call."

"Happy humping," I shouted into the phone, trying to be as encouraging as possible.

"Thank you." And she hung up.

I stared at the blinking cursor of my laptop. It seemed to be mocking me and my fallopian tubes. A baby? This was incredible. I was so far from even thinking about babies. I had never really had a boyfriend even. I didn't count my two and a half lovers (eeew, I was going there, too) as boyfriends. But Jamie? The girl who used to dance on the table and make me be her lookout in high school when she hooked up in empty classrooms? She was going to be a mother? I might need "just one beer" on my own.

I've always sort of felt like everyone else was in on something that I couldn't quite figure out. It's not a joke necessarily, but it's kind of like maybe there's this guide that everyone read, that I didn't get. Part of it might be that English is my second language. Even though I picked it up quickly, I didn't really learn it until kindergarten, and one of my first memories is sounds coming out of everyone's mouth that I didn't understand. But, it's more than that. I'm suspicious of people.

I just don't trust them. Maybe that's why I like being a writer so much. It's a solitary job for the most part and it's sort of a one-sided conversation. I don't have to see another side looking at me like I have a bird on my head. I'm more confident communicating through written words than trying to make myself clear in person. But, it was always different with Jamie.

Almost fifteen years ago, Jamie and I met at Stuyvesant High School. I don't know why she took to me, but I'm forever grateful that she did. Jamie opened up a whole new world for me. I was a nerd and still sort of am, and before I got into that school my world was limited to Astoria, Queens, and the trips to Cyprus my family took every other year.

Jamie's family was all-American while my parents spoke to us in Greek. There were no secrets in her family like the ones my sisters and I kept from our strict parents. Jamie's parents were fine with her dating; we were forbidden from dating anyone, and then he better have been Cypriot, or at least Greek. It was Jamie's mother I went to when I had questions about my changing body. My mother thought that if we didn't talk about it, I wouldn't realize what breasts could be used for.

From the beginning Jamie's family wowed me. The first time I went over to her house in Park Slope, the phone rang and no one bothered to answer it. *They were having too much fun with each other!* They treated me like one of theirs. They found out things about Cyprus and asked me how to say things in Greek. They took an interest in me, not like I was some kind of freak but like I was an interesting person. I'd never felt so relaxed before. In my apartment, someone was always on edge.

As soon as we met, Jamie and I were inseparable. Well, except for when she was with whatever boy she was dating. We hung out at her place all the time and watched *Donahue* after school and ate melba toast and cream cheese. We shared clothes and scoped boys. With Jamie, my life seemed almost normal.

We met when I was fourteen, right after the summer that my oldest sister, Cristina, died in a moped accident in Cyprus. I can't say that I had ever had anything close to a functional family, but nothing was the same after that. It was as if my parents switched personalities. My mother, who had been given to constant yelling and hysterics, just shut down. My father, who had rarely said anything, started slamming doors and picking on us whenever we were in his presence. I retreated to a fantasy world of trash TV and books, both of which I still rely on. My middle sister, Helen, finally got to run with the bad crew Cristina had always stopped her from being around. Without Cristina, we fell apart.

It was Jamie who kept me tied to reality. She was the one I studied to find out how regular people responded to things. She seemed like she had it all figured out. Everyone wanted to be her friend, and for some reason she wanted to be mine. I was afraid of a lot of things that didn't seem to worry other people. I always imagined the worst. Tragedy seemed to strike whenever I let my guard down. Jamie "got me" and never minded my blue moods or my sarcastic comments. Jamie pulled me out of my chair and got me to dance.

She'd been married for two years, but now she was really settling down. What was I going to do? My social circle was on the small side, and working from home didn't really help me network, which I wasn't good at anyway.

Maybe this was all happening because of the article I'd written for *On the Verge* magazine. The idea was to get to the truth about what I'd considered a baby backlash—the media warnings about dropping fertility levels after the magic age of twenty-seven. Granted, you aren't as fertile after twenty-seven, but it's not like your eggs shrivel up and rot. The editors peppered my article with photos of Susan Sarandon and Madonna and the babies they'd had as older women. I thought it was a pretty good piece that let them put "The Truth about Your Fertility" on the cover. Everyone had been happy when it came out six months ago.

Jamie had asked me a bunch of questions about the facts I'd gathered. I'd thought she was just curious about the real story because we enjoyed uncovering all the ways the media lied to us—but maybe she was starting to panic.

She was three months shy of thirty at the time, so perhaps

that was adding to the pressure. Her younger sister, Ana, often joked about turkey basters and artificial insemination, but Jamie always said she was in no rush. Raj had gotten a pretty sweet promotion and was a few years older than us. Could *he* be behind the baby push? It didn't seem possible that all of this was what Jamie really wanted.

This felt like when Jamie decided to go to Amherst and I went to Columbia, like we were hurtling in two opposite directions, and I worried that our days of giggling and sleep-overs and (even back then) just one beer were coming to an end.

But our friendship had survived that distance. I continued to go with her family to Block Island in the summers. I learned what skunked beer was and how to tap a keg. I met her roommates Morgan and Alice, whom I continue to have a love-hate relationship with. The trips from my mother's apartment in Queens to Amherst were just another part of our friendship. Now, instead of the Olsen Twins—my affectionate name for the roommates, and their histrionics and body obsessions—I would have a bouncing, drooling, shitting baby to get to know. I wasn't sure I was ready.

I should have known this was coming. Ever since Jamie met Raj it was like she was no longer just Jamie. Now, she was part of a unit. Jamie had made me co-maid of honor with her sister when she got married and I really liked Raj, but I admit I was also a little jealous of him. Jamie appreciated having her girlfriends (as different as we all were), but more and more it seemed like Raj was the person whose opinion mattered the most. Once again I looked to Jamie for clues about the world, and I guessed that was just the way it was when you got married.

"Ciao, bella," Armando said, coming out of his bedroom. He was just getting up. It was two in the afternoon. He was shirtless and filled the tiny room I'd commandeered for my desk and laptop with the smell of his cologne.

"Hey, Armando," I said, trying to stifle the blush I often had when he traipsed around the house without his shirt on. Armando was from a small village in southern Italy, right at the arch of the heel. He often told me of how fresh the produce was because of the soil in his *paese,* and I believed there was something in that soil that nurtured men who were unbeliev-ably handsome. Several of Armando's fellow villagers had stayed with us over the years for short stints and all of them seemed to have been bred on another planet. I had had a crush on Ar-mando for a while. After a year or so it had turned maternal, but that first glimpse of him in the morning (or early after-noon) always got to me. Jamie and I had often joked that it hurt to look at Armando he was so hot—and even after living with him for three years, it still did.

"Vou-lah, I mus' go in a leetle early this morning, but I wan talk to you."

I turned away from the work I wasn't doing and didn't re-mind him that it was way past morning. Armando managed the front of an Italian restaurant in the West Village and he kept completely different hours than I did. It worked out well; for my job I needed as few distractions as possible.

"What's up?"

"Okay, 'Arry cannot live here anymore."

"Why?" I asked, wondering if our latest roommate, Harry, had done something to annoy Armando. I liked Harry because he was barely around. He traveled for work and he had a boyfriend he stayed with a lot. I didn't like roommates who spent too much time in the apartment. I'm territorial.

We lived in an area near Penn Station that I liked to call Chelsea Heights because it really didn't seem like a neighbor-hood at all. Armando had lived here for five years, and I'd moved in three years ago despite my mother's objections. We had lived with no fewer than twenty-five roommates in that period, including, but not limited to: the many Italians that came in and out of the apartment and the restaurant; the UN intern with the crush on Kofi Annan; the guy who was track-ing the Asian long-horned beetle in Jersey City, but then got reassigned to Michigan; the woman who insisted her puppy was house-trained even after it started pooping in the middle of the kitchen and peeing in my bedroom (we banned pets after that); our pre-September eleventh roommate who'd fled the city for a sheep farm in Idaho; and the couple that rented both of our extra bedrooms, then got married in city hall, then divorced the next day after deciding they couldn't live together or in our apartment.

There were also at least two women who'd moved out after falling prey to Armando's charms.

Armando, though a player, was always pretty honest with women about not looking for a relationship. Our former roommates had said they were okay with a casual affair, but Armando brought women home several times a week. I'd learned to sleep through these escapades, which often got pretty loud, but the roommates who'd slept with Armando couldn't handle it, and I don't blame them. I've seen Armando in action. He's a flirt, but he makes you feel like you are the only person in the room. Sometimes I melted when he said my name in his sweet song of a way.

We actually could have had two extra bedrooms, but after the married couple, I worked enough to pay more for the tiny windowless room I used as an office. In any other city, it would be considered a closet, but in New York people settled for whatever they could afford.

"'Arry came to the restaurant last night wit his fren, you know?"

After five years, Armando was finally getting used to same-sex relations. He often treated Christopher Street like a tourist attraction, taking his compatriots there when they got off the plane. "He say me, he wan live with 'im. He pay to de end of the mounth."

"Great. Now we have to get someone else."

"You put in ad," Armando said, half request, half assumption that I would do what was necessary to find that perfect roommate—one that would stay out of my way, and not succumb to Armando.

"I'll do it. We still have to the end of the month."

Armando looked at me with his otherworldly dark eyes. I knew he was thinking about the two occasions I hadn't placed the ad right away. Those had been lean times—both Armando and I had budgeted our months pretty tightly—although my budget always included squirreling a lot away into savings, a habit instilled in me by my frugal family.

"Okay, okay," I said, procuring the perfect smile from Armando. "I'll do it today."

It would help me procrastinate, after all.

2

I got one of the little booths at Murray's so I would have a clear view of Jamie when she entered. I wanted to see if she looked any different. I thought I might be able to tell if she was preggo.

Jamie arrived looking done up as usual. Working at Flirty Cosmetics had totally changed her style. In high school and college, she rarely wore makeup and didn't do anything to her light brown, pin-straight hair.

But once she graduated from college and completed her internship at Flirty she had had a complete makeover. Now that she was VP of marketing there was never a stray hair on her brow line, her hair was highlighted and twisted into elaborate buns, and her outfits told the world she was an exec who meant business. She could recognize who did the highlights on celebrity heads and knew all about spa treatments. I wondered if she would be one of those super-moms with nannies and play dates and pictures of her offspring in beautiful frames on her desk.

"The usual?" she said after kissing me hello.

I already had my coffee, but she got in line to order our

toasted whole-wheat bagels with low-fat chive cream cheese and a tomato on the side.

She slid into the booth following her gigantic Kate Spade briefcase.

"Did it take?" I said, scraping some of the massive amounts of cream cheese off the hot bagel. No matter what you asked for, they gave you enough cream cheese for at least three bagels.

"What?" How could she drop a bomb like "trying" and then not follow me when I asked about it?

"You know," I said, searching for a glow. "Do you think the puck made the goal now that the goalie's been pulled?"

"Jeez, Voul, I don't know yet." She started to eat her bagel.

I found the whole thing kind of disturbing, but I had spent all night thinking about it. I couldn't help but compare myself to her. Okay, nothing in our life was really comparable, but I couldn't help feeling even *more* behind if she was already at the "trying" stage. I wanted to know what was ahead for her. I wanted details. I wanted someone to come and tell me the future. I hated uncertainty. I was scared of surprise. My jaw began to clench with anxiety.

I decided on another approach. What had once been Jamie's favorite subject, her favorite metaphor, what her mind always went back to…sex.

"Was the sex any different?" I saw I'd hit something. When she wasn't having sex, she wanted to be talking about it. It was lucky for me, because some of my best pitches for women's magazines came out of her knowledge and expertise.

"Well, when we first started trying, you know, halfheartedly, it was really exciting. But now, there's a certain lack of spontaneity. And…oh, forget it."

Already this baby thing was making her less forthcoming. I prodded. I'm good at that.

"And what?"

She took another bite of her bagel. I noticed her eyeing my coffee. It had to be hard to give that up. Why was coffee bad for "trying" women anyway? I offered my cup. She took it guiltily and gulped some down. I was heartened. She was breaking rules already. That was the push I needed. Leaning closer, I repeated my question. "And what?"

"Well," Jamie started, continuing to chew the bagel unbearably slowly. "You can't really get creative on positions."

There was a time in Jamie's life when she felt a true boyfriend was one who could sustain all positions from the Kama Sutra. When she met Raj, he made the cut and then some.

"So, missionary?"

"Yeah."

"Was that satisfying?"

"Well, not exactly. The thing is, orgasm supposedly helps your fertility. I read that somewhere. Did you write it?"

"No, my only fertility article was the one debunking the myths." I tried not to convey that I wished she'd read it more carefully and had waited a little longer. I wondered if I could pitch an article about strange methods of baby-making. "Pulling the Goalie" would be the perfect title.

"Oh, right," she said. Now she was ready to tell all. "So, I didn't, you know, come. Usually if I wasn't going to, Raj wouldn't either."

In my wildest dreams I could not imagine a man as perfect as Raj. He was as sensitive as Armando was good looking, but also quite sexy. It wasn't so much his looks, which were fine, but his confidence.

"I guess he kind of had to, though," I said. "You sort of need that. For a baby."

She nodded and reached out for another sip of my coffee, looking guilty again but quickly getting over it.

"So why didn't you do it again or do something else?" My notebook was in my bag—would it be impolite to take notes?

"Because, I felt like I needed to lie still for a while."

"Give those boys a chance to get where they needed to be."

"Uh-huh." She laughed and looked around. "Also, I had a pillow under me to kind of angle myself, you know, up."

"This sounds far too clinical."

The laugh came again, the *"you, my friend, are so ignorant of the sacrifice one makes for a perfect little human"* laugh. "It was, but it's worth it."

"I'm sure," I said. "So are you going to do this again tonight?"

"Yes."

"Wow. I hope you get more out of it."

"I think we'll try more foreplay. I think we're starting to get desperate. Last night we were a little eager."

It was possible that I was learning too much.

"Right." I had barely touched my bagel. I was about to rectify that when Jamie looked at her watch.

"I've got a meeting with Accessories at ten. Is everything okay with you?"

I could have told her about the roommate situation, but the story would have turned into a saga. Other than that everything was the same. Except for the articles I work on, nothing really changes for me. If she had had more time, Jamie might have hounded me about meeting a guy or trying Internet dating. But she didn't, so we said goodbye and she reminded me that I was invited to her parents' summer house in Block Island in a couple of months.

When I got home, there were fifty-six messages on our voice mail. Usually this would be exciting. Calls meant potential money. If editors were calling in response to some pitch I sent them, I was set. For someone like me who worried a lot about money, the future and nest eggs, the profession I had chosen was a constant and precarious struggle.

But I'd placed the ads for the apartment and I knew most of the calls would be from interested people. Each of these people would have his or her own series of questions and concerns, each would mean time I would have to take away from writing and put into small talk. Then of course there would be the interviews, and Armando would be grumpy about having to get up earlier than usual. The task was daunting.

I listened to all the messages in case one was from an editor. It was just past ten and I doubted the ads had been up for that long, but people were desperate. I sighed. Fifty-five of the messages were from interested potentials; one was from my mother.

Dealing with my mother was possibly more disturbing than dealing with all of the potential roommates, editors and twinkles in Jamie's eye combined. I tried to imagine who my mother was when she was younger. By my age she already had three daughters and a husband who was disappointed that she couldn't produce a son. It was an amazing revelation for me in seventh grade when I realized that men determine the sex of the baby. I told my mother and she ignored me; I wouldn't have dared tell my father.

You wouldn't know it from the annoyance that punctuated every Greek word of my mother's message, but at one time she was happy. She had to have been.

I remember my older sisters telling me that my parents had always planned to return to Cyprus. They had moved to New York right before Turkey occupied the northern area, their homeland. I was born the following year—another disappointing girl—but the first in my family to be an American citizen.

We went back every other year to visit, but my mother was embarrassed that we had to stay with relatives who'd moved south. Year by year, she got more tense. Two years after Cristina died, my father moved back by himself and found an apartment near where my uncle had relocated in Cyprus. My parents talk as much as they ever did—which is not much—and still consider themselves married.

To simplify things, I tell people I'm Greek. It's the language we spoke, and screamed, at home. Most people don't even know that the island nation of Cyprus exists, but because of Cyprus's prime location in the Mediterranean Sea, close to Asia, Africa and Europe, it has been invaded by just about everyone at some point in its history. My features represent that: medium brown hair, fair skin that tans dark, eyes that are almost black. I've been mistaken for Puerto Rican, Italian, Arabic, and Raj, when I first met him, assumed I was half Indian.

I decided to call my mother back first. Guilt always got the better of me. My mother was alone and she couldn't help but be the way she was. She'd already lost one of her daughters, and the other one, my sister Helen, had abandoned her (well, she had been sort of kicked out). I was all she had.

"Ti kanis, mama?" I asked when she answered the phone.

"Oh, it is time to call your mother at last," she said in Greek.

I closed my eyes and didn't say anything. My mother continued with a litany of health complaints. I imagined her with her graying hair up in a loose knot and her back stooped over after years spent hunched at her sewing machine, making gowns she could never afford.

"Are you coming home this weekend or do you have plans with strangers?"

For the most part I led the life of a nun, but my mother suspected I was disgracing her somehow. Once, Armando answered the phone without checking the caller ID and I had to make up elaborate lies about why there was a man in my house.

I told my mother that I lived with two sisters who worked with Jamie. She didn't know how wild Jamie was. She had always thought of Jamie as smart and respectable, so I figured the Jamie association would legitimate the imaginary roommates. But the lie didn't matter, my mother wouldn't have believed me even if it were true. Fortunately for all of us, she never came to my apartment. She rarely left Astoria, where the owners of the shops she frequented and the bankers who helped her save money spoke to her in Greek.

My mother disapproved completely of an unmarried woman not living in her parents' house, no matter how old she was. She had thrown a fit every time I brought up moving out, but when I'd finally had my fill of living in Astoria and sharing a home with her constant criticism, that's what I did. I was twenty-six. I cried for two weeks in my new place. Jamie came over every day. I'm sure Armando was convinced he was living with a psycho. Logically, I knew I wasn't doing anything wrong, but I felt just awful for leaving my mother alone. She didn't speak to me for three months. Eventually she must have realized that without me, she was alone except for my father's sister in New Jersey, because she began talking to me again. Of course, she always made sure I understood I'd disappointed her. I placated her by going home almost every weekend.

"*Nay, mama,* I'll be home."

"Bravo. I'm glad you're not too busy writing about disgusting things."

I had made the mistake of showing my mother one of my earliest book reviews in a women's magazine. Unfortunately the word *sex* was on the cover twice, along with a photo of an embracing couple. My mother never even got to my review. She dismissed my job as yet another disgrace.

Jamie's mom, Maura, once asked me if I thought maybe my mom was going through menopause. If so, it was the longest menopause ever. Maura also delicately broached the subject of my mother being mentally unstable.

"Well, she has a right to be," I'd snapped. "Her daughter is dead."

It was one thing to complain about your family, but it was another to let other people disrespect them. I couldn't help being protective of my family, fuck-ups and all. My mother would be furious if I questioned her sanity; I knew that counseling was not an option for her.

Sometimes I burst into tears when I got off the phone with my mother. Feeling a little sorry for myself made me feel a lot better. But, after this call, I worked for four straight hours on a piece for *Breathe.*

The phone rang repeatedly as I tweaked the article, but I ignored it. When Armando woke up, I decided he should return some phone calls for a change.

"I no know what I mus ask," Armando pleaded.

But I had decided to be immune to his charms this morning (well, afternoon). I just didn't want to deal with anyone after talking to my mom.

"Look, Armando. Find out if they smoke, if they have any crazy habits, what kind of hours they keep, et cetera. Pick five who sound nice, tell them to come for an interview tomorrow. Let's just get this settled." Even though I was comfortable having him make the initial inquiries, there was no way he was going to do the interviews on his own. I knew he would be swayed by a pretty woman, they would sleep together, and we would be back in the same boat.

"What about my Englis?"

"You're English is fine." My parents pulled this too, when they were feeling lazy about things. An accent wasn't a get-out-of-jail-free card. He had to pull his weight.

I paid no mind when, minutes later, I heard his sighs as he paced his room yelling questions into the phone at perspective roommates.

I decided to sneak out for an early dinner before he finished. This way, by the time I got back, he would be out at his job. One thing I really enjoyed about being freelance was the freedom. I had no real contact with the outside world for hours and occasionally days at a time, and I could have a sweet or savory crepe any time of the day without incurring disapproving looks from bosses or co-workers. If I failed to produce an article by the deadline, an editor would probably never use me again. But the only person I had to answer to at the end of the day was me. I really cherished this about my job. Sometimes I heard people complaining about their bosses and co-workers and I knew that I had made the right career choice. I didn't owe anyone anything. I could rely on the person I always had—me. I was just starting to feel like my life was normal and my hang-ups were manageable. Even my money concerns and the constant hustle for articles paled against the happiness I felt being a writer.

I went to the Le Gamin on 9th Avenue and 21st. It's a tiny French restaurant packed with about fifteen tables where the servers aren't in a rush and nor is anyone else. There were a couple of other people in the café. When I worked at the non-profit, my first and only "real" job, I always wondered who all the people were that I saw out on the street during the day. I was envious of their time. Now, I felt camaraderie with them. We were free.

I scanned the menu and then ordered a chicken ratatouille crepe and a large iced coffee. It was around four, and this was the time I usually started to fade. The first sip of coffee hit me quick and I pitied Jamie her self-imposed kick.

I went over to the magazine rack to grab something to read while I waited. Sometimes I told myself that everything I did was billable, like I was a lawyer. Sure, I was shirking calling other editors, but flipping through magazines meant I was boning up on formats and what types of stories were selling. I was being…productive.

I was studying my possible employers when my crepe came. I loved how they served it with a salad. For just under ten bucks I had a relatively balanced dinner.

Some people are scared to be out alone, I actually relish it. My mother thought decent women didn't go places by themselves. She thought only prostitutes did things like that. I guess I used to wish I had someone with me, but now I've sort of accepted the way things are. I like the fact that I make my own rules and have my own pace.

The idea of going through the whole roommate search again was daunting. Maybe it was time to search for a new place instead of a new person. But I liked my location, my rent and most importantly I liked procrastinating. I doubted I'd ever motivate enough to move out.

I felt the breeze of the door open, and a group of six mothers came in pushing strollers. They chattered loudly, oblivious to the quiet they were invading. A couple of the kids were crying. The mothers bumped into chairs, including mine, and muttered insincere apologies before settling the posse into the two long tables right behind where I was sitting.

"Travis, put that fork down," I heard one mother say. I couldn't see what was happening, but it was already distracting. I had only eaten half my crepe. I heard the same voice explain "He's discovering everything."

"Wait until he starts walking, we can barely keep up with Shelley."

"Lynn has taken her first few steps. She's been crawling all over the place. I bet walking will be worse. Is Shawn crawling?"

The women were yelling between tables, completely oblivious to everyone around them. I began cutting bigger pieces of my crepe.

"Shawn hasn't started crawling," I heard a nervous voice say.

"You have to give him some more belly time."

"I try, but everyone's always picking him up. He's very vocal, though," the mother offered, obviously trying to compete with the rest.

I waited for these women to start talking about themselves, but the conversation continued to revolve around the toddlers. Two of the people who had already been in the café when I got there, settled their bills and left.

The waitress finally meandered over to the mommy cult.

"We haven't even looked at the menu yet," one of them said.

I wanted to tell her to look now, because she might not see the waitress again for twenty minutes.

The mothers began to discuss the menu. At last, I thought, something else could occupy them. But I was wrong, of course. They all began talking in weird high-pitched voices, asking their kids what they wanted, even though I doubted the kids would know the difference between lemon and sugar, or orange crepes. They continued to list off facts about their kids by pretending to talk to them instead of each other.

"Lynn, would you like to get a baguette with jam or fruit salad? I think you want some fruit salad, I think you do. Yes, I think you do."

"Travis, do you think you want to eat a Nutella crepe with Mommy?"

"Shawn can't eat Nutella, can you, honey, because you are allergic to nuts. We're going to have a nice savory crepe with yummy spinach and cheese."

"Shelley, you know Mommy can't eat cheese because she's still breastfeeding, and dairy makes you gassy."

I looked to the lone survivor from before the mommy invasion. He was desperately waving for the waitress, who was leaning against the counter sipping a gargantuan cappuccino.

I tried to catch his eye, to smile and show him that I knew how horrible it was, but I think he was scared to look my way.

"Oh, he's spitting up. Honey, are you okay?"

When the waitress finally brought the guy his check, I asked for mine, too. I needed to get out of the crossfire of baby non-sense. I had lost my appetite. It took five excruciating minutes for the waitress to bring it to me. In that time Travis got Nu-tella all over his hair—but wasn't it *adorable?* Shawn continued to spit up, eliciting all kinds of advice from the other mothers. And from what I gathered, Shelley nursed happily at a breast. I sensed the other mothers disapproved of nursing an almost-one-year-old, but I couldn't tell why. I didn't know enough about their strange culture.

Back out on 9th Avenue, I glanced in at the tribe. Who were they? I wondered if any one of them could have had a con-versation with me about the celebrity couple breakup. Could they have talked about anything but breast milk or allergies or the color of poop?

I am easily amused by observing people. I enjoy embellish-ing little stories to Jamie to make her laugh. I planned to tell Jamie about the mommy invasion the next time we talked, but then it occurred to me: as soon as the missile hit the target, Jamie was going to be one of those women too.

3

I was impressed that Armando had pulled it together so quickly and got the interviews squared away. But I wasn't surprised that all five of the people he'd narrowed it down to were women.

The interviews started at one p.m. The first one didn't show up.

"I hope you have a B-list," I said to him.

"Che?"

"Forget it." It was forty-five minutes until the next one got there. Karin, candidate number two, arrived early, and I knew immediately that she was a lesbian—and not someone who dabbled either. This was a wife-beater-shirt-wearing, many-earringed, combat-boot-stomping lesbian. In case there was any doubt, she had two women signs tattooed on her substantial biceps and a rainbow patch sewn onto her baggy jeans pocket. It was a check in my book. Armando wasn't her type and she wasn't his. Also, she worked in construction and said she liked overtime. That meant she would be out of the apartment while Armando slept and I wrote.

"I liked her," I said when she had gone.

"She no look like she sound" was all he said.

I put a star next to her name in my notebook.

The next woman, Kelly, arrived twenty-five minutes late. I wrote that down. When she finally got there, she was a bit wound up and apologized profusely. Apparently her train had gotten stuck. She was a freelance camerawoman. She was kind of hot. She also sported a wife-beater, but was braless and beaming. Her jeans rode extremely low.

"She nice, I think," Armando said after she had left.

"I don't think so."

"Why you no like? Because she no like girls?"

"Listen, I'm just being realistic. She said she works three to four days a week and has slow times. We don't want someone who might not make the rent."

"She make lot of money. Dose people in TV, you know, like Raj."

"She was late for us—that says irresponsible."

"Was de tren. C'mon, Vu-laaa."

"Don't think with your dick, please."

"No, I jus appreciate."

"You'll appreciate us into having this same problem in a month. Besides, I don't want a roommate who is going to be here as much as I am. I need space."

The next woman was even better looking. Her name was Jill. She was a buyer for Bloomingdale's. She traveled a lot and didn't seem to be fazed by how hot Armando was. I liked that she looked us both in the eye when asking questions about the electric bill.

"Well," I said to Armando when she had left. I was a little nervous about him going for her, but she seemed like she could handle it.

"She okay."

"You don't think she's pretty." I didn't want him to. I was just surprised by how nonplussed he appeared.

"No, the other one better."

I would never understand men's taste. Did it all really come down to boobs and exposed skin?

"I think Jill is the front-runner. I totally oppose the one before her. I wish you had picked some men. Did you call *all* those people back?"

"No, I mus work yesterday."

"Great, so now they're going to keep harassing us."

"Was too many," he argued.

"Welcome to my world," I said.

"Eh?"

It wasn't worth getting into.

Our last prospect was in her late forties. She had recently divorced, and worked as a salon manager. She was nice enough but didn't make a big impression on me. She had two children in college who were spending the summers in their college towns. They might come down to the city for a weekend or two, but mostly she wanted to travel on her own over the summer. Her schedule worked for me, but I preferred Jill.

"She very old, eh?" Armando asked.

"She's probably in her forties."

"Sound different on de phone."

"I still like Jill best."

"What about—" He paused and held his hands up to his chest.

He had such a one-track mind. I swatted him.

"You pick 'Arry. I no like 'Arry."

"You did like Harry, except that he had a penis."

"Maybe he like me."

"Surprisingly, Armando, I don't think he did."

Armando smiled at me. But I had been a victim of the smile before. He may have found this place, but now it was my home too. I was not going to let him get his way on this.

"Look, the last one, Delilah, she makes the most, but she's also got kids, and who knows what kind of debt she might be in from her divorce?" I could tell I was confusing him, which would work to my advantage. "Jill makes almost as much. I think we should get her, and if you agree, I'll run the credit checks and call the references. What do you think?"

"Managia te" is what I thought he said. He said it a lot. I had no idea what it meant in Italian, but for me it meant yes.

★ ★ ★

When I called Jill a few days later, after doing all her back-ground checks, she was very excited.

"Hector and I will be able to move in at the end of the month."

"Great. Wait. Who's Hector?"

"My cat."

"Your cat?" I wanted to cry. Ever since the diarrhea dog, we had banned pets.

"He's great. You won't know he's there."

It didn't sit well with me that she hadn't told either of us about the cat. I'm sure that Armando would have mentioned it in an attempt to get his favorite to live with us. I knew that cats could be independent, but they could also rub themselves over your legs seductively while you were trying to concentrate on not procrastinating. One of the Olsen Twins had a cat and cats reminded me of her. I would have done almost anything to avoid going through the whole rigmarole of reference checks for someone else, but I didn't think it was fair to violate our house rules just because I liked her best.

"I'm sorry," I said. "Armando is allergic to cats."

"Oh," she said. "That's too bad."

"Yeah," I said. "Take care."

I looked at my notebook. Karin had two checks. I called her to see if she was still interested before starting to do reference checks, but by the time she got back to me, she had just signed the lease on a place in Chelsea proper.

"Maybe next time," she said.

"Yes," I said, fearing that next time would probably come soon enough.

I left Delilah a message and waited. We'd pulled the ad and I had deleted the messages from other interested parties. I *so* didn't want to go through this again. If I could settle it without getting Armando involved, I would be happier, but of course he asked when Jill was going to move in.

"Actually, she has a cat. She can't move in."

"She lie," he said.

"Yes, she lie," I said in his accent. I have this strange habit of taking the accents of people I talk to. I can't seem to help it.

"So now, de one I like."

"I left Kelly a message," I lied. "And Delilah. We'll see who gets back to me first."

What he didn't know wouldn't hurt him.

Finally, Delilah got back to me. She was still interested. I checked her references, and by the end of the week told her she could move in the first weekend of the month.

"Kelly no call," Armando said.

"No, Kelly no call."

"Porca butane," he cursed, or so I thought.

He would get over it, I was sure, and I would have what I hoped would be an unobtrusive pet-free roommate who would not sleep with him and who would stay for a long, long time.

I relayed the whole saga to Jamie over veggie burgers at Trailer Park, another one of our midway meeting spots. I liked how they had cans of Pabst Blue Ribbon, no matter how ubiquitous the beer was becoming in hipster hangouts across the city. Jamie decided against the beer.

"If this woman is recently divorced, the Italian Stallion might be just what she needs."

I had my suspicions that Jamie had slept with Armando on one of my overnight visits to my mom. It was during my crush phase, but I never asked. I just didn't want to know.

"Well, I'm hoping for the best." I gestured to her lemonade. "Any reason for the abstention tonight?"

"No," she said, looking down. "No dice. I'm on the rag yet again."

"I'm sorry. 'Maybe your womb is a rocky place where his seed can find no purchase,'" I said doing my best Nicholas Cage in *Raising Arizona*.

She was unimpressed.

"You spend too much time with Netflix. I think I'm going to see a doctor."

"Don't these things take like a year sometimes?"

"Sometimes, but I don't know if I can wait that long."

"You've really got the fever, huh?"

"Yeah," she said, taking a big bite of her burger. "I do."

"Okay," I said. I didn't ask anything else. I just started eating my sweet-potato pie.

"Hey, there's something I've been wanting to tell you." She looked nervous.

What now? What more? Was she flying somewhere to adopt a baby because she just couldn't wait?

"What is it?"

"It's Dan the Man."

I rolled my eyes at the sound of his name. "What about him?"

"Well, um, he's, um, getting married. I'm sorry."

I rolled my eyes again and shook my head and laughed. Jamie laughed too, but I noticed she was watching me, kind of studying me.

"Does the wife know about me?"

"You mean, that you're still going out? I don't think so."

"Well. Someone should tell her to stay away from my man."

Jamie laughed and took a sip from my beer. "That's what I said to Raj."

Dan the Man was Jamie's only pseudo-successful setup. He had gone to college with Raj and had come down to visit and meet me. We hit it off, sort of, and he had returned to the city almost every other week for a total of five weekends. We had sex seventeen times, which surpassed anyone else—the other two—I had ever been with by sixteen. Jamie and Raj were really excited about it. I imagined they stayed up nights discussing our wedding. I mean, at first I wasn't too attracted to Dan the Man. But I wanted to see what it would be like to actually date someone, even if that someone lived in Providence, Rhode Island.

Jamie polled me periodically on my feelings for Dan the Man, and when I questioned where it was going, she encouraged me to keep dating him. I had been all set to ask him to come with me to Jamie's family's place in Block Island, when he decided to stop calling, just like that. I left him a couple of messages and e-mailed him, but he never responded. He avoided Raj for a while too. When they finally saw each other at another college friend's bachelor party, Dan said he wasn't sure why he had behaved that way and he was sort of embarrassed about it. Raj spread it around to all of their friends, and Dan was ridiculed for being such a coward.

Jamie had been really upset about it and had told Raj that Dan was never welcome in her house again. I laughed it off, and called Dan the Man my boyfriend when his name came up. I said that since we had never officially broken up, we were still together.

"Honestly, Jam, did you really think I would be upset?"

"No, but I didn't know if you were just making jokes because you were covering up how you felt about him."

"Tears-of-a-clown style."

"Exactly."

"Why? Don't I deal with my issues head-on?" I smirked. She sort of sighed, and I wondered for a second if maybe there was a tiny bit of her that pitied me. I covered it up myself. "Honestly, Jamie, I think I *wanted* to like him more than I actually *liked* him."

"I know that. I mean, I know you said that, but I knew it wasn't normal for you to be involved with someone, and when it finally happened, it ended badly, and oh, I don't know—"

"Trust me, I'm not going to cry any tears for my boyfriend. I think it's kind of funny that he's a coward, but believe me, I wish him the best with his new wife."

"Okay," she said. "But we don't have to close the book on this conversation if you want to talk about it again…"

"Really, Jamie, I'm fine."

She looked back down at her plate and starting eating the rest of her fries.

"Do you want to split and get some Krispy Kreme?"

"Yeah," Jamie said. "I have one more thing I want to talk to you about."

"I can only imagine," I said, bracing for the worst.

"Do you mind if I go to the wedding?"

"Only if you promise to stand up at the appropriate point in the ceremony and demand he come back to me."

Jamie giggled and shook her head. I motioned for the check.

No one was home when I got back. I wondered when exactly Harry was moving out and if I would see him before he left. I got ready for bed and thought about Jamie's expression when she told me about Dan the Man. Did she really think that I cared about him? Was it easier for her to imagine that I had been pining away for someone than to think I never really cared about Dan?

Dan was all right. We didn't really have the same sense of humor. Like, I would say something sarcastic and he didn't get that I was being funny, so he'd respond as if I was serious. Then, I would have to explain my joke and he would look puzzled and I would question why it was so important for me to make him laugh anyway.

The thing about Dan was that I had been kind of getting used to him. I'd never slept with anyone so many times, and sleeping with Dan the Man was becoming familiar to me, you know, I was growing accustomed to it. It wasn't predictable— it was just starting to be less awkward.

But, no, I didn't care that Dan the Man had found his woman. I was happy for him. Sure, he was a coward, but the world is full of cowards. Maybe Dan had taken the easy way out with me, but it was bound to happen sooner or later.

My history with boys is basically nonexistent. I didn't date in high school. I wasn't allowed to. My mother would call to make sure I was at Jamie's, which was like the only place I was allowed to go. She was so strict it was embarrassing, but by then it was only her and me in the apartment in Astoria. Cristina was gone, my dad was in Cyprus, and Helen had already been kicked out or had run away, depending on how you looked at it. I was only allowed to go to Jamie's after Jamie's mother called and assured Mom that I was welcome. Finally, junior year, my mother let me join the drama club because my aunt Effie convinced her that the more extracurricular activities I had, the more chance of a scholarship for college. I loved drama troupe. I was really into set decoration.

Jamie was always the lead. Senior year, we did a production of *Bye Bye Birdie* and Jamie had several show-stopping numbers as Rosie. She convinced me to join the chorus and I did, even though I preferred to be backstage. I still find myself singing "I've Got a Lot of Living to Do." My favorite part of working on the play was the hours I spent ogling Leon Cullen. Leon was an androgynous, skinny sophomore whom I wouldn't have looked at in the hall, but when he got on stage as Conrad Birdie he exuded a strange mix of Mick Jagger meets Tom Jones meets Johnny Depp post-Wynona. He was a sexpot.

I told only Jamie of my crush. On the phone late at night we concocted all kinds of crazy scenarios where I would seduce him in the music room, but of course I never did anything about it. Until Jamie decided to host the cast party…

It was perfect. I had a reason to stay out overnight. Jamie's mother even called mine to make sure I could sleep over. She didn't say that boys in the cast were allowed to sleep over too. We all camped out in the backyard. What Jamie's mother might not have approved of, but probably sort of suspected, was all the alcoholic concoctions that I drank. I only remember pieces of the night. I remember giggling in the double sleeping bag I shared with Jamie. I was daring her to call Leon over to us, and she did. She urged him to climb in and told him that we both wanted to kiss him. We put him in between us and laughed and laughed. In all my childhood I had never felt as happy and free and safe as I did with Leon lying between Jamie and me under the stars in a Park Slope backyard.

Leon may have hoped to kiss both of us, but Jamie quickly climbed out of the sleeping bag after suggesting I go first. It was my first kiss and my first everything. Kind of.

Unfortunately, I had combined too many types of alcohol. In the morning Leon smiled at me like something big had happened, but I only remembered portions of the big event.

Later I wasn't sure if we really did it right. I told Jamie that it only counted for half a sexual experience when we were tallying the guys we'd—really she'd—slept with. I always wonder if I'll hear about Leon starring in some Broadway show or on *Law & Order* or something. No one knows what happened to him. Of course I questioned whether or not he could be gay. I've Googled him plenty of times during periods of procrastination. As I did with Dan, I wish him all the best. More than Dan actually—I think he deserves to be famous. He sure knew how to shimmy in those Elvis-esque white satin pants.

When it comes to men, I think I'm pretty realistic. There was Leon and Dan—and Warren, a boy I met in Block Island who set a high bar for all future paramours. Unless Warren comes back into my life, I'm not sure my prince is ever going to come. I don't necessarily think I need a prince, but just once I want to be comfortable with a guy. I want to hang out in socks together, and put on his shirt over my underwear, and laugh. I don't know—I think I watch too many movies, or maybe I've been influenced by too many ads.

I turned on my cell phone to see if anyone had called while I was at dinner. I was hoping to hear an approval for some copy I wrote for a fashion spread. I had one message. It was Delilah.

"Hi, Voula, I'm sorry I couldn't find your home number. I have some interesting, rather surprising news." She giggled self-consciously. "Could you call me? I don't care what time of night it is. I'll be up."

I was intrigued so I dialed her number. It was eleven-thirty, but she had said anytime. She sounded extremely alert when she picked up on the first ring.

"Delilah, hello, it's Voula. You said I could call…"

"Yes, Voula, hello. You aren't going to believe it. Hell, I practically fainted in the doctor's office. I'm pregnant."

"Pregnant? I thought you were divorced." Not to mention that she had two college-age kids.

"I am and I am. But I've been dating again. It's been so long. I was sort of easing back into it, you know."

More power to her, I thought and wondered how a woman pushing fifty could be doing so much better than I was. "I thought it was just menopause. I am forty-seven. Imagine my surprise. Those little eggs keep on producing."

"Well, congrats, I guess." Congrats? I wasn't sure what I should be saying. If she was telling me about it, I assumed she must be planning on having it.

"Yeah, I know, it's crazy, but I figure it's cool, you know. It'll be good."

"So does this mean you're—" I didn't know what to say. We had banned pets—what was our stance on babies?

"Well, I think I'm actually going to move in with the father, I believe he's called my baby-daddy."

I laughed hard, remembering how Delilah had looked like a sweet soccer mom from Greenwich. I had to laugh before I thought about looking for a roommate again.

"That's great, Delilah. Good luck to you." I hung up the phone and sighed.

It was a sick joke. It had to be. My best friend couldn't get pregnant, I didn't get dates, and most likely Armando was going to fuck our new roommate. Or worse, we were going to have to do the whole search over again.

Babies, they screwed things up.

4

Kelly moved in the day I went to my cousin Georgia's engagement dinner with my mother. The dinner was in the city, but my mother insisted I come to Queens first to get her, so we could go together.

I figured it was either look for a new roommate after finding out Delilah was knocked up or look for one when Kelly slept with Armando as she inevitably would. As usual, I procrastinated.

Armando tried to conceal his excitement when I said Kelly was in, but I knew he was psyched for a new challenge. Would he ever learn?

"Could you please just try, Armando? Try not to do anything with her. Please."

"Vou-laah, what you dink. I no want noting wit dis girl."

I shook my head. "I've heard it before. Can you please just not work your charm on this woman?"

"*Cosa* charm?" Armando was like Antonio Banderas— cheesy at times but also really hot.

I tried to convey it in the little Italian I knew. "*Basta con* the roommate fucking."

Armando clucked his lips as he did when he thought I wasn't being ladylike. For such a slut, he was awfully traditional. I fostered the Madonna role of his Madonna/whore woman complex by never having any boys over. I just wanted to make an impression, before I left him alone in the apartment to help her move her bedroom furniture.

"I'm serious," I said. "Keep your shirt on."

So, when I arrived at my mother's apartment, I was already slightly impatient.

"We are already late" was how she greeted me.

"Well, we wouldn't be if you had just met me in the city."

"Too much trouble to pick up your mother."

I didn't reply. I saw my mother look me over and knew what was coming next.

"Where did you get those pants?"

It was a trick question. There was no right way to answer. If I answered truthfully, she would question me about the price, which she would claim was too high. I would be accused of selfishly spending too much money. If I claimed I forgot, she would say I bought too many clothes. If I made the pants cheap, she would say that she thought they were ugly or inappropriate or any number of negative comments. That was my mom. And Jamie wondered how I could be so pessimistic.

"Mother, let's just go, if you think we're going to be late."

"See now, we have to rush."

"I'm not that late."

She didn't say anything, she just got her coat. Silence was the worst possible reaction.

On the subway she didn't talk to me, but as we got off at our exit, she muttered, "I could make you pants of much better quality."

It was true, the clothes my mother made were nicer than anything that was in fashion magazines. She'd even made Jamie's wedding gown. But if I let my mother make my clothes, I would be giving her back control that I had fought too hard to establish. I just couldn't do it.

Back in the day when the Greek Orthodox church was a

bigger deal, getting engaged was an official religious ceremony. The priest would bless you, your fathers would shake hands and after that you could live together. This is because Greeks didn't really date. They decided they liked each other, got engaged, were allowed to live together and "do it" and then married.

I always questioned what would happen if you decided you didn't want to marry the guy after you took him on a test run. I asked my mother that once and she looked at me in disbelief.

"You? You should be happy to find a man who wants to marry you. What kind of question is that?"

I took that to mean that most women accepted their lot once they got engaged.

These days the engagement is much more casual. There's still a handshake, but now moms shake too. There's no official church ceremony, just a dinner. Even though Georgia and Victor have been living together for a year, now it's more accepted. Georgia's mother, my aunt Effie, will admit they live together instead of ignoring it. Last year when Georgia went with Victor on a Caribbean cruise, Aunt Effie said she was on vacation with "friends."

Throughout dinner, my mother was on her best behavior. Aunt Effie was my father's sister and my mother always wanted to put on a good face with his family.

"So," Georgia said after dinner when our mothers were talking. "How is she?"

Even though I thought Georgia had it easy, she insisted on harping on the Greek thing: the unique hand we were dealt by being born into strict Cypriot families. In her case it meant that her mother was a little more traditional than most, but in my case it meant truly unstable.

"You know, the usual. Nice job going and marrying a Greek," I joked. "Way to set the rest of the cousins up for disappointment."

"At least he's only half Greek. Of course as my mother says—"she switched to Greek, imitating her mother "—the better half."

We laughed. Why did we put up with these weird rules and beliefs? We didn't know any other way, I guess.

"There is something I've wanted to talk to you about."

I smiled. The last time she'd said that, she wanted to set me up with one of Victor's cousins who was almost fifty. The time before, she had given me a terrific pitch idea based on one of her graduate psych studies.

"What now?"

"Helen called us."

I wasn't expecting that and I glanced over at my mother to see if there was any way she had heard. Luckily, she was immersed in a conversation with my aunt Effie and Victor's mom. I hadn't heard my sister's name spoken by anyone in our family in almost fifteen years.

"She called you?"

"She called my mother, yes. Of course Mom was too much of a chicken to call back, so I did."

"When?" My jaw tightened.

"About a year ago."

"And you didn't tell me before now."

"She didn't really want me to. She misses you a lot, but she knows your mother and she didn't want to get you into a situation that would make you uncomfortable."

I was in shock. So many times I had wanted to try to find Helen, and something had always stopped me.

"How is she?" I asked, after checking that my mom was definitely still talking to her sister-in-law.

"Well, she had another baby. A daughter."

I wasn't even sure what the first one was. "With the same guy?"

"Yeah. He's now her husband."

As quietly as possible, I put my wrist on my forehead. I didn't want to attract attention from my mother, but I just couldn't believe it.

"They live in Brooklyn in Boerum Hill."

I looked back up at Georgia. I wanted her to tell me she was joking, but she wasn't. I wondered if it was possible that

I had walked by Helen on the street, that we had ridden the subway together. I wondered why I had never bothered to Google her.

"Believe me, Voula, I don't like being in this position, but I figured you had to be told."

"Why? Why now?" But then it occurred to me, and my mouth dropped open. When I spoke my voice was a whisper, not because I was trying to be quiet, but because I couldn't make it any louder. "The wedding?"

Georgia nodded and started to say something, but my aunt Effie called her over to show my mother her engagement ring again. It had been our grandmother's.

I followed dumbly.

"Oh, *mana mou,*" my mother said, smiling. Georgia got a term of endearment for making her mother proud. I wondered if my mother would stop smiling when she found out our whole family was going behind her back.

I wanted to get more details from Georgia, but as it was her dinner she was pulled in other directions. When we kissed goodbye, she whispered that she would call me.

I didn't say anything on the subway home. I just listened to my mother gossiping about our family. Basically all the women were divided into two categories: the ones who didn't disgrace the family (meaning their mothers) and married well or didn't marry but remained obedient, and the ones that she whispered about, the ones who seemed to me to be a lot happier. My cousin Zoe who lived in Paris and worked as a journalist; Victor's sister who was married to (gasp!) an Eastern European; and even Georgia, who might have caused shame had she not been saved by her half Greek knight in shining armor.

"You see, Voula, you see how much happier Thea Effie is, now that she will not have to worry. Now she will be a *yiayia.*"

I wanted to tell my mother that she was a grandmother. I wondered if the presence of descendants would make any difference to her. It certainly would have quieted her for a while, but I couldn't bring myself to devastate her like that. The father of her grandchildren was not Greek, but Puerto Rican, and no matter how nice he might be, my mother had prejudices that were set in stone.

Instead I closed my eyes as she said, "Instead of spending money on pants, you should spend money on finding a husband."

"Are you saying you want me to marry a gigolo?"

"Listen to the way you talk to your mother," she gasped.

I couldn't take any more of this. In spite of how much of a disgrace I was, I knew that my mother still wanted me to stay over. She hated being alone, even though in many ways she had placed herself in this position.

I dropped her off at the front of her apartment and kissed her goodbye, but walked only a block before hailing a cab back to our apartment. I couldn't stand the thought of her saying I was wasting more money.

5

I'd planned on taking the cab to Jamie's apartment, but she wasn't home when I called from my cell phone. I didn't want to be alone. Usually, I knew what she was up to on the weekends, but I couldn't remember what she had said she was doing when we talked. For all I knew she was home making a massive attempt at conception.

Instead, I went to Better Burger and bought a tuna burger. I had one more stamp left on my card before I'd be able to get a freebie. I was working on a story for *NY BY NIGHT* about the proliferation of cards, so I was collecting them. I had a nail card, the burger card and a coffee card. I sat in the window and watched the cute gay boys of 8th Avenue walk by as I dunked my fries in karma catsup, which tasted of curry.

I was reluctant to go home and see how the move had gone. I didn't want to get involved with Kelly. She was sure to be just another roommate that passed through our apartment. First, she'd probably see me as a rival for Armando's affections, then she'd confide in me about the ways he flirted and try to get me to speculate with her on a relationship with him, and finally, when all was said and done, she'd be gone just like everyone else in my stupid life. Why even bother? I hated people.

I realized that all of this anger was protecting me from thinking about what I didn't want to think about. After Cristina died, my sister Helen went a little wild. Wild is good when you come from parents like the Jacobses who admit to smoking pot and still have sex. Wild isn't good when you come from the Pavlopouloses. I covered up for Helen so many times, even when I knew she was dating guys and bringing hair spray bottles full of booze to school.

My mother searched Helen's room constantly, and broke her silence to scream and yell when she found notes from boys. My mother planned such elaborate methods of spying on my sister that she might as well have worked for the government. She'd walk by places where she thought Helen was hanging out. She'd pick up the phone quietly whenever Helen was on it. Years later, when Georgia was first studying psychology, she said she thought my mother was looking to release all the tension she felt over Cristina's death.

I tried hard to be good during all this. Georgia psychoanalyzed me too, and said that I was trying to deflect what I knew was an explosive situation. It didn't matter, though. My mother never bothered to praise me, she just continued to go after my sister; to spy and scream and sometimes to hit. I dreaded being in our apartment back then. My father stayed out of these battles between my mother and sister—until the night that Helen didn't come home.

It was the first night that I'd slept over at Jamie's. Maura Jacobs came into Jamie's room and said that my mom was on the phone. I figured that she was checking up on me as she did with Helen. I remember feeling confident when I picked up the receiver. I knew I had done nothing wrong, and maybe my mother would be ashamed of herself.

Instead, my mother was hysterical. Helen had been forbidden to leave the house. Other people got "grounded," we were "forbidden to leave the house." We didn't know what the penalty was if we disobeyed—none of us had been that brave—

but Helen had finally decided to test the boundaries. My mother had gone to the store, and when she returned, Helen was gone. It was unthinkable. I knew without asking that I had to come home immediately.

My dad was sitting at the kitchen table drinking strong Greek coffee out of a tiny cup. My mother, crying, had searched Helen's room again, this time uncovering notes to her boyfriend, Andre. If anything, my parents had returned momentarily to the people they were before Cristina died. My mother asked me to translate certain words—usually slang or curses—that she didn't understand from the notes spread before her. Even though I created benign definitions, it didn't matter. I worried that my parents would be upset with me for some reason, but they weren't. My father didn't say a word, which wasn't unusual for him, but something about the set of his lips and the look in his eyes made me more afraid than I had ever been.

"It's the Puerto Rican," my mother said over and over again.

Each time she said it, I looked at my dad and became more and more convinced that they were going to kill my sister when she came home.

That night when I finally went to bed around midnight, I realized that not even my bed felt safe anymore. Cristina was dead, and now who knew what was going to happen to Helen. There was nowhere for me to be at peace. Everything could be taken at any second.

I stared into the blackness of my room, my heart pumping fast, for what seemed like forever. Eventually, I must have dozed, because when I woke up it was as if the house were alive. I could see all the lights on outside our door. I could hear thumps, screams, crying and cursing. Cristina would have taken the beating quietly, crying just enough to satisfy my parents, to show them that she was sorry, but not defying, not yelling at them. Helen was much tougher.

She ran into our room and my father followed with the belt, my mother shrieking and wailing, all three of them playing out some kind of crazy scene. My sister jumped back and forth across our beds. I don't think either of my parents even saw me. It was all about my sister. Then she said her damning words.

"Leave me alone, I'm pregnant."

Time stood still. We were all frozen, waiting to see what one statement could do. Then my father was pulling my sister out of my room, my mother screaming louder than ever, and the sounds I heard coming out of my sister didn't seem real. It was worse than the usual punishment.

After that, our world changed again. The police came and got my dad, my sister went to the hospital and my mother seemed even more empty than she had been before.

We didn't visit my sister in the hospital. I didn't even know where she was. My father spent the rest of the night in jail, but was out in the morning thanks to Georgia's dad. When Helen came home a few days later she brought her boyfriend. They cleared out only the stuff that she'd bought with her own money. My mother yelled about things she was and wasn't allowed to take. It was awful. I have to admit, I'm ashamed about the way I handled it. I didn't know what to say to Helen. I couldn't quite comprehend that she was leaving for good. My father left the apartment cursing in Greek about Puerto Ricans.

I went to sit outside on the stoop.

Finally my sister came out, gave a plastic bag of belongings to her boyfriend and asked him to wait in the car.

"Voula," she said, but I didn't look up. "Okay. I just want you to know that you saved my life. Two lives, actually. So, thanks, and I guess I'll see you around."

Then my sister was gone. What she meant and why I didn't run after her and hug her I don't know. I think I was just too scared.

But I didn't see her around—not for almost fifteen years.

I never caught a beating like that. I never did anything to deserve one. And my father moved to Cyprus that summer....

When I finished my burger, I tried Jamie's apartment again

but got the machine. I almost left a pathetic pick-up-if-your-listening message, but I didn't. I walked up 8th Avenue back to my apartment.

I heard laughing as I put the key in the door. It was starting already.

Kelly and Armando were standing in the kitchen holding glasses of red wine and smiling at each other. I so couldn't deal with this.

"Ciao, bella," Armando said.

"Hey," Kelly said, reaching out and grabbing my hand to shake. "It's nice to see you again, Voula."

The way she said my name was a little too slick, like I should be impressed that she remembered the name of the person she was living with. Raj was a TV person—I knew how slick they could be.

"Hi, how was the move?"

She sighed and kind of smiled at Armando. "Well, getting movers was the best money I ever spent, but moving is still a pain in the ass."

I smiled. She was wearing an obscenely short skirt, but from the looks of it, she had a bra on this time.

"Yeah," I said. I kind of wished they would just skip the wine and cut to the sex scene. I wanted them to go into Armando's room and leave me alone. Maybe they could get all the drama out of the way quick, so Kelly wouldn't have to unpack her boxes.

"Do you want some wine?" Kelly asked. "It's great. Armando has fantastic taste in wine."

"No thanks," I said, ignoring Armando's smirk. "I have some work to do."

"On a Saturday?" Kelly said.

"Yeah," I said quietly, and went into my office.

I closed the door behind me and turned on my laptop. The cursor blinked at me, mocking me. It said, "auntie, auntie." I was an aunt to two kids somewhere.

I was also still a sister.

I put my iPod on shuffle and swiveled once in my chair. Then I focused and wrote, *"There is no greater sense of accomplishment than getting the free cup of coffee at the end of the coffee card."*

Okay, I was in. For the next hour or so I wrote. I stopped to check whether a song was Audioslave or Sound Garden, but other than that, I was in the perfect zone. I came up with a halfway decent rough draft that accurately portrayed something that everyone could relate to, with enough inside New York references to make commuters on subways smile as they sipped the coffee that might have been free or at least leading them to a free cup.

I always hoped articles like this made life seem better, even if just for a minute. I knew they were fluff, but I could also picture the readers smiling in recognition. Obviously it wasn't going to change their lives, but it could take their minds off the fight they had with their boyfriend, the fabulous or dumb job they were headed to, or the stinky-breathed guy on the subway reading over their shoulder.

I used to work as an administrator for a nonprofit agency that raised money for international sculptors, but I had always wanted to be a writer. Since I was a girl I dreamed of leading a writer's life in New York City, working from home in my pajamas, waking up whenever I wanted, and writing exposés about injustice in the world. I was a long way from exposing war atrocities, but everything else came pretty close.

I started writing reviews online for various Web sites to get clips, and then I got my first assignment for *NY BY NIGHT.* It was four paragraphs about the etiquette for running into an acquaintance on the subway in the morning, but it paid. I made a dollar a word, I popped my cherry, I was a paid writer. And after that I got assignments here and there. I kept working at my day job because I was scared I wouldn't be able to support myself (and truth be told, I got a lot of writing done during my downtime).

Then *My Big Fat Greek Wedding* came out and I wrote a

scathing review. It was hard not to. I mean, I guess it could be argued that it was a good movie if you like innocent extended sitcoms, but what bothered me was that it really glossed over the Greekness of it. I mean, Toula's family could have been Jewish or Italian or any safe ethnicity, but they weren't—they were Greek. And where were all the Greek traditions? And who has Greek parents that wind up being that accepting at the end? I just felt diminished, and I wrote my most emotional review ever. *On the Verge* magazine published it and I started getting steady gigs.

Sometimes I had to travel or do research, which made it harder and harder to keep my day job. So I did the riskiest thing I'd ever done—probably will ever do—I trusted my talent and quit my job. My mother couldn't believe it, and maybe that made it sweeter. I believed. I had to. And it worked. I made a living—not a fabulous one, but a decent one.

The one place in my life where I seem to have done all right is my job.

There was a knock at the door of my office. I pulled the door open expecting Armando, but it was Kelly. She smiled and inched her way in. The office was tiny. I had garbage-picked a desk off the street and it took up most of the room.

"It's so cool in here," she said brightly. "I didn't get to see this the last time."

"Thanks," I said. I felt myself growing protective of my space. It was one thing to move into my apartment, but another to come into my work area.

"I was wondering if you wanted to go get a drink."

"Oh, um, thanks, but I really have to do some work." To her credit, she actually looked disappointed. She could drop the act. "I'm sure Armando will go."

"Actually, he went in to cover a shift at the restaurant. So I guess I'm not going to get to know my new roommates to-night." She smiled, her tone was even a little self-deprecating. "I'll let you get back to work."

She closed the door, and I turned back to my draft and spell-checked it. It wasn't due for another couple of days. And honestly, it was one of those pieces they could run at any time. I had a good enough relationship with the editor to know my deadline on that story wasn't hard. I felt a little bad about being so curt with Kelly. I mean, she was reaching out. But she was too cute and perky, too up, plus I knew she was going to screw Armando, and then it would be more agita for me.

I tried Jamie again—still no answer. I started to read over my article. I knew I had lost the thread. I kept imagining my mother's face when she found out that people in her family were talking to Helen.

I got up and knocked on Kelly's door. She was playing Joni Mitchell—at least I think that's who it was. It sounded folky. She opened the door and smiled a toothy smile.

"Come on in."

I entered cautiously. She seemed the type of person who is always at ease. How did she do it? Why couldn't I ever muster this kind of calm?

"Sorry about the mess," she said. "I decided to get a jump on unpacking. Since you dissed me for drinks."

I waited for her to say "just kidding," one of my pet peeves. The secret to good humor is knowing your joke may not go over and not really caring if it doesn't. I may not have been comfortable in my own skin, but I was comfortable with my sarcasm. She smiled at me, but didn't qualify her statement.

"I'm just a working girl," I said.

"You do it all for the cheese."

"I do." I smiled and felt my shoulders drop a little. "But the booze helps. Do you still want to grab that drink?"

"And not spend a Saturday evening unpacking…"

I laughed. Something about her didn't seem so bad. I liked her even more when she said, "I'll just put jeans on."

We went to a bar near Penn Station called Tier Na Nog. It was my first time there. I guess I had always assumed anything that close to the train station was off-limits, as in serious commuter haven.

"This place is super crowded during the week," she said. "My sound guy and I come here before he catches his train. Although, sometimes I make him miss it."

I looked up from my Guinness.

Kelly's eyes sparkled and she winked. "Probably not the healthiest thing I've ever done, but definitely one of the most fun."

"What shows do you work on?" I asked.

She named a few and a couple of indie films—one I had just watched last month. It was a vanity project of an Oscar-winning actress who had a soft spot for animal rights. Kelly told me how the woman had this thing about always having brown M&M's somewhere on the set, but never in her line of vision.

"Did she ever eat them?"

"I never saw her eat them, but they had to be available. And she'd check. She'd make them get the bowl between takes, just to show her."

"Wow! I wonder what would push her over the edge, and need to eat them."

"I don't know." Kelly laughed. "But I kind of wish I'd seen it, and then, I'm kind of glad I didn't."

"I wish I could write about it for *Who?* magazine."

"You can't," Kelly said, grabbing my hand and looking mock horrified. "It could be my career."

"Okay, I'll take it to the grave." I took another sip of beer. "Man, brown M&M's."

"Peanut," Kelly said.

I nodded. I, too, preferred peanut.

"I think if *I* could get a rider on *my* contract…"

"Oh, God!"

"It would be for Marie's blue cheese dressing and brown rice chips."

I nodded again, impressed.

"What about you? What would you put in your rider?"

"It's a great question," I said. "Feels like one of those games people play in college, but a good question."

Kelly giggled and signaled for another round.

"Okay, original Baby Belles."

"The laughing cow," she said, smiling. "Is that what you're talking about?"

"Yeah."

"Cool." She nodded.

I have to admit, I was glad to elicit her approval. I told her about Raj and some of the funny shows he worked on. His latest reality thing was called "Mr. Right…Now." It involved lots of fornication and catty women.

"I think I've heard he has a great deal of integrity, which in this business—and by 'the business' I mean the industry—" she joked, "means a lot."

"Yeah, he's a nice guy."

"Don't we all need a nice guy?"

I shrugged. *I* certainly did. I needed *something*.

Kelly cocked her head and then leaned into the table a little. "Are you and uh…Armando hitting it?"

"No," I said, looking down at my beer. I wondered if this whole get-to-know-you outing had been to feel me out about him.

"You never did?"

"No," I said, looking her in the eyes. "And I'm glad, because all the other roommates that slept with him couldn't hack it."

"Is he that irresistible?" Kelly asked, and it was clear that she couldn't see why. I was surprised. I thought Armando's appeal was a given. I thought no mortal woman could refuse him.

"You don't think he's attractive?"

"I guess he kind of is, if you like that sort of thing. He's definitely handsome, but he seems cheesy to me, you know. Kind of like Antonio Banderas."

"I like Antonio Banderas," I protested. "Have you seen *Tie Me Up, Tie Me Down?*"

"Have you seen *Original Sin?*"

"What about *Zorro?*"

"*Spy Kids?*"

"C'mon, he was trying to be campy in that. How about *Mambo Kings?* He learned to speak English phonetically. Do the words 'beautiful Maria of my soul' mean anything to you?"

Kelly laughed. "Yeah, what about *Femme Fatale?* Does that mean anything to you?"

"Oh." I groaned. "I did see that. I wish I hadn't. You got me."

She nodded. "So, Voula, do you think we should get one more?"

It was after midnight, but I felt a great sense of relief that Kelly was not into Armando and might actually last as a roommate. I believed her.

"Okay," I said. "Just one more beer."

6

When Armando covered Saturday nights at the restaurant, he generally slept through Sunday. I got up early, put some coffee on and went to the corner bodega for fried egg with bacon on a roll, and the Sunday *Times*. I bumped into Kelly coming back in. She had her own Sunday *Times*.

"Maybe we should start planning this better," she said.

"Well," I said, feeling like I could joke with her. "That depends on what your order is for reading."

"I go front to back," she laughed.

"Really," I gasped. I figured everyone would start with Sunday Styles, move to City and then see what struck their fancy. "It just might work."

Sundays were the only days I really hung out in the living room. Sure I spent nights there watching DVDs, but weekdays I forced myself into my office at all costs. Well, most weekdays. I wondered how a Sunday would be with Kelly, but she followed my lead and plopped on the couch when I sat in the easy chair.

We had been reading our papers for a while when the phone rang. It was closer to Kelly, so she looked at the caller ID and read Jamie's number.

"I'll take it," I said, and she tossed it to me.

"Hey, J. You pregnant yet?"

There was a pause on the line. I saw Kelly smile and then look a bit disturbed. Maybe I wasn't supposed to joke about this, but there had never really been a limit on what we could and couldn't joke about. Jamie could give as good as she got.

"No, but your number came up on the caller ID a zillion times. Were you drunk-dialing me?"

She was back to her old self, but I decided to be more careful about making pregnancy jokes.

"Where were you guys?"

"Well, it was so nice out and Raj has been so busy that we decided to take a drive. We went to the Delaware Water Gap, did some hiking."

"Tossed his salad?"

Jamie laughed, but across the room Kelly raised her eyebrows. Then she got up and went into the bathroom.

"Something like that. How's the roommate? A slut? Did she and Armando keep you up all night with their squeals of delight?"

"Like you and Raj last night? Actually, the situation is better than I thought." I kept my voice low in case Kelly could hear me.

"Wow! Are you making a new friend, Voula?"

I giggled.

"Are you gonna get like best-friend charms or something?"

"No, shirts." Jamie was one to talk. There was a time when the two of us had both.

"Wow. Do you feel like going to Togi tonight for some chow?"

"Sure," I said. We arranged to meet at eight.

Kelly came out of the bathroom as I hung up.

"It was my friend Jamie."

"Sounds like she can take a joke."

"Yeah, we've been friends for a long time. Forever."

"How cool," Kelly said.

I felt like kind of a dork. I wondered what Jamie would think of Kelly. It was rare that I felt almost comfortable with someone so quickly. I rarely was in situations where I had to be with people. Maybe it was a snow job. If anyone could spot a faker it was Jamie.

"We were going to meet for sushi tonight in Chelsea proper. We have these places we go to that are almost equidistant from our apartments." Now I was really starting to feel like a loser. "Do you feel like going?"

"I would love to, but I can't. I don't eat sushi. I had an allergic reaction once."

"Actually, this place has Korean food too. It's cooked." Was I beginning to sound desperate?

"No, sorry." She laughed. "That was two separate statements. I would love to go, but I can't because I have other plans. I'm continuing my very unhealthy relationship with the sound guy, despite all signs that I should know better. Then I was just letting you know that I didn't eat sushi."

"Oh, okay."

"But another time."

"Sure." I guess it *would* have been pretty strange to hang out two nights in a row with someone I barely knew.

I got to Togi first and ordered a green tea. Togi has the best spicy crunchy tuna roll I have ever tasted. The place had the misfortune of having opened with another name on September 10, 2001. It lasted three months, shut down and reopened as Togi. They added Korean food to the menu. It was never crowded.

In a way I was glad that it hadn't been discovered. But every time I went in there, I worried it would be the last. I feared that Togi would close down and I would never be able to eat such good spicy crunchy tuna again.

"Hey," Jamie said. "Sorry."

I stood up to kiss her. I wasn't sure why she was apologizing. She wasn't late. We didn't bother with the menu. When the waitress came back I got an eel roll, a spicy crunchy tuna roll and a couple of pieces of sushi. Jamie ordered bi bim bop, a Korean specialty.

"No spicy, crunchy?"

She shook her head. "No, just in case."

"Just in case, what?" I asked, and then remembered. "Oh, right. Was last night the night?"

"Well, I was ovulating again. We'll see how it goes. I hope it takes, because my next ovulation should be right before Memorial Day."

"Oh, just in time." Every year on Memorial Day the Jacobs family went to their parents' summer house in Block Island. They brought all kinds of boyfriends and girlfriends, but I was a staple.

"Yeah, it could be a real family affair."

"Well, at least you'll be able to drink some Dark and Stormies if it hasn't taken."

Then Jamie gave me that laugh, this time it was the *"you are so dumb, of course I would sacrifice ever again tasting ginger beer and dark rum mixed in an amazing concoction if I could only get Raj's wayward sperm to find my egg"* laugh.

Our salads came—seaweed for her, house with ginger dressing for me. I ordered a Sapporo. "So give me the dirt on the latest installment of *Three's Company.* How is she, really?"

"Not bad, honestly. We went out for drinks last night."

Jamie looked shocked. "Wow!"

"What?"

"That's pretty big."

"What do you mean?"

She kind of laughed. "I don't know, you just don't usually, like, like people."

"I know, but she seems nice." I didn't say that I was probably so open to it because I didn't want to be alone.

"I'm sure she is, but I rarely hear you say that about anyone."

"Maybe I'm changing," I said, twisting my face from side to side so she could see the possibilities. Our meals arrived before she could say anything else.

"Hey, how was your cousin's party?" Jamie asked, stirring up the egg in her bi bim bop.

"Can I get a fork?" I asked the waitress. I never learned to use chopsticks. I figured, I'm a westerner, I use western silverware. "Fine," I said to Jamie.

"So, how was your mom?"

"She was…herself. You know, I should be more like Georgia or my other cousins Roula, Toula, and Sula—I know it's ridiculous—and marry a Greek man."

"I can't believe she actually can mention men to you."

"As long as it could be sanctioned by the church and I promised to only use sex to give her male grandchildren, it would be all right."

"Jeez."

I thought about telling her about Helen, but for some reason I never talked about my sisters to Jamie anymore. And since I didn't talk about them to her, I didn't talk about them to anyone. If she had been home when I called, I probably would have told her. But it was a new day and I didn't think I had the energy to mess with my emotions again.

"How's Georgia?"

"She's good. You know her. Well, you don't really, but you know that she brings it all back to mental illness."

"Right." She continued to play with her meal. "So, I looked at the tapes of the finalists for Raj's show."

"Oh, I love those." There was nothing better than seeing how far people would go to get on TV. "Do you have any left for me to see? Has Raj agreed to let me write about them yet, anonymously?"

"Well, you're going to have to take that up with him, but I do have one." She reached into her bag and pushed a VHS across the table. I picked it up. The name on the sticky was "Warren Tucker." My mouth dropped. It had been so long since I had thought about that name, and yet, somehow I think I thought about him every day. Mr. Number Two of my two-and-a-half.

"Wow!" I couldn't quite get my voice back to say anything more.

"I know, I couldn't believe it. Remember when you had that crush on him? Remember that night?"

"Yeah." I nodded. "I think I do."

"Now, he wants to be Mr. Right…Now."

"Oh *panayia mou,*" I exclaimed in Greek. "Can we get some ice cream tempura?"

"Sure." She ordered it. "Voul, are you okay?"

"How was it?" I asked, gesturing to the tape.

"Well, he is almost as cute as he was when he worked at the pub with us. I don't know. I didn't watch the whole thing, just saw the intro. The weird thing for me was thinking this guy, you know, pushing thirty guy, wanting to be on TV like everyone else in America is Warren Tucker. *The* Warren Tucker."

"Oh." I dropped my face into my hands. Was everyone deciding to resurface in my life all at once? Dan the Man, Helen, and now, oh, now Warren.

"Are you sure you want to see the tape?" Jamie said, reaching across the table to take it back.

"Yes!" I practically screamed. "I'll watch it…when I'm ready."

We got our fried ice cream and talked about what the weather would be like on Block Island. I was glad that she didn't bring up the baby stuff, because I wasn't really hearing anything she was saying and I don't think I would have been supportive. I was too busy thinking about Warren Tucker.

Back home, I stared at the tape. I didn't feel like bringing it out into the living room where Kelly and her bad-boy cameraman might stumble across me. I wasn't sure I *could* watch it.

Warren Tucker.

I wasn't prepared for this. Warren bartended at the pub where Jamie and I waitressed the summer after our junior year of college. We lived in her parents' Block Island house for the summer. All of the Jacobs children got the house for the summer after their junior year, and I tagged along. Jamie's parents took themselves on a cruise those summers and only came out for Memorial Day. It was the longest I had ever been away from home. After the traditional Jacobs reunion that Memorial Day, Jamie rented out the extra rooms and we lived with four other girls. I imagined that that was what going away to school must be like. It felt like I was having a normal life, even though I still maintained all my abnormalities.

But there was Warren Tucker. As soon as I showed an interest in him (and it took me to the Fourth of July to admit it to anyone, including myself), Jamie declared him off-limits to everyone in the house. It wasn't really a problem, because almost everyone but me had paired up with someone. Jamie had a constant stream of boys that she dated.

There was just one night with Warren Tucker. Oh, I didn't want to think about it. I never talked about it. It had been my thing. My moment with the boy I'd wanted all summer.

Now that boy was going to be cheapened on network television. I couldn't, I just couldn't watch Warren Tucker pandering to nameless producers.

I climbed into bed and read the last of *The New York Times Magazine.* I should have fallen asleep dreaming of writing for *The New York Times Magazine,* but instead I thought of sitting on the jetty with Warren Tucker....

Warren smiled as he opened his picnic basket. It seemed pretty loud for Block Island. It sounded like New York City. I was wearing a heavy wool coat even though the sun beat down on me. My face was sweating, but Warren didn't seem to notice. He just gestured inside the picnic basket and I saw rows of beautiful spicy crunchy tuna. Before I knew it, Warren had lit a match and set the sushi on fire. I smelled it burning. There was a lot of smoke—

I woke up, disoriented. There was smoke in my room and Armando was screaming and banging on my door.

"Our apartment is on fire!"

I grabbed a sweatshirt and slippers and opened the door. Immediately, my throat filled with smoke, and Armando grabbed my arm and led me through the hall.

"My laptop, my laptop," I said.

"No, Voula, no. I call fireman. They coming. We mus go." Armando pulled me out of the apartment. The sirens were so close they seemed like they were inside me.

"Kelly! Kelly's still inside," I screamed.

"No, she not here. I open door, I look. *Non preoccuparti.* Let's go!"

As we started down the stairs, crouching to avoid the smoke, we saw the firemen. There must have been four of them with axes and giant backpacks running up the stairs to the fire. They were so fearless, running toward what we were fleeing.

"Go right downstairs," a voice behind a mask boomed.

And I ran with Armando still pulling on me—all the way down the four flights that the firemen had raced up.

Outside, it was cold, and a blond woman came up to us immediately. She was wearing a thin T-shirt and a pair of Armando's silk pajama pants.

"Voula, dis is Nadia."

"Hello," said Armando's latest conquest. "Nadia."

"Hi," I said. I was still kind of in shock. I looked up to our floor. There were flames in Armando's room and smoke coming out of my window. I watched as the firefighters fought it out. In addition to the men that had run up the stairs, firemen hustled up the fire escape pulling hoses from their giant backpacks. On the street, some firemen sprayed hoses to back up the firemen on the fire escape. Other people in the apartment building ran out onto the street where passersby gathered. It was close to two in the morning, but the fire gave the street a new light. The air was filled with the sounds of beeping horns. We had blocked 32nd Street. Armando was cursing in Italian.

The whole thing was unbelievable. There were three fire trucks, and another one arrived just as I saw Kelly walking up the street.

She looked up at our building, not sure what was happening. I yelled her name, and when she saw the three of us standing there, she ran over.

"What the hell happened?"

"I don't know. Fire."

"Is all that smoke in our apartment?"

"I think so," I said. "But at least it looks like the fire is out."

Soon firemen began to spill out of our building. The minute they stepped outside they lit up cigarettes. The street was full of men in heavy jackets smoking and looking up. When one of the trucks pulled away, I took this as a good sign.

"What time is it?" I asked Kelly, noticing she was wearing a watch.

"It's two-thirty."

I couldn't believe that much time had passed. One of the firemen came up to me.

"Do you live there?"

"We all do," Kelly said.

"I think the problem was a candle."

"Porca butane," Armando cursed.

I looked over at him and his Swedish import. Was this his fault?

"Do you have apartment insurance?" the fireman asked.

"Do we?" Kelly asked me.

I looked at Armando, who shrugged and shook his head.

"No," I told the fireman, my voice shaking.

"You should never leave a candle unattended," said the fireman.

"I didn't," I said defensively. I immediately regretted it. The man had just risked his life.

"There's an office in there. A room with a desk and a file cabinet."

"Oh, my God," I said. I felt a knot forming in my throat. "My office, my computer. It has everything."

"It's fine. There's some smoke damage. Your health," the fireman said. "Your life. That's everything."

Another fireman came and stood beside us. He was wearing a backpack, and I was pretty sure he was one of the guys who had run up the stairs. The backpack looked like something out of *Ghostbusters.* For some reason when I looked at him, I felt like an idiot.

"I know, but what happened to my office?" I said to the first guy.

"Part of the desk is shot," the new fireman said, adjusting the backpack and taking a cigarette out of his jacket.

His voice was kinder. "The files in one of the drawers are ash because it wasn't shut all the way. The computer, I think, is okay."

I closed my eyes. I knew that I should have been happy for my life, but all I could think was, Why hadn't I shut the filing cabinet drawer? Why hadn't I shut the office door?

"What about the bedrooms?" Kelly said.

"Who's got the one with the candle?"

"Me," Armando said.

"Gonna be lots of smoke in that one," answered the new fireman. "You might want to stay somewhere else tonight. We can try to hook you up with a deal at the Marriott down the street. Who's next to you? With the purple chest of drawers?"

"Me," Kelly said. "I just moved in."

"Well, the drawers ain't purple no more," the original fireman said. "Everything is going to smell like shit for a few days, but considering the stupidity of leaving a candle out, you guys are lucky."

"Yeah," added the second fireman, who I noticed was quite cute.

"Let's go, Torrisi," the first fireman said.

Torrisi put out his cigarette and looked at us, in various stages of dress, standing there in shock. He met Kelly's eyes. "It's going to be okay."

I looked down at the ground and then I felt a hand squeezing my shoulder just above where it was beginning to hurt from Armando's grip. I looked up into Fireman Torrisi's eyes.

"For real," he added.

"Thanks," I said.

Then all of the puffy-coated firemen climbed back into their various positions on the truck and drove away. The crowd dispersed and traffic began to move down the street again.

None of us could bear to be in the apartment. The whole place smelled the way Georgia's kitchen had when her brother Spiro decided to cook his G.I. Joe in the microwave. I had an awful hacking cough as I picked up my shoes and put on my jeans. I didn't bother to turn on my computer. I didn't want to think about what I might have lost.

Nadia went home, and Armando, Kelly and I went to The Blarney Stone. It was us and a bunch of old men who looked like they'd been there drinking since the seventies. We got a booth and settled in to drink beer all night.

"I so sorry," Armando said to us. "I lit candle." He looked like he might cry. His room was in the worst shape, worse than my office.

Kelly seemed really annoyed, but I was too exhausted by the whole situation to be annoyed. I had no idea what to say. I just drank can after can of beer until I knew I could go home and pass out despite the smell.

Even though it wouldn't help us, we got apartment insurance the next day. Actually, I called, but I made Armando swear that he was going to deal with our management company. I wasn't going to accept any of his excuses about not speaking English, and he wasn't offering them.

It was over a week before the apartment stopped stinking like smoke. All of our clothes reeked of it; the inside of the kitchen cabinets that had been closed were blackened by it. That fire had been powerful, but from what I gathered from the insurance company it could have been a lot worse.

I was lucky that my computer was fine. It almost made me reconsider backing up stuff on disks. But then the disks could get burned. My desk was in pretty bad shape—but it had been a street find after all. A lot of old invoices and several of the magazines where my articles appeared were lost. Luckily I kept the magazine with my first paid story in my room.

Kelly was pretty bitter at Armando for being so careless, but I thought he was beating himself up about it too much, so I went easy on him.

I ordered in a lot that week. I didn't want to turn on an oven. Heat and fire of any kind freaked me out. Armando told me he had trouble going into the kitchen at the restaurant. Kelly said that she was having trouble smelling matches. I guess we were all pretty spooked.

I started fantasizing about living alone. As much as I was happy that night to have my roommates with me and to not have to be on my own, I couldn't help but think that I never would've been in that situation in the first place if I lived alone. Maybe that would send me into my shell forever, completing my transformation into a hermit, but I wanted to be the one responsible for everything that happened in my life. Never again did I want to be running out of an apartment because of someone else's negligence. I wasn't ready to actually move, but the thought kept gnawing at me.

I also kept thinking about the firemen running up the stairs. They had been fearless. It didn't make any sense to me. How could you risk so much for people you didn't know? I didn't know anything about those guys, but because of them I still had my computer, which, while it wasn't as valuable as my life, still meant a lot.

I caught myself daydreaming about those firemen—good-looking men coming *to* my rescue in all sorts of ridiculous circumstances. I felt like a walking cliché.

7

Every day for almost a month I stared at the Warren Tucker tape, which had survived the fire, but didn't watch it. Then, when Jamie and I were leaning over the railing of the New London ferry, Block Island-bound, she told me that Warren had made the first cut. There would be one more cut before they brought the guys on air, which meant that Raj's schedule was going to get super busy once the Block Island trip was over. When would he find the time to impregnate her?

I had left the tape at home for our Memorial Day weekend trip. I half expected the place would be burned down when I got back and I would never see it, but obviously I wasn't prepared to face the image of Warren Tucker anyway.

"My temperature has been up for fifteen days," Jamie whispered as we grabbed some seats.

"Do you think you should be going to Block Island with a fever?"

"No, silly." The laugh came again, the *"haven't you figured out yet that everything I say revolves around procreating?"* laugh. Jamie pointed down. "My temperature down there."

"Oh." I nodded. Did she expect me to remember her scientific lecture? She knew I struggled through AP bio. "What does that mean again?"

"It means—" she looked over at Raj, who was smoking a cigarette against the railing "—I might be pregnant."

"Really," I said. I felt a bit queasy, but I was certain it was from the sharp dips the ferry was taking and not her revelation.

"Yeah," Jamie said, smiling but clutching the back of the seat.

This kind of turbulence was not uncommon, but it was certainly a pain in the ass.

"That's terrific," I said as my stomach flip-flopped. I smiled over to where Raj was, to prove how excited I was. The horizon rose and fell behind him.

"He's going to quit smoking the moment I get the EPT results. I figured I would take a test on the island."

"How nice," I said, pretty sure I smelled vomit. I wasn't looking forward to finding out that Jamie was pregnant on the island. I guess I had sort of been hoping she would put all this stuff aside for the weekend. Block Island could be so much fun. I loved getting drunk on Mudslides or Dark and Stormies and sitting on the big chairs getting too much sun. Right about then I would have given anything to be on solid land.

One of the women who worked on the boat came around handing out bags. I took one and so did Jamie. Raj made his way to our bench, holding on to anything he could grab.

"Hey," he said.

"I just told Voula our news," Jamie said, trying to smile but starting to look a bit green.

"About Warren?" Raj said.

"No, silly, about us and the baby."

It was a baby already? I thought we were just talking about a very warm cootchie.

"Don't jinx it," Raj said.

"Come on, Raj. You just don't want to stop smoking," Jamie said, and then she puked.

Raj rubbed her hair as she filled her bag, and then I gave her mine. I felt bad for her, but suspected she might be happy about the symptom.

"Are you okay?" I asked.

"Yes," Jamie said. She smiled at me, then puked again.

The sea calmed as we spotted land. Jamie felt well enough to get up as we slowed and coasted into the harbor, past the jetty where I had once sat with Warren Tucker.

"There's Mom," Jamie said.

I looked over to where Maura Jacobs was standing in a long white linen dress. She wore a floppy sunhat and sunglasses. She waved furiously and so did the three of us, laughing.

We gathered our luggage and were the first ones off the ferry. I was thrilled to be on solid ground. Then, I had that familiar feeling I had when I returned to Block Island: I immediately had a sense of slowing down and relaxing. Still, *I always* worried that I was tagging along. It had nothing to do with Maura, who wrapped me up in a big hug.

"How are you, Voula? You look great."

"Thank you. And thanks for the package." Maura had sent me a bunch of funny little presents after the fire, including a water gun and a pair of thong underwear with a flame on the front.

"You deserve it, honey. Tell me you got one of those big beefy firemen's numbers."

Sometimes I thought there was a gay man trapped inside of Maura. The only word I could think to describe her was *flamboyant*. She enjoyed drama, but at the same time knew when to take things seriously.

"I'm working on it," I lied, as the image of Torrisi in his giant Ghostbuster-type backpack flashed through my head.

"How was the trip?" Maura said, after she'd kissed everyone and we'd loaded our junk into the Jeep. Maura pawned the car keys off on Raj. She hated driving because she had trouble staying focused on anything for too long.

"Your daughter hurled," Raj said.

Maura looked back at Jamie and raised an eyebrow.

"I don't know, Mom, but I think this could be it."

Maura gave a little yelp and Jamie laughed.

"We haven't taken any tests yet," Raj said.

"We're going to do that tonight," Jamie added, sounding defensive, even though Raj was just being practical.

"Are you late, honey?" Maura asked.

"No, but her twat's hot," I interjected, knowing that Maura would enjoy that.

Maura yelped again and threw her head back, laughing, so her big hat fell into my lap. "What does that mean?"

"My basal temperature, Mom." Jamie sounded as if this was something everyone should know.

I wondered if, perhaps, every normal woman did. Was this something else I had missed out on thanks to my uptight, old world mother?

"Jamie, honey, what the hell are you talking about?" Maura asked, turning completely in her seat and unwittingly reassuring me.

"My temperature—you know, to chart my fertility."

Maura looked at me and I shrugged. It was an old routine we had.

"I have a special thermometer."

"Well," Maura said, looking really surprised. "I never heard of anything like that. A special thermometer."

"It's pink," Raj said.

"It's pink?" I asked, squinting at Jamie.

"Well, yeah. It's for fertility."

Was it suddenly a given that everything for fertility was pink? What kind of cult was Jamie getting involved in?

Just then we pulled up to the summer house. Compared to some of the other houses on the island, it wasn't much, but to me the four bedrooms, three bathrooms and front porch were heaven.

"Ana and Crystal are already here. Don't say anything, Jamie, but they've already grabbed the big guest room. You and Raj will have to take the pullout."

Jamie pouted a little. I always got the guest room with the daybed. If someone else wanted to crash in there, they could. Before she met Crystal, Ana used to.

"What about when Mike gets here?" Jamie asked.

"Well, so far it seems that he's flying solo and will get the basement guest room." Maura winked at me.

Jamie smiled, and because of her delicate condition I took her bags out of the car and up the steps. Crystal, Ana and Mr. Jacobs were sitting on the porch. They made quite a picture. For all of Maura's flamboyance, Mr. Jacobs was a quiet solid rock. I winced imagining the kinds of things Crystal had said in his presence. Not that she was crass, she was just kind of self-obsessed and she never stopped talking.

"Hey," I said, putting down the bags and hugging them.

"Margaritas are in the fridge," Mr. Jacobs said. "Just worry about the bags later. I'll bring them up."

"Just water for me," Jamie said, clearly hinting.

I wasn't sure that she should be telling everyone about this yet. But she didn't even have the chance to elaborate, because Crystal heard Raj telling Mr. Jacobs that the water was rough.

"Rough," Crystal said. "You wanna talk about rough. We took the Montauk ferry this morning and I swear I lost twenty pounds in the toilet."

Crystal also liked to tell you things you didn't want to hear. Her allergy to wheat was one topic she went on about non-stop. Drinking only made the endless chatter worse. And she liked booze and cigarettes. It was a good thing there was no wheat in either of those things.

I went to the kitchen to pour some drinks and Ana followed me. I refilled her glass.

"That's a jones about the fire, huh?" she asked as we went back to the porch.

"Yeah, it was really scary." I was about to elaborate when Crystal started a long loud story about a fire in her dorm room when she was a freshman. We listened politely. I finished my drink. I would have gone back into the kitchen to refill and escape the description of Crystal's charred stuffed animals, but Mr. Jacobs was on it. I was halfway through my second (strong) margarita when Jamie managed to get a word in.

"Well, I think Voula and I should head into town. I need to

get something at the drugstore." She grinned and looked around, waiting for Ana to quiz her.

"Honey, you just got here. Let Voula enjoy her drink."

I wanted to kiss Mr. Jacobs, but I'm sure he was already too embarrassed as always by Crystal.

"I figured we could rent a bike for Voula, too."

Great, just what I wanted: a drunken bike ride. Block Island, despite its relentless drinking, was full of people on bicycles trying to avoid the cars that were going about five miles an hour to avoid *them*. I always had to go on at least one ride, just to be a sport. The Jacobses could spring it on you at any time. I usually hung back, hoping no one would notice if I decided to get off and walk, fighting off thoughts of Cristina. She had been on a moped in Cyprus when she died. She must not have seen the car barreling toward her. Ever since, anything with two wheels freaks me out. I held on to the brake every time I went downhill, no matter how small the incline. I was scared that if my speed picked up, I wouldn't be able to stop.

"It's almost six, honey," Mr. Jacobs said. "By the time you get the bike, the drugstore will be closed."

"Should we really be biking?" I asked, letting my eyes drop. If Jamie was knocked up, maybe she'd think biking wasn't a good idea and I could get out of it.

"Why, what's going on?" Ana said, immediately suspicious. Ana always felt like people were trying to put one over on her. She had to be included.

"Nothing," Jamie said quickly. "I just still feel queasy from the boat."

In the morning, Mike arrived with Maura, who'd managed to pick up a pregnancy test when she got him at the ferry.

Mike looked like he'd stepped out of a Polo ad. I'm sure he never would have bought Polo, though. His clothes probably came from some obscure Boston tailor.

Like his big sister Jamie, Mike had been a really smart teenager. He had been accepted to Stuyvesant, but went to Bronx Science. Everyone had assumed he was going to be a scientist or a doctor or something. He was kind of a nerd, but once he got out of high school he shirked the full rides he had to places like MIT and Cooper Union and decided to be a font designer.

A what? That's what I said, but apparently Mike was really good at coming up with new ways of making letters. He started working in a font firm and within two years had done so well that he started his own company.

While your average person (myself included) really had no idea what he did, a select few art directors in everything from magazines to ad agencies considered him a god. What had been socially inept, nerdy behavior in high school, had turned into too-cool-for-school eccentricity. He was the quietest of all the Jacobs children, and I wondered if he was a bit disdainful to have to hang out with people who didn't understand him.

We exchanged some quick greetings with Mike before Jamie pulled me into the bathroom for the pee test. I feigned revulsion, but I was secretly thrilled to be the first person to find out if the bun was actually in the oven. I sat on the corner of the tub and averted my eyes. She went through the process and I felt like we were on one of those pregnancy test commercials."

When Jamie finished peeing, she put the stick on the sink, closed the toilet and sat on it. We looked at each other and smiled.

"Hey, how's it going in there?" Maura called, banging on the bathroom door.

"C'mon!" Raj called.

"Another minute," Jamie yelled, smiling.

"Am I going to be an aunt or what?" Ana yelled. She had interrogated Maura and gotten the information she wanted.

Then Crystal chimed in with, "I was once certain I had chlamydia based on my discharge, but luckily it was a yeast infection. It was before I came out."

I heard Mike say that there was another bathroom downstairs.

I panicked. Jamie was already too invested in this. Raj had tried to be the voice of reason, but what if it was negative? We were all there. Raj, me, Maura. And then I got a little sad: her mother was there. Regardless of the outcome and whether or not she knew it, Jamie was going to be okay because she had so much support.

"Okay, it's time," Jamie said. Her left eye twitched the way it did whenever she was nervous. "Voul, I don't know if I can look. Can you do it?"

"Okay," I said. I picked up the stick that my best friend had just peed on. This was a true test of friendship.

I stared at the little window, unsurprised by what it showed. I looked up at Jamie; I didn't have to say anything.

"No," she said, her voice soft and incredulous-sounding. She took the stick from my hand and looked for herself.

I held onto her wrist.

"I can't believe it," she said.

"I'm sorry," I said, stupidly.

"What's going on in there?" Maura asked, banging on the door again.

"I just don't get it," Jamie said. She looked at the stick again, as if she was hoping the results would be different. "My temperature was up. According to everything I read, it means I should be—"

Jamie had always been good at making everything seem okay for me. I wanted to make this seem okay for her. I wanted to be there for her.

"We'll be out in a minute," I yelled toward the door, to Raj and her family, who still had hope. I pried the test from Jamie's hand, wrapped it in toilet paper and buried it at the bottom of the trashcan.

Jamie didn't look like she was ready to leave the bathroom, so I sat down, with my back against the door, and looked up at her.

"What?" she said.

"Nothing. I was just trying to think of the right things to say."

"Yeah? What did you come up with?"

" 'Don't worry, Tiger, you'll get 'em next time'?" I said.

She looked at me, and for a second I thought she was going to cry. But she started laughing. And it wasn't one of those *"oh, you don't understand"* laughs. This was a real laugh, a Jamie laugh.

8

I got home late Monday night after three days with the Jacobses. I loved hanging out with them, but after three days of Trivial Pursuit, getting drunk in the sun, and taking hesitant bike rides, I was ready again for my own space and my own schedule. The Jacobses seemed to thrive on pretending they had a dysfunctional family. But they wore their quirks like a badge of honor. However much they labeled Ana as the paranoid one or Mike as the snob, they loved it. They loved being a part of their own little Jacobs group, but although they considered me a part of the family, I wasn't. It was something I was always conscious of when I was with them.

The music was blaring when I opened the door. In my living room I found a cosmopolitan crew of people who worked at Armando's restaurant. I winced as I spotted the chef cooking stuff up on our stove. I had spent the weekend trying to avoid being by the barbecue grill. Fires still scared me.

"Voula," Armando said, getting up and sending Nadia tumbling off his lap. "Howah you, *bella?*"

"Fine," I said, looking around at the well-dressed group. I

didn't like feeling out of place in my own apartment. "Looks like you're having a party."

"Yes, nothing big, little come-together."

I smiled. It was always funny hearing Armando use expressions that he hadn't quite mastered.

"Pino is making some pasta. You must have some wine."

That was all I had been drinking with Jamie. Once she got her period she started drowning her sorrows in alcohol.

"Actually, I'm kind of tired."

"Oh. How was de trip?"

"Very nice, thanks." I smiled at a couple of the other waiters I knew. "Hello, everyone. I think I'm just going to do some work in my room."

"Okay, Voula," Armando said, and walked me over to my door.

My office still had the slight stench of smoke and I didn't want to be in there.

"Is it okay they here?" he asked.

"Sure, Armando, no problem."

"Well, come eat someding when you finish."

"Okay, thanks. I will if I don't fall asleep."

I went into my room and shut the door behind me. Was it too much to ask for a little downtime? A little quiet? I don't know that I was meant to live with roommates. Maybe I was meant to live in a cave.

I flopped on my bed and pulled off my sandals. On the top of my bureau I noticed a stack of newspaper. I grabbed it and saw a note on top from Kelly.

Hey Voula,
    Don't have a call 'til Thursday, so I went to the Hamptons for a few days. Thought you might like to see the paper.
K

Well, that was thoughtful. I felt a pang of guilt about my anti-roommate thoughts. I had to try to stop being such a loner. But, couldn't I be social and still not have to deal with other people? Maybe not *not deal* with them, maybe just not have to worry that what they did could affect my home base. I wasn't blaming Armando (okay maybe I was), but the whole irresponsible candle thing had rubbed me the wrong way. And even though Kelly seemed like a cool woman, how long before I had to go through the whole rigmarole of a roommate search again?

I started looking through the Styles Section of *The New York Times*. After finding no one I knew had gotten married and skimming an unsatisfactory Vows story, I went to pick up the City section, but then I changed my mind.

I never looked at the Real Estate section. Like the Sports and Automobiles sections, I put Real Estate directly in my recycle pile. Maybe I could just take a look, get an idea. Real Estate was a big game in New York—supposedly it was a good investment. I was curious. Was someone my age even equipped to start looking?

Maybe I could get an article out of this. If I didn't know anything about it, I bet a lot of New Yorkers didn't. We all just rented less-than-perfect apartments, moving like nomads when some aspect of our lives changed. Maybe instead of giving money to a faceless management company that waited too long to fix the leak in the bathroom, I could give the money back to myself. What was it called? Equity. I wrote the word in my notebook. I wanted to find out more. It was like another language. I didn't invest, didn't really know the first thing about stocks, but I had opened a savings account in kindergarten. I always remember my teacher saying responsible people saved thirty percent of their salary, and since then I have.

I opened the paper and looked at the highlight section— how much certain key apartments were going for and how long they had been on the marker. A one-bedroom with a doorman and roof rights in Chelsea was going for something absurd like $899,000, a Brooklyn two-bedroom was now $425,000 after starting on the market four weeks ago at $455,000. I had $28,000 in the bank and I knew that somewhere I had about $7,000 in bonds that my extended family had been giving me since birth. These places were way out of my league, but maybe if I was going to do an article about it, I could get a taste of what these top-notch apartments were really like.

But was it just an article? My interest was piqued. I flipped to the back of the section where the actual listings were. When I had researched renting an apartment, before I moved out of my mother's place, the one thing I had found was that you needed to isolate a neighborhood. The West Village would have been ideal, that's where Jamie lived—but it was too pricey. Chelsea was starting to be really popular, but the apartment I found in what was then still midtown and is now obnoxiously Chelsea Heights was cheaper.

I liked the neighborhood and Chelsea. I didn't want to leave the 212 area code. I liked telling editors I lived right in the city. I thought it gave me some bizarre street cred.

I decided I would look at a bunch of apartments—some would be just to get an idea for an article on buying a place, but others I would actually be looking at. I found one for $250,000. I could get a mortgage, right? Who knows how these things worked? I had missed the open house on Sunday, but there was another one on Thursday night. I was in the game. I was on assignment. (Well, I would be after I pitched the story). I was entering a new world.

I arrived at eight p.m. at the building on West 20th Street. It was just west of 8th Avenue, where the buildings were a lot prettier than those to the east. There were several people marching through the tiny space. It was just a small kitchen with a squat, square living room, and I assumed there was a bedroom behind the door. A classy looking blond woman stood like Art Garfunkel, hands clasped behind her back, in the center of the room. She reached one hand forward and shook mine.

"Daria Hayes-Gelsimino, senior sales agent for Corcoran."

"I'm Voula Pavlopoulos."

She blinked and smiled. This was a woman who was "on" for a living. In a minute, she'd forget my name.

"Please sign in."

I looked over to the coffee table she gestured toward. There was a white sheet of paper that demanded all kinds of info about me and the name of my real estate agent.

"Um, I don't have a Realtor."

Daria smiled even more brightly, but I could tell by the looks of some of the other interested parties that I was an amateur.

"Even better for me," Daria said.

I didn't quite understand what she meant, but I complied when she said, "Just sign yourself in."

For about half a minute I considered giving a fake name, but then remembered that I had already introduced myself. Plus, I suspected this was in my price range. Next to the sign-in sheets was a pile of papers that had a floor plan and some figures.

"Could I take one of these?" I asked.

"Of course."

I wasn't sure what the protocol was. Did I study it or just refer to it later? No one else seemed to be looking at their sheets. I wasn't sure what they were looking at.

I walked into the bathroom, where a man and woman were inspecting the inside of a medicine cabinet. There was hardly space for two people, let alone three. I wondered if I should come back.

"The hot and cold water are reversed," the woman said to me.

"Oh."

Then the man and woman squeezed past me into the main area. I stood dumbly in the small bathroom. Actually, I had to pee, but that didn't seem appropriate. Then I suspected that maybe the couple really liked the place and was trying to downplay it. I turned on the hot and cold water faucets and after a minute realized they were, in fact, switched.

I went back into the living room. There was the cutout of a fireplace where the owners had stuck a few candles. The ad had mentioned a faux fireplace as if this was a selling point, but I didn't really get it.

"Is the building pet-friendly?" a woman in a bright yellow jacket asked.

"With board approval," Garfunkel said.

Does that mean the pet has to meet with someone? I wanted to ask, but I didn't want to betray myself as a newbie.

What I thought at first was another couple seemed to be a Realtor and her male client. He seemed kind of uptight, but I wondered if this would be a good place to meet men. That could add a whole new dimension to my story—that is, if I was the type to approach random men at open houses.

"It's a really tiny kitchen," the guy was saying.

"I know, but you could work with it," the Realtor said.

I thought I saw her wink at Garfunkel.

"It's in your price range," she added.

"I don't know," the guy said, shaking his head.

"What I would do with this space," Garfunkel said, "is turn the fridge."

"Why, that's a fabulous and creative option," the other Realtor said.

"Excuse me. Turn the fridge, I don't get it," the uptight guy said.

I was happy he asked, because I didn't get it either.

"Yes, I've seen it done," his Realtor said. "You could pull it out of the kitchen a little."

"Right, and face it this way into the living room."

The Realtors were tag-teaming now. Was it a setup?

"And then you'd have so much more room in the kitchen."

"Yes," the uptight man said. "But I'd also have a fridge in my living room."

He made a good point.

Garfunkel looked crestfallen and his Realtor seemed to know that he wasn't going to be persuaded. They thanked the host and left.

"Sometimes, you just have to have vision," Garfunkel said to me.

"Yeah," I said. I wasn't sure I had vision.

I went into the bedroom. Someone really liked those photos where they dress babies up like flowers or stick them on top of trees. That someone lived here. I smiled at the two women who were already in the room.

"Not much light," one of them said.

"I know," her friend replied.

But I didn't. It was after eight o'clock at night. The sky was dusky. How could they tell how much light it got during the day? I figured I had to learn something from this experience. I didn't think the apartment was as bad as everyone else did, but maybe I was blinded by the exciting new experience.

"How can you tell?" I asked. They looked confused. "About the light, how can you tell there isn't much?"

"Oh," one of them said. "Well, it faces north."

I nodded, still unsure but not wanting to press it. This is why I could write pieces but didn't really consider myself a journalist.

"South facing," said the one whom I suspected wasn't the buyer. "That's what you want for light."

"Oh," I said, betraying that I really hadn't had a clue. "I get it."

We did a little dance and they squeezed around the bed. I stared out the window. I could see the Empire State Building, barely—even though the ad had mentioned Empire State Building view (or had it said vista?). I wasn't sure then or now what the allure was. It was a cool building, but even if I loved it, I still wouldn't exactly consider this a view.

I went out to the living room to say goodbye to Garfunkel. What was the thing to say? *I'll call you.* No, too one-night stand. *Great place, too bad you decorate in weird baby photos.*

I decided on "Thanks."

"Sure, take my card if you are interested."

"Great, I will," I said, perhaps too eagerly. But I took it.

Out on the street, I felt overwhelmed. It was only one apartment and yet I had had no clue what to ask or what to look for. It was scary to even think about spending that kind of money when I was so uninformed.

If only Jamie had bought a place. Why couldn't she have done this first too? She was having a baby—didn't she think it needed a home of its own?

There was one person I knew who owned her own apartment, and that was the woman who waxed my body, Diane. I decided my eyebrows were getting a little dense and made an appointment for the next week. If anyone could give me the lowdown it would be her.

I also decided to send out a pitch to all of the possible editors that might be interested. I looked at my calendar. Tomorrow I was writing copy for an article on antique lamps for the shopping section of an in-flight magazine. I hated some of the assignments, but it paid really well. And if I wanted to have whatever percentage of the price I was supposed to have for a down payment, I needed to take any assignment I was offered. Beggars couldn't be choosers and neither could young real estate moguls on the make.

Friday night Jamie invited me over for dinner. Raj was working late, so I knew it was going to be just the two of us. I wouldn't have to worry about looking good for any random guy she wanted to set me up with. I caught myself thinking that, knowing it was the wrong mentality if I ever wanted to have a date again, if I ever wanted to wax more than my eyebrows.

She greeted me at the door to her apartment with a glass of wine. She was dressed down in jeans with bare feet. No one I knew could put themselves together as well as Jamie, but without makeup she looked five years younger. She was blocking her dog, Sparky, a Westie with a barking problem, from getting out into the hall.

"On the bottle again, are we?" I asked as I kissed her hello. I allowed Sparky to jump all over me.

"Sparky, off!" Jamie screamed, to no avail. "I just finished my period. Raj is doing final casting. I need something. And I'm sure I won't be having any procreational sex this weekend."

"Well, as I've always said, alcohol often leads to babies… How was your workweek?"

"Awful. A four-day week only means longer workdays." She looked at me and shook her head.

Statements like that made me glad I worked from home. Jamie thought that just because I worked from home, I didn't really work. Sure, I got away with a fair amount of procrastinating, but the truth was, I was good at buckling down when I needed to.

"Did you even change out of your pj's once this week?"

"Actually, three times," I said, laughing. "Hey, smells good in here."

"Thanks. I made some cheesy veggie lasagna."

"Awesome. I'll take some wine. So how was your mom's postmortem of the weekend?" I asked. I wondered if Maura played favorites with everyone, if she said things about Jamie to Mike and Ana the way she gossiped about them. I wondered if she said stuff about me.

"As usual, she doesn't know where Mike comes from. Didn't he seem completely horrified playing Trivial Pursuit?"

"He likes to have that air of having something better to do."

"It's like he gets mad because I don't understand the kernels of letters or whatever. But why should I? I don't ask him to try on makeup."

"I believe it's called kerning. And I only know that because I listen to him sometimes."

"Kiss-ass," Jamie said, and stuck her tongue out. "And Crystal—Jesus. I can't. I just can't."

During dinner, Jamie told me that she was certain that Warren Tucker had made the cut. "So that means one way or another, he'll be at the wrap party and you'll see him. Maybe he can be *your* Mr. Right Now. Did being on Block Island bring back any memories?"

I didn't tell her that it always did. I had spent, all told, maybe thirty hours alone with Warren Tucker and I could pretty much tell you everything we ever said to each other. In fact, I could bring myself back to those moments on the jetty whenever I wanted. I suspected that was the reason I never really cared about anyone else or wanted to be set up. My memory, my vision of Warren Tucker was just too good.

"Not really," I answered, and blew on the lasagna even though it was pretty much cooled off.

"What did you think of his hair?" she asked.

I shrugged.

"Come on, Voula, you watched the tape, didn't you? You've had it for weeks."

"Remember the fire?"

"Yeah," she said, getting more excited, or perhaps the lack of drinking was lowering her tolerance. "I don't think your VHS got burned."

"I have to rewire when I watch DVD," I said, reaching for an excuse. "I haven't had a chance."

"Well, what have you been doing?"

I didn't want to talk about Warren Tucker anymore. I didn't want to learn anything. I didn't want details on why I should note his hair. I pined for him and I didn't want watching the tape, seeing the real him, to show me I had wasted time thinking about him, comparing all the people Jamie tried to set me up with to him. I didn't want to find out that Warren Tucker wasn't worthy of all the thought I had put into him. But I knew that saying it wouldn't get her off my case. I knew she would never believe me.

"I've been looking at places," I said.

I hoped it was a dropped bomb, like her "trying." It was high time I had some news other than domestic disasters. I could see the shock spread across her flawless skin. I tried to put it in the most sensational *E! True Hollywood* story way.

"I'm in the market for some real estate."

Then we both exploded with laughter.

"I can't believe it," she said as she served me more lasagna.

She looked around her apartment, and I thought I saw a strain of envy cross her face. When she and Raj first got engaged they talked about moving out of Raj's rent-controlled apartment in the West Village. They looked at places, but in the end their jobs got too busy. Jamie told me they were going to hold off until they decided to move out of the city.

"That's big. That means you'll actually own something? Do you have enough for the down payment?"

"Well, I don't know. I haven't done all the research yet. I've been saving."

"You should talk to Alice."

"Why?" I had no idea why I should talk to one of the Olsen Twins. I had heard enough about their perfect lives while Jamie was in college with them.

"Voula, do you ever pay attention? She's a mortgage broker."

"Oh, right. I knew it was something with money." It's true I had a tendency to tune people out when I didn't think they were saying something I could use as a story.

"She could totally help you figure out what's what."

I wasn't sure I felt comfortable asking a favor from someone I secretly mocked so much. Also, I didn't know if I wanted her telling Jamie how fiscally responsible I was or wasn't.

Jamie got up from the table and went across to the cordless phone. "Let's call her right now."

"Jamie, don't worry, I'll call her when I figure things out a little better."

"No, this way you'll know what you really want to do. It'll be great."

"It's Friday night. I don't think she wants to hear about my issues."

"C'mon, she's married. What the hell else would she be doing?" Jamie started dialing the number.

Our roles were switching and she was living vicariously through me.

"Doesn't she have a summer house or something?"

"Voula, that's Morgan. They are two different people, you know." She shook her head at me.

"Alice, hey, it's me," said Jamie. "I wanted to ask you— You were? Why? Oh, really, what? What? Wow! I didn't even know you guys were— That's awesome. When? Wow! That's great."

Jamie's face didn't match her tone of voice. She left the kitchen and walked into the living room. I wondered if I should follow her. I picked at a little bit more of my salad and stared at the kitchen clock. After about ten minutes, Jamie returned to the kitchen. Her eyes were red like she had been crying.

"Hey, what's wrong?"

"Nothing," she said. "It's stupid."

"What?"

"Ugh." Jamie sighed and sat back down. She put her head in her hands. "I should be happy about it, but—"

"What's up?" Alice could be a little self-righteous at times, but I didn't think Jamie ever really noticed.

"Alice is pregnant."

Jeez, was everybody on this baby kick now?

"I know, I know I should be happy for her, but— Oh, I'm such a bad friend."

"Why?"

"Well, they weren't even trying. She got off the pill—you know, because of the mood swings—" oh was that the excuse they were giving now? "—but she was using condoms mostly. She said they drank too much when they were away and she didn't get up to pee after they did it. That's what she thinks caused it—can you believe it? The next thing she knew she was late and she didn't even really think about it. You see. I mean, how could she not think about it?"

"It's okay," I said. "You're going to have a baby soon."

"Thanks. It's just so tough. I mean, I think maybe I'm doing this all wrong."

"Maybe you're just too stressed out about it."

"We've been trying for almost eight months."

"Yeah, but maybe you need to relax."

"I know, but it feels like I'm a total loser if I can't do it. How can it come so easy to some people?"

I had felt that way about so many things throughout my life, but I had never in my wildest dreams expected to hear that sentiment from Jamie.

9

"The thing about buying apartments in Manhattan is that they can charge whatever they want and someone's gonna pay," Diane said in her thick Staten Island accent as she bent in front of my face and ripped the hairs out of the bottom of my left brow.

Diane was one to talk about overcharging. It cost me forty bucks (fifty with tip) every six weeks to get my brows re-shaped. That was a discount price I got because I had referred her to Jamie, who had referred her to Raj's co-workers and her own, and now all kinds of makeup executives, television producers and C-level reality-TV stars were charged triple what I was to have their brows arch just right. Diane believed, as I did, in networking. She referred me to beauty editors who came to her through Jamie's co-workers' friends and they referred me to features editors at the magazines they worked for. It was all one big happy circle.

I knew I was lucky for my bargain. No matter what she charged me, I would have kept coming back to Diane. I didn't really wear a lot of makeup. I occasionally threw on some lip gloss if I met with an editor. But whenever I got my eyebrows done just right by Diane, I felt attractive. I felt more put-to-gether, almost sexy. Now, she was advising me on what I should be looking for in an apartment. Maybe I should be listening to her.

Apparently, most places in the city required you to put down twenty percent. She said you could get away with putting down less, but you would have to pay more in interest. A lot of places wouldn't even show you something without a preapproval letter, and a lot of mortgage companies wanted to know more specifics about the place you were buying before they worked out your preapproval. Diane told me about how she wound up losing the first place she bid on, to someone who paid in cash.

"Can you believe that?" she asked, ripping, then taking out the tweezers to get the tiny hairs that hadn't come out in the wax strip. That was my least favorite part.

"No," I said, and winced.

"The thing I would do is figure the absolute top you can spend. And look for places much lower in case you have a bidding war. A lot of those places— Are you okay?" she asked, seeing the way my hands gripped the spa chair.

I nodded. I wanted her to hurry up and get it over with.

"Let's say it lists for like 299 or 349, you know what I mean, they do that so they can just make it into some people's budgets. Like if it was 300 or 350, some people might think it's out of their range."

"Uh-huh," I grunted, still bracing. That certainly wasn't my budget, but what she was saying made sense.

"And then you have a bidding war and then—" she was back to waxing and ripped a little too hard to emphasize her point "—it's over."

"That would suck."

"Yeah, you won't believe how stupid people are until you buy a place. Well, you'll see."

I couldn't wait, although the thought of it was daunting.

"You should write about it."

"I think I probably will." People said stuff like that to me all the time. Once they found out I made my living writing, they thought that any story they had would make a good story for me. Sometimes they were right, but usually I just smiled and nodded. If it's a good idea, chances are I have already pitched it.

"You're all finished, hon," Diane said, and held out the mirror for me to inspect her work.

I smiled at my reflection. I spent the six weeks between visits trying to clean up my own brows with tweezers, but only Diane had the magic touch. "They look beautiful. I don't know how you do it. You're an artist."

"Thanks, sweetie."

I handed her the envelope of money.

"Listen, I'll give you the name of my girl. She can help you find a place. I've got her card right here."

"But I was thinking more West Village/Chelsea." Diane, though she kept her accent and her terms of endearment, had long ago moved out of Staten Island and on up to the Upper West Side.

"They all get the same listings. Sometimes they try to push their exclusive stuff on you so they won't have to share the commission, but she's good. She's just got a mouth on her. Tell her I sent you."

As soon as I got home from the spa, I pulled out the card Diane had given me. It said: Maureen Soltero, Senior Experienced Realtor. Well, I guess that was comforting. I called and left a message about meeting up for some info on available apartments. Maybe before I got all crazy with mortgage brokers and how much money I had, I needed to see what was out there.

I checked my messages. I had missed a call from Eve Vitali, an editor at *On the Verge* magazine. I was anxious to pitch my idea about friends being pregnant, but so far Jamie still wasn't knocked up. It didn't really matter, because I played constant phone tag with Eve. I knew she liked my pieces, but she was so busy all the time.

I was okay, though in terms of work. I was paying the bills.

Financial Woman had liked my pitch about searching for real estate in New York City. They were kind of a stuffy magazine that wanted to hook a younger reader. Fortunately, the editor-in-chief was an overweight white guy who would have believed me if I told him that women my age liked to have their toenails pulled out. It was another instance of the editors of a magazine not really being in touch with the intended reader. But it worked in my favor.

I called the stuffy editor and talked the talk. I was hired to write the series as soon as I finished another one for them on car insurance. I considered the insurance assignment quite a score because I didn't own a car and had only driven maybe five times in my life, all of them in Block Island. I never even got my license, but growing up in the city meant I never really had to drive: I took the subway everywhere. So basically the article involved a lot of running around and phoning the DMV and various insurance companies. I threw in some gory tragic accidents for the readers to salivate over. Between that and another article for the in-flight magazine that kept calling me, I stayed busy for a few weeks.

I had moved back into my office, and kept spraying it with air freshener to get rid of the smell. I still refused to light candles. And because it was summer and my apartment was already as hot as an oven, I didn't cook.

Diane was right about Maureen: she was a talker. After our initial conversation, where she revealed to me how difficult it had been to get pregnant—mind you, I had said *nothing* about being interested in pregnancy—she called me every other day.

Because I needed to finish the research on the car insurance article, it took me two weeks to be able to even go out with her. And then, it was as if I'd signed on to some kind of roller coaster I couldn't get off. In about four weeks, I saw at least fifty apartments. I saw one-bedrooms that were way over my price range, but I got talked into going because they had fireplaces. I saw studios the size of broom closets that somehow had really expensive kitchen appliances. I learned that a junior one-bedroom is really just a studio that someone separated with a cheap wall or partition. I wondered whether I could really sleep in a loft or whether I would break my neck on the ladder when I went for my nightly pee.

Maureen Soltero talked the entire time. She was exactly what I imagined she would be. She wore blazers and long beaded necklaces. Her hair was a red not found in nature. She talked constantly about her triplets and gossiped about her nanny. She said things I would not have tolerated from anyone else. When I said I didn't have a boyfriend, she awkwardly suggested I might like women. She wondered aloud when I said space was important to me if I might be a spinster for the rest of my life. There were times I almost gave her my mother's phone number so that they could just gossip about what a failure I was.

So why did I tolerate Maureen's incessant chatter as I tried to imagine myself putting groceries into various cabinets all over town? That's easy: I was hooked. From the moment I stepped into the first apartment I realized that I was in the real estate game. And I liked it. I've never been a gambler, but with each new apartment I imagined the life I might have there. It was hard to decide which place would suit me best. There were too many possibilities.

"You just have to have vision," Maureen said whenever I questioned some feature of an apartment.

But I didn't have vision. I didn't think that I was going to move into a place and turn it into something it wasn't. I wanted a place to speak to me. Like the way they say you just *know* about a man. I wanted to just *know* about the apartment.

"I don't know," I said to Maureen again and again.

"Well, I know they probably have a bid," she said sometimes, trying to force me to action. Or, "A place like this isn't going to be on the market forever."

Things did move quickly, though. The studio on West 18th with the dressing alcove, for example, went quick and for twenty thousand more than the asking price. I didn't like it because it had no closets. But the duplex on Grove Street that was cool looking, but not practical at all, stayed on the market and even went down twenty-five thousand. I worried that it didn't have enough light with the bedroom in the basement. I felt like Goldilocks.

I didn't think I knew what I was looking for, but Maureen was confident that she did. She would say things like "you are adverse to basement apartments," "you prefer places that have fireplaces or at least decorative fireplaces," and my favorite, "for you a kitchen need only be functional, you're the type who likes to eat out." I wondered if that was another poke at my sexuality. I was amazed that someone was keeping track of what I wanted. It would be fantastic if I could have someone like Maureen for every aspect of my life, someone whose job it was to listen to what I said, tabulate it, and then clue me in to what I wanted. I said as much to Maureen as we huddled together in a tiny apartment after opening a dusty Murphy bed.

"Well, I guess that would be a therapist, dear," Maureen said.

It was one of those times when I wondered if I seemed like as much of a freak to the outside world as I felt to myself. Then she sneezed and it echoed through the small room, and we laughed and went to our next apartment.

Miraculously, I was told by a mortgage broker that I would be approved for a mortgage of $250K. Of course if I went that high I would have to pay PMI, which was something you had to do when you couldn't afford twenty percent, although I had seen the rare place that would let you finance for only fifteen percent.

The whole thing seemed over my head at times, but I enjoyed having this project. I liked announcing to Jamie that I was in the real estate game. She was busy at work and we barely had time to talk, but I could still sometimes make her laugh. They hadn't "succeeded" yet. Her voice had started sounding frayed around the edges.

As I saw what seemed like every one-bedroom and studio in the city, the summer slipped by me. It was the end of July, seven weeks since I'd last seen Diane, and my brows were a mess. I tolerated her scolding and then updated her on my outings with Maureen. She squeaked when I told her about the triplets. She had just pressed the wax down. I felt it start to harden. I hoped she was going to pay attention.

"So, she *did* do the in vitro. Wow! That's big."

"Yeah," I said. I felt my hand gesturing up toward my eyebrow to remind her, but Diane seemed really shocked about the turn Maureen's pregnancy had taken.

"Can you imagine—you want one, you get three? And what do you do?"

Her accent was so strong I almost heard the landfill.

"Mmm," I said. It was definitely time to pull off the strip.

"Oh," she said, looking down at me.

It was not something I wanted to hear from my aesthetician. She ripped the strip off and it hurt more than ever.

"Sorry," she said.

"No problem," I lied, feeling my eyebrow start to shake a little.

Minutes that felt like hours later, when I got out of Diane's, I pulled out my compact. Sure enough, the skin under one of my brows was bright red. What was it about pregnancy and babies and all that shit that made grown women lose track of what they were doing? I just didn't get it.

As if her ears were ringing, Jamie's work number came up on my cell phone.

"Hey," I said.

"Hey. What are you doing?"

"I just got my eyebrows done. Diane ripped the shit out of them."

"Yuck, but it's cool that you are up here. I was calling to see if you wanted to meet me in Central Park. Raj worked all night last night and has the day off. He's playing soccer in the park and I want to get the hell out of here and enjoy a summer night for once. Want to go watch them with me?"

"Sure," I said. And then I hesitated. "You're not— This isn't going to be a setup, is it? Is there going to be some surprise guy that you happen to think I should hook up with?"

"You know, it isn't easy trying to set people up with some-one so positive."

"So stop trying, I'm perfectly content being on my own." It was the truth, sort of. "Besides, don't you find my cynicism and negativity refreshing?"

"Unfortunately, I do," Jamie said. "It just doesn't make it easy to get you matched."

"Like I said, stop trying. This isn't one of Raj's dating shows. Who else is going to be there?"

"I don't know, honest. It's a pickup game. I know two of his associate producers are going to be there. One is gay. One is engaged, so calm down." Jamie started talking to me in a mat-ter-of-fact tone that betrayed her annoyance. "I just wanted to hang out with you. No setups, just me and some food. I've learned my lesson, believe me."

The last time Jamie had tried to set me up with someone was a disaster. I had gone over to her apartment expecting a normal dinner party and preparing to laugh at whatever the Olsen Twins said. But later that evening Jamie's colleague's brother, my prospective paramour, had decided it was funny to make loud grunting noises while he was in the bathroom just off Jamie's kitchen.

"Fine, I'll see you there."

"Don't do me any favors," she said, and hung up.

Would there come a time when I was too much for her?

A half hour later I was at the soccer field on the Great Lawn. I spotted Jamie sitting on the grass on an old blanket with an-other woman. She was clapping, and I followed her gaze to where Raj was playing with a bunch of guys.

"Hey," I said as I got to the blanket.

"Hello, Voul, this is Jackie Bynum, Troy's fiancée." She pointed to the field where Raj was doing some fancy footwork.

"Nice to meet you," I said, shaking her hand. "Voula."

I slipped off my sandals and sat on the blanket. I should have gotten a pedicure. My old nail polish was chipping.

"Let me see the damage," Jamie said, gesturing to my eyes. I took off my sunglasses and turned so she could see.

"It's not that bad," Jamie said. Her voice was level and sweet. I knew she was lying so I wouldn't feel bad.

"At least it isn't somewhere else," Jackie said slyly.

"Yeah, I know." I laughed, and tossed a plastic bag at Jamie. "Ice cream sandwiches. Jackie should eat Raj's before it melts."

"That's so sweet of you," Jackie said.

Sweet was a word that rarely described me. We ate our ice cream sandwiches as Jamie occasionally burst into applause for Raj.

"I have no idea how to follow this game," Jackie confessed.

"Americans aren't big on it," I said. "My dad and my uncles were crazy for soccer, so I grew up with it."

"Are you Indian too?" Jackie asked. I guess the *too* was because of Raj.

"No, Cypriot," I said. "It's an island in the Mediterranean."

"Oh, of course, that explains your Greek name." It was nice not to have to explain my origin.

"I figured we could order pizza when the guys are done," Jamie said. "Jeez, I guess we should have got some wine. I only brought Snapple. You want one, Voula?"

I took a bottle and turned back to the game. It reminded me of my dad. Evenings spent watching soccer games were usually good times in our house. We got to stay up really late. If my father's team won, he was in a terrific mood. If it didn't, my uncle was there to make sure that he stayed in line.

I watched Raj crash into one of his opponents. They toppled over each other and lay on the ground for a minute.

"Oh, *panayia mou,*" I yelled.

"Jesus," Jamie said, getting up.

"Wow," Jackie said, as if she hadn't really expected the game to get this intense.

Raj got up off the field. He waved to Jamie, who sighed and plopped back onto the blanket. Then, he offered his hand to the opponent. When the guy stood up, he looked really familiar. He was broad with medium-brown hair and tan skin.

"Who is that?" I asked Jamie.

"I don't know," Jamie said. "I think he was playing when they got here."

"He's cute," Jackie said. "I love those shoulders."

I tried to place the guy's face as he limped off the field and closer to where we were sitting. He was wearing those baggy Umbro shorts and a faded red T-shirt. He stood in front of us and contorted his leg, pulling the shorts up to expose the muscle that he rubbed. He seemed oblivious to us and in a lot of pain.

"Wow!" Jackie said, still enjoying the view. Then she yelled to the guy. "Are you all right? I'm a nurse."

I thought Jamie had said she was engaged. I couldn't believe she was trying to pick up a guy with her fiancé so close by. I looked at Jamie, but she nodded and smiled, so I knew that Jackie actually was a nurse.

"I'm fine," the guy said, looking up. "Just an old injury."

"Well, let us know if we can help," Jackie said. Nurse or no nurse, she was definitely flirting.

"I will. Thanks, ladies," he flirted back. He smiled at us, and when he met my eye he said, "Hey."

"Hello," I said, still confused, because he recognized me, too.

"How's it going?"

I could feel Jamie and Jackie staring at me.

"Fine." I think my voice betrayed my confusion.

He smiled and winked a light brown eye at me. "335 West 32nd Street."

It was my address! Next to me, Jamie gasped. I squinted, trying to figure it out.

"I think I put out a fire at your house."

"Oh," I said, finally remembering.

Next to me, Jackie mumbled, "I'll say."

I felt myself blushing and wished I had put my sunglasses back on. "I remember you, too. You're—"

"Paul Torrisi."

I had had elaborate fantasies about this fireman, but I would never have recognized him without his gear on and his face covered in soot.

"Right," I said. "Thank you, again. You saved us."

"Hardly," he said.

He was still rubbing his thigh, and now I was compelled to look at it.

"You were already out of it. Is your place okay, now? What was that, a couple of months ago?" he asked.

"Yeah, about three. It took a while for the smell to go away."

"Have you cooked anything yet?" he asked.

It stumped me. I'm sure a lot of people had the same fears I did, but I hadn't told anyone about it and it was weird to have a stranger know something so personal.

"Not really," I said.

"Well, you will," he said.

I remembered how he had squeezed my shoulder the night of the fire and how it had felt so calming.

He took a sharp breath in and squeezed his thigh.

"Um, we're going to order some pizza, actually," Jamie said. "Why don't you sit on the blanket and have some with us."

"You should definitely take some weight off that leg," Jackie, the expert, said.

It was like they were working in tandem to help me keep talking to him. I would have hemmed and hawed and tried to think of a way to keep him there, but for them it was easy to talk to men.

Paul looked at me and smiled. "Seems like a good idea. I rarely get such enticing invitations."

The other women slid over on the blanket and Jamie grabbed my shoulders and positioned my stunned body to give Paul room on the blanket, but not too much.

"Thanks," he said, sitting down.

The hurt thigh was pressed right up against my leg, and unfortunately he had the perfect vantage point of my reddened eye area. He smiled at me. Jamie immediately called for pizza and gave them directions to get to us in the park.

"I have to return a call," Jackie said, getting up off the blanket (to make an imaginary call?).

With Jamie occupied and Jackie gone, Paul could only talk

to me. He kept rubbing his leg, and I wanted to ask him if he needed help. Instead I just asked if he was okay.

"Yeah," he said. "I'm just being a baby. By the way, what's your name?"

"Oh, right," I said, laughing. "Voula."

"Voula. That's beautiful." He squinted, trying to read me. "Italian?"

"No," I said, reaching up to scratch (cover) my yucky eye. "I'm Greek."

"Ah, Greece," he said. "That's somewhere I'd like to go. The closest I've been is Cyprus."

"Oh," I said, feeling silly for not just coming clean. "That's actually where my family is from. Why were you there?"

"I have cousins who live in Italy. They vacation there. One time I went with them. You ever been?"

"Yeah, almost every other year when I was growing up. My father lives there now."

"Let me guess—you grew up in Astoria?"

"You're right."

"An Astoria girl," he said, smiling.

Are there rumors about us? Because I'm sure I didn't live up to any of them.

He looked at me again. "Hey, what happened to your eye?"

"I told you not to use that eye shadow," Jamie said, popping back into the conversation. She winked at me and handed me my sunglasses, which had been on the blanket. "You know how allergic you can be— Pizza is on the way."

"Just in time," Paul said. "It looks like they're done."

The boys came barreling off the field. Paul stood up, putting his hand gently on my shoulder for balance. I wanted to reach up and hold on to it. With all the guys off the field, I doubted I would be able to talk to him much.

"Hey, man, sorry about that. You okay?" Raj asked.

"No problem," Paul said, shaking his hand in one of those silly macho ways. "I made a stupid move, you made a great play."

All of the guys, including Paul, started talking about the

game, and as I suspected, Paul got lost in the crowd. When the pizza delivery guy biked by us, Jamie and I ran and flagged him down. As we walked back with the boxes, she smiled at me.

"You are devilish," I said.

"Be a sport, Voul, and play this right. I can tell you like him. And I didn't see a wedding ring." She looked back at the guys and Jackie and shouted, "Pizza's on."

After the group had finished stuffing our faces, people started meandering off. It was a perfect summer night and it made me realize how I had been too busy running around and being annoyed by the heat to enjoy it. A few times Paul caught my eye and winked. I smiled back without opening my mouth, because it was usually full of sauce and cheese. He was hanging out, but not eating. Maybe he had someone at home cooking for him.

Eventually, I saw him pick up what looked like a giant gym bag. It was time for him to leave. He came over to say goodbye.

"Well, I'm glad you're doing so well, except for the eye thing," he said, gesturing to my sunglasses.

"Yeah, well thanks, you know, for everything you all did." I actually did go to college and have been known to complete sentences without saying "you all."

"I bet you'll be cooking in no time."

"Oh, she's a great cook," Jamie blurted.

She seemed to cherish these moments of ambush. I can boil water, but it isn't like I'm a secret chef or anything.

"You should eat some of her food sometime," she said.

"Maybe she'll invite me over sometime," Paul said, smiling.

"Well, you know where I live." I managed to follow this with what I felt was a coy smile. "Take care."

"You too," he said.

I watched him walk away until Jackie and Troy said goodbye. Jackie wished me luck with Paul, like there was even a chance we would meet again. I smiled in attempt to be the good sport Jamie asked me to be.

When the group had thinned, Jamie and Raj came up to me and asked if I was ready to go home.

"Maybe we should walk," Jamie said.

"Yeah, that would be nice," I agreed.

Raj didn't want to. "Do you really think it's a good idea?" he asked Jamie.

"Why not," I said. "It's such a good night."

"Raj is being a baby because his feet hurt," Jamie said quickly, kissing him. "We'll get the subway."

On the way to the subway, Jamie congratulated Raj on bumping into Paul and called him my new boyfriend.

"As usual, your wife is getting way ahead of herself."

"You should have seen her, babe. Not since Trigonometry have I seen Voula so flustered."

"It does happen," I said, shaking my head. "Though it might have been the heat."

"He seems like a nice guy," Raj said when we were on the C. "I think he's a firefighter."

"Der, Raj. He put out her fire."

Both Jamie and I giggled, but I continued to shake my head at her.

"Speaking of fires, did you tell her what we've got cooking?" Raj said. He looked at Jamie. She smiled and put her arm through his.

Then I got it: she was going to ambush me again.

"You tell her, babe, I think I might cry."

"Well," Raj started as both he and Jamie beamed at me. "We're pregnant."

The Family Way

10

I had an idea that being in her apartment might add to the tension between my mother and me, so I invited her to dinner in a restaurant.

I should back up, because I make it seem as though I casually chose a restaurant and called her up and that was that, but relations with my mother, like the politics of the country we came from, were never as simple as they could have been.

I knew that the idea of us going to a restaurant would be met with immediate suspicion. My mother had a strange paranoia about paying for things. She was always convinced that people were trying to take advantage of her. I chalk this up to her being an immigrant and for a long time not being sure what people were saying, although Georgia's parents were nothing like this.

I couldn't choose any food too exotic, because my mother wouldn't have liked it and probably would have made some racist comment about the country where it originated. I definitely couldn't have picked a Greek place, because my mother would have taken offense at this and accused me of not liking her cooking. Also, the place had to be convenient, close enough not to put her out, but not so close that she could suggest we go upstairs to her apartment instead. It was just dinner, but I put more thought into it than into most of my pitch letters to magazine editors.

I picked an Italian place in Astoria. I asked my mother to meet me there, because it was right near the train station and close enough to her job for me not to have to escort her from home.

I got there first and stood in the entrance waiting for her to come in. The place was empty when I arrived, but as I stood there, more and more couples started coming in. I began to fear it was a date place. But it was too late to change location. My mother approached the door, walking in her defiant way, as if she had something important to tell anyone who would listen.

"Hey, Mom," I said when she got in. I kissed her on the cheek and watched her eyes dart around the dimly lit dining room.

She spoke to me in Greek. "How are we going to be able to see what they're feeding us?"

"It's very highly recommended, Mom," I answered. "Zagat gave it a good score."

She sneered at me. I knew that she had no idea what Zagat was. The red guide made no difference in her world. I ignored her and told the maître d' that my party was ready. He glanced over his shoulder, squinted and then looked back down at his book. My heart began to beat faster. I hoped there wouldn't be a problem. When I'd called I was told they didn't take reservations. If we had to wait for long, my mother would get cranky. It was such a small, stupid thing, but if we had to leave I would feel like a failure.

"Just a few minutes," he said.

I stood at the desk, not wanting to turn and see my mother's expression. The man said something in Italian and I wished that somehow Armando would emerge from the kitchen and get us seated. (But then, of course, I would have to explain how I knew him and that would cause all kinds of other grief.)

"Right this way, miss," the man said.

I couldn't believe our luck. I turned to my mother, beaming. She looked as if something had just dripped on her head.

"Right this way, Mom," I said.

"So I heard," she said.

It wasn't a mood. If someone was constantly in the same awful state, it was a personality disorder. But I was going to persevere.

We sat down and I took both the menus while my mother pulled off her jacket. The maître d' asked her if she would like to check it and she looked at me for translation. Though she spoke and understood English almost as well as Greek, she was rarely in a situation to have her coat checked. Like Zagat, it was foreign to her. The idea of losing sight of one of her belongings would have distressed her.

"We're fine, thank you," I said.

"Ti eipe?" she asked me.

"He just wanted to know what we wanted to drink," I said. I could have used a nice stiff drink, but it was out of the question. "How about some wine?"

"The wine is too expensive here."

She hadn't opened the menu, and I was certain that she had never been here. I swallowed.

"Well, I'm going to get a glass." I held my menu up in front of me so as not to see her expression.

I ordered for both of us. I got orecchiette con rapini, homemade pasta with sausage and broccoli rabe. She chose a chicken breast with lemon and capers. She pushed most of the capers off when it arrived. I decided not to ask her how it was. I tasted mine and told her it was delicious, and decided to order a second glass of wine.

I was worried about telling my mother that I was thinking of buying a place. For almost three months I had been searching for apartments, and though I stayed up nights fretting about her reaction, I thought no matter how scary it was, I should bite the bullet. My mother was going to have to learn about it sooner or later. I would need to get access to my bonds. Ever since Jamie had told me she (or excuse me, she *and Raj,* who seemed to suddenly share a uterus) was pregnant, I had felt as though I needed to make a real change, not just speculate or research an article. It didn't hurt that the editor of *Financial Woman* gave me a six-month stint, which meant a little secure money coming in.

As we ate, I told my mother about some of the places I had seen, specifically the ones that had doormen. I figured I would appeal to her sense of security. I didn't tell her my price range.

"Apartments in the city are too expensive," she said matter of factly, between chews of her chicken, "but real estate is a good investment."

I looked at my mother. Was it possible she was going to approve of something I was doing? I had planned out many arguments to show that I was making the right decision, but I'd never figured on her going for it. I didn't know how *not* to defend myself.

The waiter cleared our plates and listed the desserts. I ordered a cappuccino, and when he brought it I thanked him.

"You really like this stuff, don't you. You like having people serve you."

I didn't understand how two sentences about an insipid transaction with a waiter could make me feel like shit. How did my mother have such power over my feelings? Just as I readied for a particular battle with her, she abandoned that road and went for the jugular about something I hadn't prepared for. She was the queen of taking me by surprise.

"Jamie's pregnant," I said, to distract myself from wanting to cry.

"Na zisoun," my mother said, pleased for Jamie and wishing her and the baby long life.

I nodded. I had prepared for that, and for my mother to say something about my single, barren status. This time she didn't disappoint.

"It must be nice for her mother to be a grandmother. That we all could be so lucky."

"But you already are that lucky mom," I said before I could stop myself.

She looked up at me, and for a minute I think she thought I might be knocked up—she had put Helen so far out of her mind. Then she realized. She looked down at her napkin and folded it into a perfect square. My mother touched fabric in a way that made me envious. She put so much care into the designs she stitched, but her children…we never received such attention.

My cappuccino was too hot; I wished I could drink it quickly to get us the hell out of there, but no matter how hard I blew it didn't cool. I sipped about half and signaled for the check.

My mother didn't say a word as I paid. Of course I had to walk her home. We were one whole subway stop away from where she lived, but I had to walk her. Even if she wasn't going to talk to me, even if every step was misery, I couldn't let her go alone. She didn't even turn to let me kiss her at the door. She just walked up the stairs and away.

On the subway platform I checked my messages. There was one from Maureen. A place I had liked with a doorman and a decorative fireplace had had a bid put on it. It was a studio, but it had a decent-size kitchen and bathroom and the ceilings were high enough that I wouldn't feel like I was living in a closed box.

Maureen had walked me through this scenario before. If you put a bid on a place, the sellers—the anonymous entities that they were—would have forty-eight hours to accept your bid or make a counter offer. If they accepted your bid, the rest of the agents could offer it up to clients and then they could try to outbid without knowing how much you bid, or maybe you couldn't know how much they bid and then either you had another chance or you didn't. I wasn't exactly sure. Now there was an accepted bid. I had a day to move if I wanted to try to outbid the nameless bidder.

My next message was from Jamie. She sounded down. She had taken the day off work, and asked me to call her whenever I got a chance. I knew production on Raj's show was really picking up and he was probably working late. Since it was only nine, I decided to call her back.

As soon as they told me "they" were pregnant, I went out and bought a pregnancy book. I wanted to read about what Jamie was going through. I wanted to be there to support her. I quizzed her about whether or not she was dizzy (nope), her breasts were sore (only getting bigger), or if she was sensitive to odors (big time!), because my book said these were all the things that happened right away.

I had this odd fear I couldn't shake, like if I didn't do what she wanted and embrace the whole thing, she would lose the baby because of me. She was only a couple of months pregnant; the whole situation was so delicate. If she had been showing, I wouldn't have been so worried, but the baby was this intangible bean that no one could see. She had told me she'd heard the heartbeat, but I was superstitious about referring to it too much—in case something happened to it.

"Hello." She sounded sleepy.

"Hey," I said. "It's me. Are you asleep?"

"No, I was just resting, watching a little TV. I can't really fall asleep. Where are you?"

"Ditmars."

"Another night in the war zone with your mother?"

"No, we actually ventured out to a restaurant." I would allow only Jamie to call my mother's apartment the war zone. And fortunately Jamie was the only person ever to have seen it.

"How did that go?"

I sighed. Did I bother getting into the whole story? What was the point? It was just more of the same. "The usual. How come you stayed home from work?"

"My stomach was feeling queasy when I took Sparky out for a walk. We went to the dog run and then on the way back in the middle of the street, in front of everyone going to work, I puked. I tried to get to a trash can in time, but they were all full."

"Ugh," I groaned.

"Yeah, and some of it spilled on the sidewalk and Sparky tried to eat it."

"That's disgusting." I felt myself starting to gag. "And I guess…sweet in a way. Have you eaten anything since?"

"When the dog walker came at lunch, she brought me some soup." She sounded pitiful.

The one thing about her being pregnant was that I felt like she needed me as some kind of crutch to remind her of what it was like *not* to be pregnant.

"Oh, Jamie, the train's coming. I'll call you when I get back to Manhattan."

On the subway, I wondered why I hadn't bothered to push my mother about Helen. I had just accepted it. Bringing it up had been daring of me, but then I backed off.

Georgia and I had been playing phone tag since she told me about Helen. Well, that wasn't really true. She had called me quite a few times after the engagement dinner, but I kept "forgetting" to call her back. We had seen each other at a family barbecue, but my mom was there too, so I hadn't pursued it.

Like my mother, I was scared to go there.

Thirty-five minutes later, I called Jamie from my land line. She told me that she was puking at least three times a day and she hadn't told anyone at work yet, so she had to make all these weird runs down the hall to the bathroom.

"They're going to suspect me of being a bulimic. Lord knows, I wouldn't be the first in that company."

"Is there anything you're craving?"

"Tuna. I would like to wrap myself up in tuna. And Reuben sandwiches."

"That's pretty intense. Aren't you supposed to want pickles and ice cream?"

"Oh, I don't know," Jamie cried. "Am I?"

"I don't know." I laughed, attempting to defuse the situation. I worried that Jamie was going to start taking this stuff as seriously as she had the "trying." I think she had strange fears of not doing it—whatever "it" was—right.

"I'm sure there isn't any right craving," I said. "What else is wrong?"

"My face is breaking out. We just came out with this new super-duper cover-up and not even that can cover it up. All the young interns are smirking at me in the hallways. I'm losing my edge."

"I think your hormones are just getting a little crazy."

"You're right," she said. Then she started to cry. First my mother's moods, now this. I was not equipped to deal with it all.

She stopped on her own but continued to sniffle.

"Do you feel better now?" I asked.

"Yes, I should get some sleep. Are you sure everything went okay with your mom?"

"Define 'okay.' "

"Voula, don't pull that with me."

If *that* was trying not to complain about everything that was wrong with my stupid family, I didn't know if I could not do *that*.

"It was fine," I lied. She was a pregnant woman who needed sleep.

"Okay," she said.

If she hadn't been feeling sick she might have pressed me, but I doubt I would have told her, even if I could have named it, even if I had wanted to.

We hung up and I heard a knock at my door.

Kelly peeked her head in. "You going to bed?"

"Not yet. It's only ten. *I'm* not pregnant."

She narrowed her eyes, confused.

"Never mind. What are you up to? Did you just get home from work?"

"Yeah, well, yeah. I had a big scene with Mr. Audio after work. It's my own fault. I shouldn't continue to sleep with him, I know I shouldn't, so I'm not going to bitch. But I am going to pop open a gift set of Amaretto Di Saranno. Don't make that face. It's like the only thing in the house. Armando drank all the wine last night with his lady friend. I got this as a gift from one of my equipment rental houses." Kelly had clued me in to the interesting life of film making in the city. Because she freelanced, she was almost more connected than Raj. She seemed to know how to network. Or maybe it was the fact that her skirt stopped at the top of her thighs. If I had legs like that, people might want to network with me, too.

"I hear it's good. Want some?" she pressed.

I followed her into the kitchen and we sat on the stools at the counter. She held the gift glasses up for inspection; I gave her the thumbs-up. She added ice and poured. I clinked a glass against hers and sipped. It wasn't bad, sort of sweet. Both of us nodded approval and laughed.

I liked Kelly. She was easy—not in a sexual way. I wished I could make an impression the way she did. We had been spending a decent amount of time together, catching up when she got home or watching the occasional talk show together when I wasn't working or running to apartments. I hadn't told her or Armando that I was looking. That would have meant I was fully committed to moving out. I still wasn't a hundred percent sure that I was.

"So what did you do tonight?" she asked. "Tell me one of us got lucky."

"Hardly. I went out with my mother."

"Your mother live around here?"

"Astoria—where all the Greeks are."

She topped off my drink and poured herself another. "You guys close?"

I snorted. "No."

"So why did you go out to dinner?"

I can see how from the outside it would be the right question.

"She doesn't really have anyone."

"Your dad passed?"

"No, he's in Cyprus. He lives there. I don't know what the story is with their marriage—if there is a marriage."

"And you're an only child?"

"No, well, now I am." Maybe this was why I didn't like meeting new people. Maybe I just didn't want to have to share my family history with anyone. "My oldest sister died when she was nineteen, and my other sister, she sort of ran away."

"Wow," Kelly said, nodding.

The few times I had said this to someone I had seen that look. The pity look. I got it from all my teachers; from kids at school who otherwise would have teased me for being too smart; and the few times that it came up when I worked at the nonprofit. Only two people hadn't given me that look: Jamie had hugged me when I told her and not asked any more questions, and Warren Tucker had kissed me on the jetty in Block Island.

"How did she die?" Kelly asked.

I wasn't expecting it, but it was a fair question. Of course she backed it up.

"I mean, we don't have to talk about this."

"She, uh, got into a moped crash in Cyprus. She wasn't wearing a helmet."

"She was driving."

"No, her fiancé was. He died, too. He was Cypriot." Now that I had started, I was going to tell the whole story. "She was supposed to be home, but she called my parents and asked them to let her stay. They only let her because they liked him. He was from a good family, that's all that mattered to them."

"She must have liked him too."

I nodded. She must have. I hadn't really thought about it. I'd never met him. She saw him on the sly for two years when we were in Cyprus before she told my parents. An image of my sister flashed through my mind. She was getting up from a table, her long red-streaked hair a curtain on one side of her face. She had spent hours on her hair; she hated when it got messed up. My mother had clucked disapprovingly at the amount of time Cristina spent on her hair. It was her only vanity.

"She was really pretty," I said.

"I can imagine," Kelly said, nodding.

I looked at her curiously.

"Well, *you* are."

"Come on!"

"I'm serious."

"This old thang," I said, teasing. I poured myself another drink.

"Really. When was the last time you had a boyfriend?"

"Greek girls don't date."

"Why?"

"We just get married."

"So, wait." Her eyebrows rose. Her eyes shot down to my crotch, then she caught herself and giggled.

"No, I'm not a virgin."

"What a scandal."

"Tell me about it. Not a virgin, but a spinster."

"Jeez," she said. "I guess we've all got our issues."

"What, do American mutts have problems too?" I was teasing, but her face got serious and I regretted being so flippant. "Sorry."

"No, it's fine."

"You don't get along with your parents either?"

"No, it isn't that. They were alcoholics. *Are* alcoholics. Sometimes we didn't even have food in the house. Boy, did they know how to go at each other. They got divorced and started their twelve steps. Now, it's like they just want to go out to dinner with me, together, and act like nothing was ever wrong."

"But you're still mad at them?"

"Yeah, but like, they don't or won't remember half of the things I do about the past. They have no idea what they were like, but I can't forget. I feel guilty because they mean well, they're trying to make a fresh start. You know, what am I supposed to do with all this shit?"

I shrugged. We were almost done with the Amaretto Di Saranno.

"Do you ever worry that you'll turn out like them?" I wondered if I was treading on thin ice, but Kelly wasn't like me. She was open.

"No, I'm so used to being in control of things, you know, being the responsible one, for them. I've always known my limits. You can't be afraid. Although, I guess I wonder if I'll ever have kids. I just don't see why people do it."

I thought of Jamie. For the first time in my life, I felt like I had more in common with someone other than her. It was unexpected. I hadn't really let myself think about having kids—I had just thought I was too far from it. But the truth was, I didn't know if I wanted kids either. There. I had admitted it to myself.

"I should get to bed," Kelly said. "I have a six a.m. call tomorrow."

I looked at the clock. It was almost midnight. I said goodnight, poured myself the rest of the amaretto and took the phone into my room. I planned to call Maureen Soltero and offer $220K on the studio. They were asking $225, but with any luck the prospective bidders had gone way low. She told me I could call her anytime on her cell, but she seemed like the type of person who answered at all hours. And after all of the amaretto, I wasn't sure I should be talking to anyone. I decided to call her office and leave a message so she would get it in the morning.

I started to dial her number. Then I stopped. Maybe I shouldn't make this kind of decision in my current state. In fact, maybe the place wasn't all that great after all. A lot of people thought that doormen really did nothing but add thousands of dollars to the asking price. The same could be said for decorative fireplaces. I wasn't even sure what the building sublet policy was. I had never thought about things like this until Maureen told me that a liberal policy was good for reselling. Also, how much of the building was owner occupied? This didn't matter to me, but apparently it mattered to banks. I should have answers to these questions before I made a move, right?

I knew I was making excuses. The truth was that most of me wanted to get my own place, but a tiny tiny part of me feared that if I didn't have people around me—if I didn't have roommates—I would turn into a recluse. I would become a cat lady. I would be dead for three days before anyone bothered to look for me. It was silly, but I had realized while talking to Kelly that I wasn't as introverted as I liked to pretend.

I enjoyed talking to people and listening to their stories; that's half the reason I enjoyed my job so much. Finding out how other people lived, what it would be like to walk in their shoes, was exciting.

I changed into my pajamas and finished my drink before washing up for bed. Kelly was coming out of the bathroom as I went in.

"Sleep tight," she said as she passed me.

I wouldn't get that living on my own.

When I finally crawled into bed, the sweetness of the drink had added a sweetness to the world. I hadn't been sleeping well since the fire, but I knew the amaretto would put me right out. My body felt heavy and I couldn't wait to drift off to sleep…

Three hours later, I jolted up in bed. For a minute, I thought that there was an earthquake going on. Animals were yelping like they had been hurt. I heard thumps and I felt my bed shaking. My heart was racing as it had on the many occasions I had been startled out of bed when I was younger. Then I got my bearings and realized that the thumps were coming from Armando's room. His usual murmurs of "shh, shh, *bella, bella*" weren't working. He had himself a screamer. This was worse than the time I was certain he was using props.

I pulled the covers over my head, but kept feeling the wall hitting my headboard. I had always meant to move my bed, but had never gotten around to it. Plus I had arranged my room like this after doing an article on feng shui. Why should Armando's sex life interrupt my long life and prosperity?

"Oh, my God! Oh, my God! You're so big, you're so amazing. Oh, my God!"

Oh, *Panayia Mou,* this one needed to stop watching so much porn. It was ridiculous. (Though I had always wondered how big Armando really was.) It sounded like they were in the home stretch. "Oh, oh, oh, I looooove yooooooooooooooouuu!"

I sat back up in bed. Then I giggled. That was a sure sign of a one-timer. Armando couldn't stand for women to be too into him. I couldn't stand the wake-up calls. He had been considerate about bringing women home since the fire. I think he still felt really guilty, but old habits die hard, I guess.

I dialed the number to Maureen Soltero's office. What would she think when she got a message from three-thirty a.m.? I didn't care. I pressed the pound key on the phone when I heard her greeting. I didn't even have the patience to listen to the whole thing.

"Maureen, hi. It's Voula Pavlopoulos. I want to bid 220 on the place on West 15th. Talk to you tomorrow."

11

When I got up in the morning, I found a note slipped under my door. It was from Kelly. It said, "Amaretto not good for six a.m. calls. Neither are wailing shrieking banshee women. Hope you're sleeping peacefully."

I smiled. I had totally misjudged Kelly, but I had learned my lesson. Maybe we could still hang out after I moved. If I ever moved out. I was edgy about Maureen calling me. I wanted her to just call and tell me one way or the other if I had the place. I was dying to find out, but still not sure what I was hoping for.

I called Jamie as I brewed a pot of coffee. I was excited to tell her about the prospect. But when I asked her how she was doing, she launched into a lengthy monologue.

"Well, my skin is worse than ever. I had to come in to work today, because I am slammed with meetings, but I feel like shit."

"You're going to have to tell them soon. You're gonna start showing."

"I know," she said in a pensive way before rattling off all the ways she was miserable, interspersed with stories of how great it felt to know there was a baby growing inside her. I realized that all she was really thinking about was the baby. I doubted she could concentrate on anything else. Or maybe she had just gotten accustomed to me not having anything interesting to say about my life. It wasn't that she was being inconsiderate, it was that she didn't know any other way—I never had any news to report.

"This morning I was brushing my teeth," she continued, "and the next thing I knew I was gagging. I crouched down at the toilet and tried to puke, and then I realized my legs were wet. I was peeing and gagging at the same time."

"Gross," I said. How could anyone choose to do this to herself?

"Oh, I wanted to tell you. Last night Raj told me Warren Tucker did body shots with the contestant. He has a strong chance of winning."

Great, I thought. I still wasn't exactly sure what the premise of Raj's dating show was, because every time I asked him he rolled his eyes. He made a good living from working in television, but it seemed to shame him somehow.

"Have you watched the tape yet?"

"No," I said. I kept it in my underwear drawer, but I just couldn't bring myself to do it.

"You are a freak."

"Thanks," I said dryly.

"Hey, Voul, are you okay?"

Sure I was okay. *I* could keep all the fluids in my body.

"Yep!"

"Is this because of dinner with your mom?"

I heard her other line beeping. It was almost ten o'clock. I was certain she had a meeting coming. She seemed to have them on the hour.

"No. I'm fine."

She hesitated. "Okay, Voula, look I have to take this call. I'll call you later. *Watch the tape.*"

"Okay," I said as she hung up. "I bid on an apartment," I told the dead air of the phone line.

★ ★ ★

After a strong cup of coffee, I got started on my article about finding an apartment. The fictional me was a lot more sure of what she was looking for and inquisitive about all aspects of real estate. I wished I could climb into one of my pieces and live the life I presented to the diverse readers of the magazines I wrote for.

Some days I felt like a mysterious force was moving my hands over the keys of my laptop. It all went so smoothly. Nothing distracted me, not surfing the Net, not unopened Netflix envelopes, not even the growl of my stomach. Sometimes I thought it was Cristina helping me write. This was one of those days. When I looked up to answer the phone it was almost three p.m.

"Voula, it's Maureen Soltero."

My heart started racing. I felt like my life was about to take a drastic turn.

"Hello," I said.

"I'm sorry, dear. The sellers went with the original bidder."

"Why?" It was a dumb question.

"Well, I think they bid significantly higher. It's a bit of a seller's market, you know."

I guess she had been telling me that all along. And I had low-balled. I was crestfallen.

"We're just going to have to get out there and find you another apartment. I'm optimistic, aren't you?"

She asked me with such seriousness, I thought I might be agreeing to go steady.

"Yes."

"Fabulous, I have a wonderful loft studio a block from Union Square. I think you would love it. We can head over tonight if you want."

"You know, I think I need a couple of days to recuperate from the whole market."

"Oh, I know it hurts, doesn't it." This was probably the same voice she used with her triplets. "But, you know, like with everything else, you snooze, you lose."

"Yeah, but I have some work to do tonight. I'll call you tomorrow." Unfortunately, I couldn't scrap the whole thing. I had to get a place, I realized; otherwise the out-of-touch editor at *Financial Woman* wouldn't be too happy with me. I had sort of insinuated I was closer and more committed to buying a place than I actually was.

"Okay, have a good night." She sounded a little frustrated with me.

I lost significant steam after that call. I checked through my Netflix. I tried to keep Daniel Auteuil movies in constant rotation. I saw the same movies quite a few times, but it didn't matter. I loved every nuance and twitch of his large French nose. The one I had this time was *The Widow of Saint-Pierre.*

I planned to watch the whole thing, but first I went straight to my favorite part where he is about to get shot. He looks at Juliet Binoche and says, "They can't touch us. I love you." But in French, of course.

It brought tears to my eyes it was so real, so perfect. Warren Tucker had said some beautiful things too. Now, he was doing body shots off E-list celebrity bottom feeders. *He* was a bottom feeder. Jesus. Only Daniel could take my mind off everything. I started at the beginning and watched the whole sad, sordid tale.

The phone rang and I assumed it was Jamie. I answered without looking at caller ID.

"Hey," I said. "I can't believe they shot Daniel."

"Um, excuse me." A voice that wasn't Jamie's but still sounded familiar said, "I was looking for Voula Pavlopoulos."

She said the last name like a true Cypriot. This time my heart didn't start pounding, I just knew my life was going to change. "This is Voula."

I heard a sob and I knew who it was even before she said, "Voula, it's Helen."

I didn't know what to say.

"Are you still there?" she asked when she had stopped crying.

"Yes."

"Georgia gave me your number. I hope you don't mind me calling."

"No." I hesitated. "No, I don't."

"It's just that I think about you all the time. I miss you. I've been determined to call you for the past year. I kept losing my nerve."

I waited for her to continue. I wasn't mad at her, but this whole thing was just too surreal. My sister was no longer a part of my life. That was a given. I had shut that part of me out. Now, there was a woman, a stranger, having an emotional breakdown on the other end of the phone. I didn't know if I was equipped to handle this.

"I'm sorry," I said, trying to get my bearings. "This comes as kind of a surprise."

"I know, I know. I'm sorry to just spring myself on you after all this time."

"That's okay," I said.

"I just wanted you to know that I love you, honey."

It was too much, now. I had loved my sister, but telling someone I didn't know anymore how I felt was just too much for me. It was too daytime TV.

"Thanks," I said. She started to cry and I had to say something. "So, Georgia said you have kids."

"Yes," she sniffled.

It was a mind-fuck to hear her voice again, to think that I was actually on the phone with my sister.

"I have a boy named Spiro and a girl. Her name is Cristina."

"Oh," I said. That made me really sad. That made it real. We shared this. I shared memories of Cristina with this woman who was now a stranger. "How old?"

"Spiro is almost fifteen, I can't believe it. And Cristina is four."

"And your husband was okay with you giving them Greek names?"

She laughed for the first time. "Yeah, I even speak to them in Greek sometimes, just like—" She exhaled. "Just like us."

"Cool," I said.

"Andre and I would love for you to come over for dinner sometime and meet them. Or if you would rather just meet me sometime… Of course maybe you don't want to see me, but I would really like to see you."

"Sure," I said. But I wasn't going to commit to anything. "Can you give me your number?"

"You'll call, right?"

"Yes," I said. As I took down the number I knew I'd call, I just wasn't sure when.

"How is your mother?"

In Greek this would have been the right way to ask, but in English I wasn't sure if she was trying to dis *our* mother. I didn't blame her, but I felt like someone had to stick up for Mom. "She's okay, you know. She's herself."

I knew she wasn't going to ask about our dad. "Are you going to go to Georgia's wedding?" It was about a year away, but I needed to start preparing for it.

"That's something I hope we can talk about when we see each other," she said. "Of course, I would never want anything to upset Georgia on her day. If you want, she can even come to our meeting, I mean, if that makes you feel better."

"I'll let you know," I said. Did we need an arbiter? "So, I'll give you a call in a couple of days."

"Okay, I really hope you do. I love you, Voula."

"Okay," I said. "I'll talk to you soon."

After I hung up the phone it occurred to me that no one had ever told me they loved me. That's why it had sounded so strange. A complete stranger loved me. I wanted to get back into bed, lie down and never get up. It was after seven and I had this sneaking feeling that Jamie wasn't going to call. I could have just called her, but she had said she was going to phone. It was a stupid game, but I didn't want to be needy and I didn't just want to be a listening post.

I wasn't sure when Kelly would be home but I didn't want her to see me like this, so I took the phone into my room and lay on my bed.

I could feel the blue black buggies coming on. I had always had these moods—well, ever since Cristina died—where I needed to sit, just sit. Maybe it was wallowing. Maybe it was detrimental to my psyche, which is what Georgia had once said, but if I just took this time, I would eventually be able to get up and feel fine.

I turned on the stereo in my room and sat down on the carpet. I let myself think about Cristina and Helen and everything. I let myself sob. That was the best part of the blue black buggies. It sucked to be in them, but if you saved up, if you only let it happen every once in a while, you could let yourself have a really good cry.

Before I knew what the blue black buggies were, before I was in control, they were awful. I remember missing a week of high school because I wasn't able to get out of bed. My mother didn't ask me any questions. She could tolerate this so long as I didn't talk about why. In college, I missed a week of exams. My professors were cool. I told them about my sister even though I felt bad about using her as an excuse. They let me retake the exams if I promised to see a grief counselor. I said that I would go, but never did.

Now the whole thing wasn't bad. It was cathartic. And naming this mood, with a term I stole from Maura after I heard her refer to an upset stomach as the bad buggies, made me feel a little more in control. It would have been pretty miserable to anyone who saw me, but it made me feel a lot better. I had it down to a system. The crying was followed by a day in bed and then a day in front of the TV watching the daytime talk shows that my sister's call had reminded me of. The wonderful thing about Springer and Judge Judy was how much better they made you feel. I knew I was going to be okay as I cried, because I could see my way out of it. I could see ahead to a couple of days from now, when I would be watching Judge Judy calling someone stupid for getting breast implants.

When I finished the sobbing part (it lasted an hour and a half), I was exhausted. I hadn't really eaten anything, but I had no appetite. It was only ten, but I wanted bed. The phone rang. I didn't know if it would be a bad idea to talk to Jamie at this point, but I answered the phone just to make sure she was okay.

"Hello," I said.

"Hello, can I speak to Voula," a man's voice said.

"This is Voula," I replied, then I sniffled.

"Hey, you didn't sound like yourself. Are you sick?"

"Who is this?" I said, getting annoyed.

"Sorry, it's Paul."

"The fireman?" I heard him laugh. "Hi. How did you get this number?"

"Well, I know your address. I work for the city. It's on the report. It's a lot easier than you might think."

"I guess so." I felt so stuffed up from crying that I could hardly breathe.

"So you have a little summer cold?"

"Yeah, I guess so."

Boys didn't call me. Men—this was a man—didn't call me either. I put out a vibe, Jamie had told me. I said it was a Greek vibe and she said it was a mean vibe anytime I didn't want her to set me up.

"Well, listen, Ms. Voula, do you think maybe you might like to go out sometime—you know, grab a beer?"

"A beer?" Was I being asked out? Hadn't he caught my vibe?

"Yeah, or a coffee, or you know, whatever."

Whatever? What was whatever? Did Daniel Auteuil ask women out for whatevers? Did it sound better in French?

"Sure," I said before I meant to. I still had two days of bad buggies to contend with and I was accepting dates for whatevers. Who was I?

"Or maybe dinner. Would you like to go to dinner?"

"I certainly prefer that to whatever."

He laughed again. "You know, you're a very funny girl."

"Thanks. I'm a regular Joe Pesci."

He laughed again.

He got it, which I liked. He did about a sentence of *Good-fellas* and then stopped just in time. I had seen enough of Ja-

mie's ex-boyfriends recite whole movies to no one in particular to know how annoying it was. I appreciated that he showed
some restraint.

"Well, I'm working tonight, but how about tomorrow?"

Tomorrow was my all-day bed day. I had no intention of
messing with that.

"You know, I do feel kind of sick—I probably shouldn't."

"How about Thursday?"

Thursday was daytime TV day, but it seemed like I was forgetting something. Thursday resonated in my head for some
reason. I got up to look at my calendar. That's it: I had two
hundred words due on Monday for *NY BY NIGHT* on a new
restaurant. It was just a short piece, but I had to go to the place.
Usually I went on my own or took Jamie and Raj. Would it
be strange to be expensing our first date? Well, maybe it would
ensure that he didn't expect anything.

Who was I kidding? I *wanted* him to expect something.

"Actually, I have to go do a sort of review on a restaurant.
Maybe you want to come? It's a pretty straight-up American
place, I think. If you don't like that kind of food, we could go
somewhere else."

"That's so cool. You're a restaurant reviewer. I love to eat."

"No, I'm a freelance writer. I just got a gig to cover this place
for *NY BY NIGHT.*"

"We answer calls at the Prescott Nelson Building all the time.
What a cool job. You must be a real smarty-pants."

I could hear myself telling Jamie that Paul was too blue collar for me and see her rolling her eyes. He seemed like a nice
enough guy. It was too soon to judge.

"I just, you know, like to write. So, you want to go?"

"Sure, it sounds terrific. I'll pick you up."

"Why don't we just meet there?" I didn't really want him
to see my apartment, even though he already had. I gave him
the address.

"A modern woman," he said. "I like it. I'll meet you there."

After we said goodbye, I lay back in bed. This day had been
just too bizarre. I had had an orderly life, and all of a sudden

there were blasts from the past and hot new (perhaps too-blue-collar) strangers. I wasn't sure I could keep up with this new pace.

My day of rest didn't go as well as I had hoped it would. For one thing, it's hard to rest when you can't stop thinking about the thighs of a really hot man you are going on a date with the following day. The other reason was that I had Maureen Soltero up my butt.

"You need to get back in the game, my dear. I know it's heartbreaking, but this town is all about movement and if you don't want to lose out, you got to be in. I have to show the place near Union Square and I have an absolutely charming steal on Mulberry Street. I know you're not into that neighborhood, but it's totally in your price range. It just needs a little TLC."

I didn't even know why I'd answered the phone. The caller ID was on the living room phone and I was too lazy to check it. Maybe I had been hoping that Jamie would call so I could tell her my Paul news and have her convince me not to cancel, which I kind of thought I should. Maybe I'd answered the phone because I kept expecting Paul to cancel. But all five of the calls I got were from Maureen, imploring me to meet her the following day to scout some places. On the last call I was losing patience.

"I don't want to live that far downtown."

"Do you have a boyfriend, Voula?"

"What?" I asked, defensively. "What does that have to do with anything?"

"I just wanted to make an analogy about being picky with men and picky with apartments. It works on a lot of my clients in your situation."

"Are you using a line on me, Maureen? My 'situation'?" I asked. I didn't even want to know what she was getting at. "This isn't a pickup bar. I don't need analogies or whatever. I'll go see the stupid apartment."

"Terrific, I'll e-mail you the info tomorrow and see you at three." She hung up before I could change my mind.

★ ★ ★

That night, Kelly stood at my doorway with a brand-new haircut. She modeled it for me and I whistled.

"If you can't change your life, change your hair," she said.

"I should think about that."

She looked at my sweats and T-shirt. "Are you feeling okay? Have you left the apartment today?"

"Not exactly. It's a little ritual I like to do sometimes." As the ritual was being cut short by my date and my apartment search, I didn't bother to explain.

"It's too hot in here," Kelly whined. "Do you want to go check out a Latin band with me? They're playing at the Knitting Factory. I bet it will be cooler than this oven."

Two hours later, I was downtown in a sweaty standing-room-only club watching five guys in multicolored suits play music like I'd never heard music played before. In spite of the heat, Kelly danced like mad. I stood at the bar watching her shoulder blades move to the rhythm as guys tried to whisper lines in her ear. She was oblivious to them and just kept bouncing. I had never been much of a dancer. Jamie would be the one with the beer over her head, howling with energy whenever we went out. I was with a different friend, but still in the same lame position.

Kelly came over to the bar to get some water. I saw men turn and follow her with their eyes. Sure, she had a great body and was working her new haircut, but there was something else about her that made her desirable: she just didn't seem to care.

"What do you think?" she asked as she rubbed an ice cube over her neck.

"They're awesome."

"Do you want to dance?"

"I'm not much of a dancer."

"It's not a contest," she said. "C'mon." She took my hand and pulled me onto the floor with her.

I danced for a while. I tried not to think about what I looked like. I just listened to the music and moved along to it. Every once in a while I clapped and gave Kelly a reassuring smile. I felt like I was the little sister she was stuck with, but Kelly acted genuinely happy to have me out with her.

After two encores, the lights came up in the club. My ears were ringing, my feet hurt and I was dripping with sweat. It was the best time I'd had in forever. I didn't even feel drunk, even though Kelly had kept handing me beers throughout the performance.

"Another drink?" she asked. Her haircut accentuated her wicked smile.

"Okay, one more," I agreed.

We sat at the bar and chilled out for a while. She told me that the smoking ban was helping her quit, but that Mr. Audio was making her crave cigarettes all the time.

"But I'm all done with him. I know he doesn't like women with short hair, so this will keep him away."

I laughed. "Has he seen it yet?"

She shook her head.

"It looks pretty damn good. I think he might forget about his hair issues."

"Well, I'm going to be strong. A rock. I need a men break. I'm going to join your convent." She winked.

"Actually, I have a date tomorrow," I blurted. I was superstitious about the date. In the same way I worried I shouldn't talk too much about Jamie's baby, I worried I shouldn't even think about this date before it came to fruition.

Kelly pulled back from the table and gasped. "You!" She feigned horror. "What kind of Greek girl are you?"

"A shitty one," I said, smiling, and put my head in my hands. This had not been the typical blue black buggie cycle. I was having too much fun.

"Hello," a voice said.

We looked up to see two guys standing behind us.

"We noticed you ladies dancing and wondered if you wanted to go do some more dancing with us. We're going to Bongo. Care to join us?"

Guys always came up to me when I was out with Jamie, but they were usually after her. These two were looking at both of us. It was absurd. I didn't even know what to say. Kelly handled it.

"You know, thanks, but we're just sort of having a girls night."

"That's too bad," the one with the long hair said. He was cute, but about five years too old for the Ashton Kutcher look. "We have a feminine side."

"I bet you do," Kelly said, "but I don't want to waste your time. I'm done with men and she is in love."

I felt myself blushing, and the guys laughed. They wished us well in a sort of cynical way and were on their way to find other women to dance with.

"And you were worried about the hair," I said, smirking.

"And you were worried about being a spinster."

"Let me tell you something," I said, pointing in the direction of the door the men had left through. "That stuff never happens to me. It's just because you were here."

"C'mon, they were totally looking at you, too."

"Yeah, as a way to get to you."

She rolled her eyes.

"Trust me. I don't date. I don't know the lingo. It isn't me."

"There's nothing to know, Voula. It's just that you don't really put yourself in that situation. And you're probably better off. Trust me."

It was confidence. That was it. People responded to her confidence. The same way they did to Jamie's. No matter what happened to Kelly on the "dating scene," she didn't give up. She was resilient. She just stayed herself. I had spent so much time hiding behind my hang-ups that I didn't realize that none of it needed to be such a big deal.

When I met Maureen the next day in front of the building on Mulberry Street, she didn't look happy.

"The other Realtor is habitually late," she said as a greeting. "I should have told you three-thirty."

"It's okay," I said. But it wasn't really. I was sort of dressed up because of my date with Paul. I had to run a bunch of errands after seeing this apartment and the one in Union Square and I hadn't been sure I would have time to go home. It was a hot August day and I wished I could strip off the summer skirt and espadrilles with the slight heel. I could feel myself sweating through the modest button-down shirt I was wearing. I wanted to look good, but not like I'd given it too much thought, lest there be any confusion between me and a casual dater.

"You look very nice, Voula."

I smiled. "I have a date tonight."

"How nice. Don't be too picky."

It amazed me that she would take such liberties with me. She once questioned my biological clock when we looked at an apartment that was being sold because of a baby.

She added now, "You might want to think about a little lipstick."

She didn't know that one of my errands was to stop at Sephora for a new gloss. Lipstick wasn't really my thing, but a nice lip gloss looked good with my naturally tan skin.

"Maureen," the seller's Realtor called out as she came down the block. They "kissed" hello, but Maureen closed her eyes in pain as she pressed her cheek against that of the other Realtor, Sandy Firestein. We shook hands, and as we walked up the stairs Sandy talked up the place in a way that only real estate agents can.

"Now it's a real charmer," she said, meaning *too small.*

"The building is prewar." *Old and run-down.*

"It needs some TLC." *A complete shithole.*

"The board is very cool." *Most likely made up of degenerates who will bring the property value down and ruin your quality of life.*

"You can't beat the price for the area." *The neighborhood is the only plus.*

"It was just reduced." *No one else liked it.*

What she didn't say and what became abundantly clear as we walked up the stairs was that it was a six-floor walk-up. No one had told me this and apparently no one had told Maureen, who was short of breath by the third floor, but that wasn't going to stop her from trying to co-broker a deal with this other optimistic jackrabbit.

"You'll certainly get some exercise going up these stairs," Maureen said brightly.

"Yeah, that's one of the great things about it. And what you aren't paying for in an elevator really makes a difference," added Sandy.

I was doomed. There was no hope of finding an apartment *or* looking at all presentable on my date. The area behind my knees was sweating.

The apartment was a lot bigger than many of the places I had seen. It had a definite sizable bedroom attached to a good-size living room. This wasn't a junior one-bedroom; it was for real.

"You don't find space like this for the price."

What she didn't say was that the place was a mess. There was trash everywhere. The cabinets in the kitchen had patches where the wood showed beneath the paint. The bathroom was missing a sink.

"They're going to replace the sink before you move in," Sandy shouted. She had been narrating throughout the apartment as if we were looking at two separate places. "All it takes is some vision."

I knew that Maureen was probably cringing. She knew that I didn't have vision. She said it to me all the time—"have vision." My vision was that for the amount of money—hard-earned money—I was going to be spending, I wanted to be able to move into my apartment and not have to do any work on it.

The light in the bathroom flickered and went out. Great. Not even the electricity worked. I went back into the living room. It was dark in there, too. I tripped on a stack of papers that was inexplicably in the center of the room.

"The owner's out of the country. I'm sure he'll be taking some of this stuff with him."

I could see Sandy's white teeth in the darkness.

"I guess we had a short," Maureen said.

It seemed only she wanted to deal with the elephant in the room.

Sandy flicked the lights on and off. "Well, you can always come back if we can't get the lights to work. I'm sure they'll come on in a minute."

"I think I've seen it, thanks," I said. I was anticipating the long walk down the six flights of stairs. But when I opened the door, the lights were out in the hallway, too. Luckily, Maureen had a flashlight key chain that seemed to double as a whistle, and Mace.

We walked cautiously down all six flights as a few people in other apartments peered out into the hall. The lights were out in the entire building.

If only the blackout had stopped there.

12

I learned from a car radio on the street that the whole city and most of the Northeast was blacked out. A crowd was gathered around it looking for the same kind of information I was.

At first, Maureen and I thought it was just the apartment building; we said goodbye to Sandy at the subway stop and then realized that no trains were running. We feared the worst. Maureen immediately tried to call her nanny but couldn't get a signal on her cell phone.

I had about two hours at that point until I was supposed to meet Paul in the West Village, so I decided to walk up to Gramercy Park with Maureen to make sure she was going to be all right. We stopped at a street vendor on Broadway so I could buy some flip-flops; my feet were blistered from the trek up the stairs. The sandals didn't exactly go with my outfit, but I didn't think I would be able to get the buckles of the es-padrilles back on my feet without some serious body rebellion.

"It could be a terrorist attack," Maureen said tearfully.

I calculated that she had been pregnant during 9/11. She seemed on the verge of an anxiety attack.

"They said it isn't. I think they would be doing things differently." I didn't believe that it was. I didn't want to believe that it could be.

"Keep smiling, ladies," a guy said to us as he motioned a car to stop so we could cross.

This wasn't a policeman. I could tell by his backpack and the bike I saw resting on a non-working traffic light across the road that he was a messenger who was just doing this to help.

"We will," I said, smiling more broadly than I usually did for strangers. There were definitely police around and they were sort of grinning too. I wanted to believe there would be some anti-terrorist plan put into effect if it was an attack. Everyone around us appeared equally confused, but not particularly scared. It would have been so like me to be scared, but what I felt was, *I'm wide awake, it's still daylight, I just wanted to take in the scene.*

"Five dollars, five dollars. Cold water. Get your water. The fridge is broke!" People were selling water out of coolers. I was parched, but five dollars was out of my budget.

"It's worse than a one-bedroom in the village," I said to Maureen, who finally smiled.

We stopped at a bus stop, but the bus was packed so we kept walking. Throughout our trek, Maureen kept trying to get in touch with her nanny. She was petrified that something was going to happen to her triplets. She started listing outlandish worries.

"What if Leona just ran out to get something while they were napping? What if she locked herself out?"

"What if they fall in the hallway because there're no lights?"

"What if she can't find the flashlights? Did I even put batteries in them?"

I had never seen this side of Maureen. She always seemed so confident. Her fears were irrational, but I wondered if that was what happened when you had kids. I wondered how Jamie was handling all of this, and hoped she was okay, but I couldn't get in touch with her. My cell phone wasn't working either. I tried from a pay phone, but it seemed her side was out of service.

Finally, we got up to Maureen's place and I saw that she lived in one of those great buildings right on the park. Despite her irrational-mother fears, she managed to tell me that hers was a key apartment—she had one of the coveted keys to Gramercy Park. She had won the real estate game. Her doorman told us that the elevator was out of service, so I found myself once again walking up too many flights of stairs.

I guess I had expected Maureen to have an illegal alien working for her, but the woman who opened the door was a few years older than Maureen with a sweet smile and a bun. Her name was Leona, and she put her finger to her lips and pointed.

I peered into Maureen's giant, tastefully decorated living room at three tots asleep on the couch. Outside people were panicking and worrying, but in there all was right with the world.

Maureen's face lit up when she saw her three cherubs. She thanked Leona and asked how she was going to get home. Leona lived in Long Island and we had heard that the trains weren't running.

"My husband drove in today. He's been driving in since he got the operation," she said ominously.

Maureen nodded, but didn't take her eyes off her kids. Leona left for the long walk down the stairs.

"I've got some champagne in the fridge," Maureen said. "It's still cool. Why don't we drink it before it gets warm."

Maureen actually had an eat-in kitchen. I hadn't seen one of those in a while. All the appliances were stainless steel. It was the kind of kitchen you had if you were a serious chef, although I remembered that when I told Maureen how I'd been afraid to turn the oven on since the fire, she said she hated to cook.

Maureen poured champagne in crystal goblets. Then she found a cooler to fill with the slushy ice left in her freezer. She filled it with cartons of formula. I hadn't even thought about food spoiling. I wondered if the restaurant I was supposed to profile was open, how I was going to get in touch with Paul, or if he would have to work tonight.

"What time is your date?"

I looked at my watch. "In about an hour. Who knows if he'll even be there."

She winked at me. "I think he'll be there."

"Why, did you hire him to seduce me?" I joked, and Maureen laughed. "Is this some sort of romantic comedy?"

"You are quite a character."

This from a woman with triplets who downed her second goblet of Moët like water.

"I wish I was young again. Don't waste it with silly doubts."

"Okay," I said. I finished my champagne. "You know, you have a great apartment."

"Don't worry. We're going to find one for you." She kissed my forehead.

I decided that it was time for me to go.

I made my way down the dark stairwell, across town and down. The vibe was even more chill. They seemed happy. It was still sweltering, but the sun was lower in the sky. There were people hanging out talking and drinking beer from brown bags. I saw a group of businesswomen in the same multicolored sandals stopping to help an elderly couple.

I caught a look at myself in a store window and saw what a wreck I was. The heat had deflated my look, if I'd ever had one. I prayed that Paul was either standing me up or working. I was not going to make a good impression.

When I got to the restaurant it was closed. It was just six p.m.—a little early for when I liked to eat, but Paul had suggested we meet early. I wondered briefly if he had double-booked the evening and had another date at nine. You might think that's paranoid, but in her heyday Jamie used to do stuff like that all the time.

There was a gourmet food shop next door and they were handing out organic rice-cream sandwiches. They were never going to be able to keep them frozen. I took two (in case Paul was hungry if he showed up) and leaned against a mailbox. I figured I should give Paul a few minutes. I ate my faux dessert and shifted from foot to foot, watching people pass. Occasionally a fire truck went by and I wondered if Paul had been called in to work.

I tried to turn my cell on to see if he'd phoned, but it kept "searching" and never found a signal. As a shadow passed over me I felt a reprieve from the sun. I looked up to a fire truck and Paul clad in all his *Ghostbusters* gear, smiling.

"You're not going to have much luck with that," he said, climbing down.

"Hi," I said.

"I didn't really dress for dinner," he said.

"That's okay, the place is closed."

"Along with every other restaurant in the city."

"Well, here," I said, handing him a rice-cream bar as he got off the truck. "In case you're hungry."

"Thanks! How'd you know I'm lactose intolerant?" He smirked and took the bar.

I was aware of the entire truck full of firefighters watching us, sizing me up, and if I had known any of this was going to happen I would have planned on going home to change before dinner—really I would have.

"Looks like you have to cancel anyway."

"I'm beat," he said. "I was getting ready to leave and come meet you and this happened. We had a false alarm and luckily I convinced DiPaolo to make a detour."

For some reason I waved at DiPaolo, whom I assumed was driving. I don't know why I did and I immediately regretted it.

"So listen, I guess we can reschedule for when the lights go on."

"Yeah, I hope my deadline gets pushed back," I thought aloud. Did that make it seem as if I wasn't excited about our date?

"I'm sure you'll work it out."

He must have been boiling in that outfit, but he held my gaze for a moment.

"C'mon, Torrisi," one of the guys called.

"Well, I'm gonna catch hell for not getting a kiss, but seeing as we haven't even shared a meal I won't be presumptuous. Unless, of course, you want to count this bar as a meal." He smiled at my expression. "Didn't think so. Be careful getting home."

"I will."

"Make sure you have enough water, and here—take this." He handed me a flashlight that he had pulled from some hidden pocket in his space suit.

I took it as if it were a bouquet of roses.

"Thanks," I said.

"No problem."

Then he was back on the fire truck waving goodbye to me. I stood to finish my rice cream and imagined how much it would suck to be lactose intolerant. Maybe if I pitched that article I would be able to interview him and force him to hang out with me even after the rest of the fire squad had pointed out what a sweaty messy awkward girl I was.

I stopped at Jamie's on the way home, but she wasn't around, then I walked up 8th Avenue. As I got close to Penn Station, I noticed the crowd was thicker. I guess people were starting to accept that they were stuck in the city. All over the place groups were just sitting on the street fanning themselves with newspapers. There was really no choice.

As I walked down my block I saw Kelly and Armando out on the street with some of the other people from our building. Someone was pulling a hibachi out of the basement storage area. Kelly waved as I approached them.

"Just in time," she said, and handed me a bottle of lukewarm white wine I recognized as wine from the restaurant. "The apartment is an oven. We're going to have a cookout."

"What?" I asked.

"*Si, bella,* I make barbecue," Armando said. He smiled at me.

Since the fire, he had been shyer around me, and I still wasn't sure I trusted him with a flame, but it seemed like a perfect thing to do on such a hot day. My stroll around the city had worked up quite an appetite.

The fire lit the area around us as the sky became hazy. Armando had taken a plethora of meat from the freezer at the restaurant and he fed what seemed like the whole block T-bone steaks, free-range chicken and tender pieces of veal. I helped myself to some of everything and there was a steady supply of good wine.

"I understand the miracle of the loaves and the fishes," I said when Armando pulled another bottle of Pinot Grigio from his duffel bag. "I think Armando might be Jesus."

"I think Voula might be drunk." Kelly laughed, and she was drunk too. "Hey, didn't you have a date tonight?"

"It got postponed, but I got this," I said, pulling out my flash-light.

"A vibrator." Kelly giggled.

I flashed her the finger and shone the light in her eye.

"You should save that," our neighbor from across the hall said. He handed me a candle.

I hesitated for a second before taking it. We were safe out here, it seemed. Nothing was going to catch fire.

We all had candles as it got darker, and all the tenants from our building and the one next door were bonding. The guy upstairs who sounded like he had brick sneakers was actually a softspoken industrial artist. The couple across the hall were getting married in the fall, and the woman on the second floor had an adorable contraband beagle puppy.

It was just chill. Other people walked by with candles and stopped and talked to us. A woman in the building next door ran into someone she went to high school with. Kelly chatted with a passing businessman. It was unbelievably hot, but it didn't seem to matter. I was happy to be hanging out. The past two days had been full of surprises, and even though I was living a strange part of the surprise I felt at peace. For once, there wasn't some Italian groupie hanging all over Armando and we could talk about all kinds of things. He told us about the blackouts that had happened in his village when he was young. At midnight, Kelly read my palm by the light of her candle, putting on an accent that was a cross between British and Transylvanian.

"I see a man with dark hair coming to take you away," she said.

"You are so full of shit," I said.

"He is going to take you away in a big truck."

"I think you know a little too much about me to be objective, if you are in fact really psychic."

"He is so close to you," she said, and I could see in the dark that she was looking past me.

"Oh, is he going to put out my fire with his big hard hose?" I was getting into her silly jokes.

"Your future is certain," she said quietly, and pointed behind me.

I thought she was kidding. It was too much of a sitcom to think that Paul was behind me and that he had heard me. I turned quickly, almost colliding with him and dropping my candle.

"Whoa," he said, taking a step back. He had changed out of his uniform into a T-shirt and jeans. "I thought you were going to be more careful with fire. That was the point of the flashlight."

"I was saving it for later," I said. Realizing that sounded strange, I added, "You know, in case the lights don't come back on."

"They should be back sometime in the middle of the night. A lot of places have gotten the power back already."

"Oh, good." I was relieved that he hadn't heard what I'd said to Kelly.

"But you should still be careful with that."

I nodded.

"I would hate to have to get out my big hard hose."

I closed my eyes and took a breath. I could feel Kelly moving away from my back. When I opened my eyes, Paul was still there, smiling.

"It's okay," he said.

"Okay," I said.

"Anyway, I am heading over to a buddy's apartment. I don't feel like walking home over the Brooklyn Bridge just now."

"They won't give you a ride? I mean, you couldn't just commandeer a fire truck or something?"

"I guess if I really needed a ride I could get it, but it's fine this way. Anyway, I wanted to check and make sure you were okay, and reschedule our date."

Had I gotten the thumbs-up from the rest of the truck?

"You could hang out for a while if you want," I said. Never in my life have I been that forward with a guy; it must have been the moderate to super-expensive wine I had been downing.

"I would really like to, but I'm so tired I can barely see straight. I need to have my A game when we hang out. I need to match you wit for wit."

He had this funny New York (Brooklyn?) accent, but I really liked listening to him talk.

"How about next Thursday?" I asked.

"How about sooner?" he asked quickly. "Like Tuesday."

I felt my eyes close again and this time I smiled and nodded.

"Okay, cool, I'll call you and we'll work it out. Have a good night. And be careful around the hibachi. Don't give me another reason to come back."

"I will—be careful, that is," I said. "Take care."

He seemed about to walk away and then turned back and looked at me. "Oh, I wanted to tell you, you look really pretty in that light."

I started to thank him, but he bent down and kissed my cheek. It was a quick, soft kiss, but he kept his cheek against mine for a minute.

"See you next week," he said against my ear.

"Yep, until then," I said, and then, even though we hadn't really shared a meal (though I think I decided to count the rice-cream bars), I turned my head and kissed him on the mouth. New York City was dark. I kissed a guy. I guess anything could happen.

This time he walked away from me, all the way down the block past Armando and Kelly who were at that point just a couple of open mouths illuminated by their candles.

I pulled out my FDNY flashlight, turned it on and illuminated myself so they could see the giant grin that spread across my face.

The power came on the next morning at six a.m. I woke up with a hangover as the light in my room flashed on. I must have forgotten to turn it off when I left to meet Maureen the day before. I called my mother to make sure she was okay. She curtly told me that she was fine and managed to make me feel guilty about not being there.

If it's not one thing, it's your mother.

I went back to bed for a few hours and when I woke up I listened to the radio and discovered that parts of the city still didn't have power and certain subways were still stuck. There was no service and no one was expected to go to work.

I walked into the kitchen, where I found Kelly drinking a Gatorade and eating a PowerBar. I could tell by her face that she was hungover too.

"Thank God it's a snow day," she said.

I plopped onto the couch and dialed Jamie's number.

"Hey," she said when she answered. "You made it."

"Yeah, how about you and the bambino?"

"We're fine. We spent a few hours at the emergency room, but we're fine."

"Emergency room?" I exclaimed. "What happened?"

She told me the whole saga. She had gone over to a colleague's apartment and had hung out there, thinking the power would come back any minute. When she finally realized that it wasn't going to, she started walking home. It was too hot for her and she puked in the middle of the street. Some guy asked her if she was all right and she told him that she was pregnant. The good Samaritan started to panic, as his wife had had a miscarriage years ago, and the next thing Jamie knew she was in the back of an ambulance, light flashing, the whole shebang. Somewhere along the ride, Jamie started fearing the worst, too. She found herself crying as she lay on the gurney, feeling like she had seen this on an episode of *ER*.

"They took me to the emergency room. Luckily it was just St. Vincent's, right across the street from home, pretty much. I couldn't get in touch with Raj, so I had to stay there. They checked me, told me I was okay, and then wouldn't release me until someone came to get me."

"Wow!"

"The only place where the air-conditioning was on was the chapel. So I was in there, with all the crazies. One of them found out I was pregnant—I guess she overheard one of the nurses—and started screaming, 'Giant flabby pussy! Giant flabby pussy!'"

"What the hell does that mean? What was wrong with her?"

"Well, I don't know what the problem was, but the nurse came over and tried to reason with the woman. She said that the—" Jamie switched her tone to one of a scientist proving a theory "—vagina does, indeed, lose elasticity in pregnancy."

"Really?" I was genuinely intrigued. I would have to look that up in my book, even if it meant skipping ahead.

"Yeah."

"Then what?"

"Raj finally came to get me and we went home and we ate bags of pretzels and chips."

I wanted to tell Jamie some of the stuff that had been going on with me over the past few days and ask her why she had never called me back. I wasn't really sure where to begin, but before I could, Jamie started crying.

"It's okay, Jamie," I said, thinking the whole emergency room experience had frayed her nerves and that I should be grateful that she and the baby were okay. "You just needed to find out if you were okay. Everything's fine now. The lights are on."

"But, Voula," she cried. "What if I really do have a giant flabby vagina?"

13

I decided to meet Helen at a Thai restaurant on Smith Street. It was close to her apartment, but *not* her apartment. I wanted to be on quasi-neutral turf.

The night before we met, I had talked to Paul on the phone to plan our date and had told him I was going to be in Brooklyn. It had been three weeks since the blackout and we still hadn't been able to keep our date: he was working so much. But we talked almost every day. Every time we spoke we made plans to get together, but were always thwarted by his responsibilities. Luckily my piece about the restaurant had been postponed, so I could keep dangling that out as a potential date. I wondered if I was going to cross the line between being a potential girlfriend and being a girl he wanted to be friends with.

The thing was that we talked all the time. He called me at random when nothing was going on at the station. I liked talking to him. He had a unique perspective on things. He just sort of seemed to know things, about the city, about people— about everything. It was easy to talk to him. We talked for hours at a time.

Even though I was worried that we might be crossing a line

into friendship, I felt that the telephone was probably an ideal way for me to get to know someone. Over the phone, I could be myself and see if our senses of humor gelled without having to worry that my eyebrows were growing out or I had spinach in my teeth. I felt like we were really getting to know each other. It was like an old-fashioned courtship or something. The only way I think I could have communicated with someone better was via e-mail. After all, I'm a writer. Unfortunately, Paul didn't have a computer. He said he had an e-mail account, but rarely got to use it, because some of the other firemen hogged the computer at the firehouse.

I had thought he was so blue collar, but he had this amazing vocabulary. I knew that he hadn't gone to college and so I figured he read a lot. Every now and then he would mispronounce a word in a way that charmed me. He had obviously taught himself things. It was hard to reconcile this witty voice on the phone with the image of the buff fireman massaging his massive thigh.

When I told him the subway stop for my sibling rendezvous, he said that it was one stop away from his and that the restaurant I was going to was one of his favorites.

"I should scope it out tomorrow and catch you with the other guy."

"It's not another guy, it's—" the word felt foreign in my mouth "—my sister."

"Aha!" he exclaimed. "I've caught you. You said you only knew Park Slope in Brooklyn. I'm totally setting up a sting."

"Listen, Columbo, it's really my sister. I do only know Park Slope. I've never visited Smith Street before."

"You would have been here if your sister lived here," he said. "I'm no fool."

"You certainly aren't," I agreed. "But I *have* only been to Park Slope."

"She just moved?"

"No," I said. I wanted to leave it at that. This conversation was only confirming my belief that letting other people into your life made things complicated.

"One of those funny family things," he said, like he knew all too well.

"Yeah."

"Well, listen, if it goes sour, you have my number. I'll be home tomorrow night. I can meet you wherever."

I wondered if he could hear me smiling. It was true that I barely knew him, but something about him seemed protective and safe. In spite of myself, I liked it.

"Thanks" was all I could think to say.

The woman at the table by the window looked like my aunt Effie looked when I was a kid. It took me a moment to get my bearings and realize that it was my sister. She got up and hugged me. I returned the embrace stiffly. I had wondered if I was going to feel the love all the talk show reunions seemed to celebrate. Instead, I felt like I was meeting a new editor to go over a story. The editor was going to be interviewing me in a sense and just happened to look like a member of my family. I sat down and we stared at each other for a few seconds before either of us said anything.

"Did you find it okay?"

"Yep."

She looked past my shoulder, as if trying to find the next question written on the wall. "How is your job going?"

"Okay," I said. I probably should have elaborated, but it seemed like it should be my turn to ask a question. Then I realized I couldn't really remember what she did. I guessed. "So you teach, right?"

"Yes."

She asked where I had been for the blackout, and I told her. She told me a long rambling story of how she had to find her son during the blackout, and I had a feeling that she was trying desperately to dispel the weirdness and realizing as she went on that she was only making it worse.

When the waitress took our drink orders, we consulted our menus in great depth. I was certain I wanted the massaman curry with chicken as spicy as I could get it, with a side of jasmine rice instead of regular, and I was definitely going to try the curry puffs. I stared at the menu for a while, though, pretending I wasn't sure.

The waitress came back and Helen ordered first. She chose the exact same thing I did, right down to the really spicy curry.

"And for you?" the waitress said.

I hesitated, but then asked for the same thing. Helen smiled, looking pleased, as if she had to prove we were really related. I don't know why I was so determined to put some distance between us.

"Look, this is really strange."

"I know," she said, sounding almost desperate.

"I know we have a lot in common, but I just don't really know how to be. I've gotten used to not having a sister."

"You had two."

"I haven't forgotten that, believe me. I just don't like to think about it. I mean, you made a choice to leave."

"What else could I have done?"

"I don't know, listened to them, served out your time."

"For how long?" Her voice rose.

I looked over at the people at the next table. They were close enough to hear us.

She lowered her voice. "I was dying there. It's no way to live. They never would have let me go away to college. I mean, did they let you go away to college?"

"Well, I went to Columbia. That's not too shabby. I lived at home to save money."

She raised an eyebrow. She knew it was bullshit. "With your grades, you mean to tell me that you couldn't have gotten a scholarship to a school that was just as good, but not in New York. Georgia told me you only moved out a few years ago. It's time to cut the cord."

"It's easy for you to say."

"It's not easy, I just did it."

"Well, what do you want me to do?"

"Nothing—"

Our food came and we pulled back from the table as the

exact same plates were set before us. When the waitress told us to enjoy our meals, Helen picked up her napkin and folded it into a perfect square on her lap.

"I just wanted us to be in contact again. You're my sister. I love you. You saved my life," she said.

I didn't know what to say to that. I took a few bites of my curry puff. It was piping hot and I felt my mouth burning. I swallowed quickly and it burned all the way down. I knew what she was talking about—one of the many nights I had woken up in a cold sweat.

"I don't know if I did. I don't remember."

"Papa would have killed me."

"No." I shook my head. "No."

Helen reached across the table and took my hand. I glanced down at our identical skin tone, the exact same jagged fingernails. I let her hold my hand without squeezing back.

"We share so much," she said. "We share Cristina."

"Please don't talk about Cristina," I said in a voice I didn't recognize. I imagined what Georgia must have told her about my methods of denial. Georgia was always encouraging me to talk about Cristina, but I still couldn't. "It wasn't all bad, you know, living there."

"No, I know," she said. "My husband always tells me that his family is mine now. He says he and the kids are my family, that we are different than they were with us and Cristina."

I felt my nose fill and numb. I wanted to defend our family.

"He's right in a way," Helen continued. "Having kids changes things, but I wouldn't change all of it. It wasn't the normal happy American family, but it was mine. You know, it made me me. It wasn't all bad. I remember watching the soccer games, late into the night. You remember that?"

"Of course," I said. I remembered being allowed to stay up really late, while my uncle and father hooted over every play, plates of *keftedes* coming out of the oven, my father picking me up and twirling me in the air when our team got a goal.

She nodded as if she was proving something to me. Maybe she was.

"Can we just—" I shook my head and looked around the restaurant "—talk, you know, just about now."

"Okay," she said. And we did.

She told me about her kids and her job. She showed me pictures of her beautiful dark-eyed children that looked like they were old souls trapped in young bodies. I told her about my writing. She said she had read a few of my pieces. She even quoted things to me from my scathing review of *My Big Fat Greek Wedding*. I was flattered and kept laughing with her, realizing that she had my uncle's sense of humor, my aunt's face, and whether or not I wanted to accept it, a smile like Cristina's. I had a wonderful time with her, but sometimes it sort of hurt to look at her.

At the end of the night, she walked me to the subway.

"Now, you're sure you don't want to come over for some Italian pastry? They make it really good around here."

"Next time," I said.

She nodded like she wasn't really sure she believed that I meant it, but I think I did.

"Okay, next time. Safe home."

We hugged.

"Thanks," I said, and went down the steps to the subway that would take me back to Manhattan.

I was more excited the following night about meeting Paul at Esme's Eatery. He was standing outside the West Village restaurant with a bouquet of sunflowers, not the small ones that you see outside delis, but four big flowers that probably needed their own seat in the place.

He smiled as I came up to him. I liked how he was looking at me. I was looking at him, too. And he looked good! His hair was cut short, so his face seemed more square. His brown eyes appeared hazel because he was wearing a short-sleeved button-down shirt that was green and brown plaid, and brown cotton pants. I wondered about his thigh. I had to force myself to stop thinking about it.

He surprised me with a bear hug. He was so much bigger

than me. He had to be about six foot two, but he was just there, you know, present, solid.

He bent to kiss me on the cheek. I flushed, remembering how I had kissed him in front of my apartment. He handed me the flowers, ceremoniously.

"Why, thank you," I said.

"You look great," he said. It was matter-of-fact.

He was much more at ease than I was. I didn't know what to say. I had already thanked him for the flowers.

"Should we go in?" I asked.

"Sure," he said. He held the door for me.

The restaurant was small and lit by candles in small brown paper bags. I find that most New York restaurants are too tiny; you're trying to have a conversation, but you can't help eavesdropping on the people next to you who might as well be sitting in your lap. This place, though, had only about a dozen or so tables. Most of them were for two people. There were a couple of four-seaters and one big round table for six. There was also a wood-burning stove that had been filled with candles. They had used the space really well and it seemed the joint was filled with people on third dates.

"What's your name, please?" the hostess asked us, after chatting with a couple near the door.

"Pavlopoulos, I have an eight o'clock." I couldn't reveal that I was from *NY BY NIGHT.* I didn't want any special treatment.

"Right this way." She helped me with my chair and handed us menus. She gestured to the flowers. "They're lovely. I'll bring you a vase. Enjoy your evening."

"Nice place," Paul said, looking at me over the menu.

I realized right then that I wanted this to work. I wasn't sure what *work* meant, but I wanted to leave tonight with this good feeling.

I put the sunflowers in the vase the hostess brought and we ordered a nice Australian bottle of wine. The food was wonderful. I had ratatouille-stuffed octopus with chickpea fries, and Paul had pea risotto. I got halibut and he ordered a steak. I told him about the assignment I had been working on about the blackout. A magazine had hired me to write captions for some photographs from all over the city. He told me about all kinds of fire calls he had been on. Neither one of us mentioned September eleventh, which had just passed, or where he had been two years ago on that day.

We ate slowly and no one rushed us. The servers were attentive without being overbearing.

"They got a real nice thing going," I said after we had been there for almost two hours.

"You think it's them," Paul asked, winking. "Or us?"

I smiled. He reached across the table and took my hand. I wasn't used to so much physical contact and yet the past couple of days had been full of hand holding.

"You want some dessert? Maybe some coffee. I bet you like coffee. You Greek types. Excuse me, Cypriot."

I liked that he had corrected himself.

"Was everything okay?" the woman who had seated us asked.

"Yes, perfect," I said.

"The food was excellent," Paul said. As he said it, a man wearing a chef's coat and plaid pants came out of the kitchen and slipped his arm around the waist of the woman.

"Great job," Paul said to the man.

"Thanks, we're glad you liked it. We hope you come back," the chef said. As he spoke, the woman looked at him smiling.

"My steak was so tender."

"Thanks. Ben's a great cook," the woman said.

"That's for sure," I said. "Are you Esme?"

"No," she said. She smiled a shy smile. "I'm Rebecca. We just named this place after someone who is very dear to us."

"Well, you're doing a great job."

"And this is her second job," Ben said.

He kissed her cheek, and I felt like they saw only each other.

"She teaches third graders all day," he added.

"Wow!" I said. "That's a lot of time on your feet."

She and Ben smiled at us and each other, and I had a feeling Ben knew how to give her a good foot massage.

"It's their first time here," Rebecca said to Ben. "You know what that means."

"Dessert is on the house," Ben said, smiling.

"I suggest his chocolate cake," Rebecca said, and winked at me.

I left the restaurant full of food and a good feeling. I felt like I'd stepped into one of those perfume ads where everyone rolls around and seems to be in love. I coveted the way Ben and Rebecca looked at each other. I had all but given up on finding that. It hadn't bothered me that I might spend my life alone. I had accepted that. I enjoyed being by myself. I wasn't full of surprises. But with Paul's solid arm around me as we walked up Hudson Street it seemed like my life was changing.

"What's on your mind?" Paul asked.

"Just the meal," I lied (sort of).

"It was good." He squeezed my shoulder. "You know, I've been thinking about that kiss you gave me the night of the Great Blackout."

I laughed at the way he said that, like he was a newscaster. I wasn't sure what to say. Should I say I liked it too? Should I blame it on the booze? Should I say that that was what had made the blackout so great?

But before I could say anything, he stopped at the Don't Walk sign on 14th Street and he kissed me. I've been kissed now by four different men, but I felt *that* kiss in the back of my knees.

He stopped kissing me to put his hands in my hair and pull my face close to him and kiss my temple. I could only squeeze his forearms. I felt drunker than I had a few minutes ago. I felt wonderful, but a little sick. Then I did something I never did: I invited him back to my place.

Of all the nights for Armando and Kelly to decide to bond it had to be that night. Armando should have been working, and Kelly? Didn't Kelly have a night shoot? But there they were sitting in the living room watching an *ER* repeat. Kelly's mouth hung open, and Armando stood and kind of sized Paul up, which I found endearing. Paul was unfazed by our audience.

"You remember Paul," I heard myself say in a shaky voice. And then all strung together I finished with "PaulthisisKelly-andArmando. Can I get you a beer?"

"That would be great."

I went into the kitchen, my heart now beating in my stomach; only one of my armpits was sweating. I took two bottles out of the fridge. Kelly was in the kitchen with me almost immediately. Another reason to have roommates: silent, delirious jumping-for-joy in unison.

"Do you want us to go somewhere?" she asked in a hoarse whisper. She was holding on to me, kind of bouncing.

Nothing like this had ever happened to me before.

"I don't know. No, no. Just stay."

"Okay," she said quickly. "Just be cool."

We went back into the living room where Armando and Paul were watching a music video. I handed Paul his beer. He thanked me and moved over on the love seat that Kelly had vacated, so that I could sit next to him. I did. Immediately he started running his hands through my hair. It was so casual. No one else seemed as surprised by it as I was. Armando offered me some wine and I accepted.

"Hey, Voula," Paul said when he had finished his beer. "Can I see your office?"

"Sure," I said, standing up a little too quickly. I glanced at Kelly, who had her lips pursed, trying not to smile. I knew if I looked at her for too long I would give something away.

In my office, Paul examined the still-dark burned walls. He put his hands against the surface and shook his head.

"You're here under better circumstances, this time," I said.

"It could be a lot worse, you know. I mean, of course, you're all okay—but it could be much worse. How's Armando's room?"

"I don't know. I haven't been in there since it happened," I said. Then I smiled. "But it must be okay, because other people have."

"And your room?"

"Oh, no one goes in there."

He laughed. "I meant, was there any damage?"

"No, no damage." I shook my head. And then, because I couldn't help myself and I felt this force pulling me toward him, toward the inevitable, I said, "Do you want to see it?"

"I'm not sure I'm that kind of boy."

"Oh, okay, never mind." I felt like suddenly I'd turned into Ally McBeal. It was so not me. Could I get a do-over?

"No, I'm teasing. Of course I want to see it."

He took my hand and led me into my room. He closed the door behind us. He stood looking around. I had pictures from Georgia O'Keeffe and a silver Greek cross. Did I seem too sexual? Or too religious? I cared so much about what he thought. Why were my walls this odd off-white color?

"I like your room," he said. "It's very you."

He smiled at me. He pushed my hair behind my ear. I wanted so badly for him to kiss me, but he just kept looking at me. It was almost more than I could take.

"You're very pretty, Voula. You're very a lot of things."

I laughed and covered my face.

He took my hand away. "Do you want me to leave?"

"No," I said. "I just never do this. I don't know what to do. I never had a boyfriend. Not that you are. I just don't know this stuff."

I was confessing. I wanted him to know he was dealing with an amateur.

"I don't want you to do anything you don't want to," he said.

I nodded. For some inexplicable reason, I trusted him.

And I didn't do anything.

He did everything. He sat me on the bed and he touched me, just touched me until I relaxed. He kept looking at me. I don't think he said anything; he just looked at me whenever he did something else, to make sure I was okay. I had this feeling that he would stop as soon as I said I wanted him to. But I didn't want him to.

He kept his white T-shirt on and his boxers. I kept my socks on, and he pulled my crocheted blanket around me to keep me warm.

I had listened to Jamie and her friends talk about all kinds of experiences they'd had, with men they loved or men they wanted or men who were so bad they were good. I never got it. I could never really relate. There was the time with Warren, but that was more about him than me. With Paul it was about me. Someone must have trained him on how to make a girl feel good. I wasn't jealous. I would just like to shake her hand.

He rocked my world.

14

I was splashing water on my face in the bathroom of the studio that Maureen had insisted I get to at ten a.m. She wanted to show it to me without the other broker. I wondered what she thought as she waited outside for me on the oversize couch she had declared "too big for the space."

My body was revolting. I couldn't blame my body. It didn't know how to handle too much positive emotion. It was used to pain. There were butterflies in my stomach and my jaw felt wired shut.

Paul and I had eaten soy yogurt and toast that morning. Well, he ate. I just pushed the yogurt around because I didn't think my stomach could take food. I was certain it was me and not the food at Esme's Eatery. I was certain I might never relax again. My world was evolving in so many ways.

Even in the morning, Paul hadn't stopped being sweet. I think it would have been a little bit easier in a way if he had been distant. I was becoming too happy. I wasn't sure what to do with it. Something bad had to happen soon. I thought about calling my mother just to get some perspective on how gloomy the world could be.

But even the bathroom was cheerful. The tile around the ceiling was trimmed with bright blue V's. The bathtub was one of those old-fashioned claw-foot tubs that I only saw in places that were too expensive. There was even a painted blue magazine bin facing me as I sat on the toilet. I imagined stuffing the bin with all of the magazines I wrote for.

"Dear, is everything okay?" Maureen called.

"Yes, just a minute."

I opened up the door and looked at Maureen, who was on the phone lining up appointments with other clients. I had a chance to assess the place.

The kitchen wasn't enclosed—you literally opened the door into it. The bathroom was perfect. There were three steps up to an area that would be big enough for my bed and dresser. I could even curtain it off if I wanted to. The living area was decent-sized. There would be room for my desk and file cabinets. I might even be able to squeeze a small eating table into the area. I opened the closet. There was only one, but it was big enough.

I studied the sheet Maureen had given me with the floor plan and financials. There was a storage unit in the basement with the laundry. There was also a roof deck. Outdoor space was a huge plus!

Maureen finished her calls so that she could talk me through the apartment.

"Now, the kitchen is small, but it does have a dishwasher."

I hadn't even noticed that.

"Also, Voula, this place is going to get great light. It's south facing."

Facing south jacked prices up several thousand dollars.

"It's move-in condition."

Maureen knew my aversion to "vision."

I looked at the financial sheet again. It was actually in my price range.

"There's no doorman," I said.

"But there is a live-in super. Besides, I thought you were willing to move away from the doorman thing."

"I am." I was. I recognized a sparkle in Maureen's shrewd eye, which I took to be a reflection of what she was seeing in mine. "Show me the roof deck."

The roof deck was at best double the size of the bathroom. There were two green chaise longues up there and a tiny hibachi. The area was surrounded by a low plaster wall and next to it was a room that looked like it had some utilitarian purpose.

We were eight floors above West 13th Street. I looked down onto the street and if I crooked my head in a quasi-uncomfortable position I could see the Hudson River. A river view? It was unbelievable. It was bliss. I knew there had to be a catch somewhere. I felt faint.

"Do you think they'll really accept 199? Or is that just a ploy to get it bought?"

"To be safe, you might want to bid a little higher," Maureen said.

"Do you think I could use the bathroom again?"

"That depends," Maureen said, grinning. "Are you going to make an offer?"

"Offer 190," I said. "And give me the keys. I need to sit on that big couch."

Three days later, I was watching Jamie get ready for the lunch that Alice was having at Alice's Chelsea Mercantile apartment. I had never been there, but talk about real estate boon.

"I feel fat and ugly!" Jamie screamed, throwing off the third shirt she had tried on.

Jamie had gained seventeen pounds in fifteen weeks. She wasn't happy with any of her clothes or her swollen ankles. I was wondering when would be a good time to pop in some info about my date. Jamie pointed to a giant ankle and shrieked. I had to ask myself again why anyone would choose that life.

"What's that?" I asked, pointing to her breasts as she changed shirts again. This shirt needed to be worn with a different bra.

"What?"

"Your nipples—they're…" Jamie had had enviably nice breasts her whole life. She had had high Bs with nice nipples and no signs of sag. Her boobs were definitely larger now, but the nipples were dark.

"I know. It happens, I don't know why. According to Raj—" she pointed down "—other things have gotten darker too. I can't bring myself to look."

I couldn't bring myself to ask for clarification, even though I needed it. I decided to let it pass, and consult my pregnancy book later. I changed the subject.

"Are we going to walk?" I asked.

"I don't think I can."

"Subway?"

"Voula, I think I need a cab. Sorry."

Unless it was after midnight, I considered it blasphemous to take a cab any less than twenty blocks, but Jamie's belly looked rounder than I had ever seen it. Her whole body was full: she didn't really look pregnant, just sort of swollen. I agreed to bend my cab rules.

As we sat in traffic up 8th Avenue, I blurted out the details of my date with Paul and that I was waiting to hear if my offer was countered. The weekend was messing with the way things were supposed to flow. For some reason no one could make a real estate decision on Sunday. As expected, Jamie didn't say anything about my real estate adventure.

"Wait! You had sex this week? And you didn't tell me?"

I wished she would lower her voice. I didn't want the cabbie to think I was a slut.

"Well, we barely talked."

"But what about yesterday?" She sounded so hurt.

I refrained from pointing out that yesterday I had listened to two thirty-minute diatribes from her. The first about the change in her hair texture, the second about how difficult it was for her to sleep. That conversation was divided into two parts—first, how often she peed, and second, how uncomfortable she was sleeping on her side since she usually slept on her back. What I said was "It just didn't come up."

"This is big, Voula," she said.

As if I hadn't thought about this.

"I know," I said. I held up my hand. "I'm almost going to have to start counting on the other one."

Jamie giggled and so did I.

"I've run out of everything," Jamie said, looking down to her swollen toes. "I stopped counting at sixty-three."

"Jeez," I said, wondering what the cabbie was thinking now. Still, it felt better to have told her. It made that night seem like it had really happened.

"Was it great? I mean, had you forgotten how to schtoop?" She elbowed me and winked.

"Is pregnancy turning you into Jackie Mason?"

"I wouldn't be surprised if it was. So, details. Namely, when are you going to see him again?"

"His schedule is so effed up. He signed up for all this over-time before our first date and couldn't get out of it. His job is awesome unless there's a fire. He basically just eats and works out."

"Sounds like your job," she said. "But without the working out."

"Shut up! Anyway, he is just so sweet. Can you believe I'm saying 'sweet'? But he is. I'm waiting for the other shoe to drop." Now that I'd started talking about him, I didn't want to stop. I avoided Kelly's questions with sly grins just because I wasn't sure I wanted her to see the full extent of my neuroses. Now that I could tell Jamie about it, the topics seemed endless.

"Don't talk yourself out of it, Voul. Just go with it. Give what you get. Don't Dan-the-Man him."

"What?"

"You know—don't act like you don't care."

"Do you really think I messed up the Dan the Man situation in some way? Do you really think I should have worn my heart on my sleeve for that one?"

"You can just pull up right here on the left," Jamie said to the cabbie. She looked at me. "No, and don't get pissy. I'm saying play it cool. Just not *too* cool. Not you cool."

"Me cool? As in frigid?"

"Don't be silly," Jamie said as she took a wobbly step out of the cab in her heels. "Just don't act like every guy is out to get something. Some of them are quite nice."

"I know that," I said. "I also know from a lot of your experiences that some of them are dicks."

"Right, but this guy doesn't have to be. It sounds like you think you can trust him. So trust him."

Alice's doorman ushered us in with a friendly wave. In the elevator, Jamie gave a deep sigh.

"So first, sex—how was it? What I wouldn't give to kiss and touch someone again for the first time. It's so amazing when it's really right. You just kind of drink him in for hours and hours."

Jamie closed her eyes as if reviewing all of the sixty-three-plus "first times" she had had. I knew then (if there was ever any doubt) that I would never be the kind of sexual person that Jamie was. I wasn't ever going to drink anyone in. But while her eyes were closed I took a look at her swollen body. For the second time in our lives, she was envious of something I was doing. It was all so hard to believe.

Alice had married well. All of the primping and exercise, the extravagant amount of money spent on clothes, had landed her a very busy, very important, very handsome—and extremely boring—investment banker. They bought a two-bedroom apartment in Chelsea Mercantile at the beginning, before Whole Foods even got there. Even though Alice said they had gotten it for a song, I was sure they paid one and half million for it. And it wasn't even south facing.

Alice had just had a baby three weeks earlier. This brunch was an excuse for us to ogle little Lucinda. Alice had a full-time nanny and planned to work part time. She was always kind to me. She didn't have to include me in her plans, but she made an effort. I liked her. I just thought she was the kind of person who didn't want you to keep up with them, that she liked to have people around who would stare at her in wonder. She was the kind of person who would happen to mention that she made her own wedding veil, that her pie crusts were from scratch and that she was next in line for a promotion at work.

She told Jamie how great she looked and let slip in her sweet-as-pie way that she had gained only fourteen pounds during her entire pregnancy. She said this in the context of how quickly the weight would come off. Already, according to her dull husband, Peter, she had lost ten.

I made my way into the kitchen to fix a drink. I checked out the silver appliances (an easy extra three grand and in a place like this, probably five) and took note of the food spread. I was certain that instead of rolling each individual wrap, Alice had just called down to Whole Foods. That was a sign to me that something was wrong.

I gathered with the rest of the women in the jumbo living room with fifteen-foot ceilings. Jamie was telling everyone about my recent bid and a select few about my recent exploits. I was embarrassed, but also kind of pleased. For once I had something to report other than just talking about articles I knew that no one was going to read. But it didn't last. Alice pursed her lips, asked me a question about Paul and then preceded to regale the group with stories of her labor and casually mention that the luxurious throws on the couch were knit by her between contractions.

The baby had been napping when we arrived, but after we polished off the light dill dip and samosas, we heard a cry.

"I'll get her," Peter said, and dashed into the depths of the massive apartment.

I was certain that if I were to look into the baby's room I would find a space bigger than apartments that were in my price range. His exit gave Alice the ideal opportunity to mention how "fabulous" a parent Peter was.

"The other day he said he wished he could lactate so he could relieve me of the nighttime feeding. Isn't that the most romantic thing you ever heard?"

I tried not to wince.

"I think I'm more scared of the breastfeeding than the actual delivery," Jamie said.

"It's really a piece of cake," Alice said, matter-of-factly. "I know some women have problems, but Lucinda latched on right away. They say it's because I didn't have any drugs."

"I think I'm probably going to have to take something," Jamie said, her voice lower than usual.

Peter came back into the living room carrying Lucinda, who was decked out in a furry pink jumper.

I felt the appropriate thing to do was follow the crowd and begin cooing at the baby. Immediately everyone was clamoring for a chance to hold the baby. I was fine to pass on it. The thing looked far too tiny to be in my arms. I could be clumsy and I wasn't going to risk dropping Alice's pride and joy. However, I alternated between telling Alice how beautiful Lucinda was with waving at the baby, as if it could even see me with its scrunched-up eyes.

I noticed that Jamie didn't ask to hold the baby until Alice's sister, Jen, offered it to her. Only then did Jamie take Lucinda, tentatively, and smile down at her.

"Just watch the head," Alice said.

Jamie immediately adjusted her arms, and I felt bad that she had been corrected. "You're a natural," I said, trying to make her feel better.

Alice's mother-in-law arrived and immediately reached to take the baby out of Jamie's arms. "I'm going to have to kidnap my grandchild," the woman said.

I looked away when Jamie passed the baby to her. I feared she was going to drop it. I was relieved when Alice took her back to her crib where the baby would be safe from all of these cooing women.

"She's ridiculous," Alice whispered to the rest of us. "She pulls the baby away from anyone."

"First grandchild syndrome," one of Alice's co-workers muttered. She spoke from experience, as she had two kids of her own. She looked at Jamie. "You should really think about natural childbirth. It isn't as bad as you think."

To me, there was nothing "natural" about anything that big coming out of someone, no matter how you looked at it. For the next twenty minutes, I listened to the three women who had already had babies discuss the perils of painkillers and male doctors and the joy one feels when pushing an eight-pound baby through the teeny tiny birth canal. According to the experts gathered, the pain was negligible.

"Honestly, once it was over, I was ready to go right back in for the next one," Alice bragged.

"I was so in awe of her," Peter said, beaming at Alice.

I felt yucky. I looked at Jamie and thought that perhaps she was getting a taste of her own *"how can you not understand how important procreation is?"* attitude.

"Well, my doctor told me I shouldn't try to be a hero."

"He's a man, isn't he?" the all-knowing earth-mother colleague said.

Jamie nodded and so did the rest of the women. She should have thought twice before picking a man.

"Well," Alice said, "it's really an individual choice, I guess." Then she got up and announced that lunch was served.

I thought I would have a break from the baby talk while we stuffed our faces, but our lunch conversation mostly revolved around a device that turned baby excrement into poop sausages and how much the women with children missed their little ones even though they had only been separated for a matter of hours.

"I know," Alice said, totally getting into it. "I don't know how I could be without her even for a minute."

I looked at Alice's sister and Jamie's other friend, Morgan, who was the other Olsen Twin. Neither of them had children or were having them, and like me, neither of them had much to say. Alice's sister looked jealous and Morgan looked like she would rather be out at a real brunch where we could tie one on.

Later during coffee, Morgan plopped down next to me on the couch. She looked at me and shrugged her shoulders. In the ten years I've known her, I don't think I have ever felt closer to her.

Lucinda was back out and shrieking. No one seemed at all

fazed when she puked up a speckled white liquid. Soon there was the distinct smell of shit, and everyone was too busy cooing about baby smell to notice the unmistakable ass smell. I still hadn't held her and this didn't seem the right time. Alice was acting as if her daughter was reciting Shakespeare and not emitting high-pitched squeals that would make a dog run for cover.

And speaking of dogs…one of the other mommy experts (I tried not to remember the name of anyone I didn't already know in the hopes I would never see them again) was telling Jamie that soon her beloved Sparky—who slept in the bed with her and Raj and who ate no less than two pieces of buttered toast a day—would be relegated to the position of actual dog, not baby substitute. Then she told Jamie that she, too, suffered from bad acne into her second trimester. It was one thing to see the acne, but another to acknowledge it.

After my second helping of lime pie, I gave Jamie the sign and happily she extricated herself from the mommy/skin/pet expert and said it was time for us to go. I said my goodbyes, exchanging an emotional hug with Morgan and bending to kiss Alice, who held an exhausted, fussy baby in her arms.

"Oh, Voula, you never got to hold her," Alice whispered. "I'm sorry."

"That's okay," I said. Realizing my voice was too loud from the way Alice grimaced, I took it down a notch. "I'll get some baby next time."

Jamie and I rode down the elevator (six thousand), walked past the security guard (at least fifteen, which doesn't include holiday tips), and landed on the sidewalk in total silence. I decided to escort her home.

"A cab?" I asked.

"No," Jamie said. "I feel like walking."

"Cool. Are you sure?"

She nodded. "What do you think of the name Lucinda?" she asked.

"It's all right," I said cautiously. I wasn't sure where she was going with this.

"It was one of my names."

"What?" As far as I knew, Jamie's middle name was Kathleen.

"I told Alice I liked it before she got pregnant. Then she stole it. You would be surprised at how many people are name thieves."

"Well, I don't think it's all that."

She nodded. Maybe that wasn't the right thing to say. I tried again.

"They really love talking breasts up there, don't they."

"Yeah."

"And shit, they like to talk about shit."

A smile spread across Jamie's face. "I'm really glad you came with me to that, Voula. Imagining your recap made it almost bearable."

She was being so sincere, I tried to stop on 7th Avenue, but nothing was going to break her stride. She seemed desperate to walk off all of her baby pounds. For the first time, I saw real doubt in her swollen, acne-covered face.

15

For seven weeks, things were almost perfect. There was a minor bidding war on the apartment I wanted. First the sellers counteroffered. They got me up to 205. Then someone else wanted to bid 210, but Maureen told me the sellers said I could have the place if I bid 220. It was just too much, so I passed on it.

I knew Maureen was losing patience with me, so I took a little break from the scene. Luckily, there were plenty of aspects of the real estate market to write about for my *Financial Woman* pieces. I waxed poetic about mortgage rates being so low and what that meant for the woman looking to buy.

At this rate, I was never going to find a place, and I had seen so many. I knew I had to go up in price. I had to stop underbidding. But, it seemed impossible to spend so much on something that wasn't all that big. It was my life savings and I didn't want to spend it foolishly. I just wanted to be wowed by something.

I think I would have felt like a real estate failure if Paul hadn't been there to distract me. I saw him almost every other night. We still talked on the phone constantly when he was at the station, but he would also come over and we'd walk along the Hudson or subway up to Central Park. Autumn had arrived, but I wanted to milk the extended days for as long as I could. I was in bliss.

I barely talked to Jamie. Despite being tired all the time, she was working like a dog. I sensed that she was busting her ass to prove that she wouldn't be affected by her pregnancy. I think she also feared what would happen when she went on maternity leave. The only real heart-to-heart we had was when she was waiting for the results of some triple screen test. I had no idea what the test was for, but I know that it was three diseases that were freaking her out. She left a message when the tests came out okay.

Kelly was dating a new guy, Joel, who seemed really into her, and we double dated a couple of times. Being in those situations, being a part of a couple with other couples, was something I hadn't ever experienced.

I felt like my feet weren't touching the ground and, despite a few nervous pangs, things were great.

I had a mini breakdown the day after daylight saving time ended because the sky got dark so early, but I think it was just a reaction to all the happiness. Luckily, Paul was working that night.

I was trying not to be "me cool," as Jamie had put it, but two things still bothered me about my relationship with Paul: We never talked about his experience during September eleventh, which I gathered for someone in his profession was probably a big deal. And I still hadn't been to his place. The former I didn't want to force, but the latter was about to be remedied. He invited me for his specialty: pasta and stuffed peppers. Even though we had spent so much time together, being let into his space was a big deal.

On my next visit to Diane, I asked her to do my bikini line and legs as well. It was only after I had my pants off that she revealed she had recently had a religious conversion. She was now a born-again Christian. She got so caught up in telling me how she had seen the light that she didn't notice she was doing the same leg twice. I was so worried that she'd be suspicious of my suddenly wanting to do my bikini line that I didn't bother to correct her.

As she poured hot wax in my most sensitive places, I told her about my real estate woes. I thanked her again for bringing Maureen into my life.

"Voula," she said, bringing her face a little too close to mine and looking me directly in the eyes. "You think it was me, but now I know it was the Lord."

She went on about all the ways that God had changed her life. And it worked, sort of, in those moments as the wax dried, I actually prayed. When she ripped it off, it hurt like hell, but I swear that once I had my clothes back on I said an "Amen."

I wanted the night to be special, so I purchased a new outfit for my trip to Brooklyn. Nothing fancy, just black cotton pants and a tight red sweater. Kelly joked that I needed to find something sufficiently outer borough since Paul lived in Carroll Gardens. It wasn't too far from the city, but it felt like a different world. When we discussed my apartment-hunting experiences, Paul told me that the yuppies were moving in to his neighborhood, where his family had lived for almost a century. When he rented his apartment, he hadn't signed a lease, he had shaken a hand.

Tonight I opened the gate and walked through the garden full of Halloween decorations. He lived in the garden apartment of a Federal brick building. When I rang the bell, he came to the door and kissed me. I was getting used to it, getting used to being with him.

"Everything is almost ready," he said.

The place smelled inviting. I walked through a long hall into his apartment. It was giant. There was a big living room with a fireplace (a real fireplace). It was cold enough for him to have a fire going. My head was filled immediately with visions of lying beside it with him. There was a bedroom and a bathroom off that room and another hall that seemed to lead to another bedroom. I followed him to the kitchen and presented the two bottles of wine I had brought. With Armando's guidance, I had a Chianti and a Barbera. Paul opened them both and poured the Barbera into a decanter. He kissed me again. I thought about how I'd never really had a boyfriend and how he had said that made him feel like I was really his.

"Do you want to taste the sauce?" he asked me.

"Sure."

He opened a giant pot and dipped some crusty bread into the sauce. He blew on it, then placed it gingerly in my mouth. It was delicious. It tasted like I imagined red sauce would taste in a small village in Italy—fresh, tangy, light.

"Did you really make this? It's great."

"Ancient Italian secret," he said. "I think I made too much. I'm used to cooking for the guys. I realized when I got to like the twentieth pepper that I didn't know how to cook for two."

I smiled. That implied he hadn't really done this before. "I can take some home and eat it for lunch."

"Yeah," he said. He seemed a little preoccupied with something. Maybe he was worried about dinner being perfect, but he wasn't meeting my eye as much as usual.

"How's work?"

"Okay. You know it's been kinda quiet. Captain Shinners' wife just had a baby. A ten-pound girl. He handed out cigars today. Shinners got captain after the Towers."

"Everyone's having babies," I said kind of stupidly, because even though that could've been just the segue I needed, I didn't know how to ask him about "the Towers."

"Yeah, it sure seems that way. There're three guys on the job whose ladies are expecting."

"Must be something in the water. We should be careful." I broke off more bread and dipped it in the sauce.

Paul stared at me. "What do you think about kids?"

"Kids?" I laughed. "Let's just get through dinner."

He barely smiled. What was up with him?

"Well, my friend's pregnant," I continued. "She's not having the best time. I keep worrying something bad is going to happen. It seems like a tough and dangerous thing."

"I mean, do you want your own? Do you want them in your life?"

I was surprised at this line of questioning. I took another bite of bread. I wished we could just start making out rather than have deep conversations about things I didn't know my stance on. I liked to have a witty retort for everything and I hadn't rehearsed the section of my program about children.

"I don't know, actually. I haven't thought much about kids. I would be perfectly happy without them, I think. I like the way my life is, you know, without mood swings, weight gain..." I stopped short of adding a giant flabby vagina and a peeing/shitting/crying brat, because something about Paul seemed suddenly strange.

"Don't you think it's more than that? Don't you think they could bring you joy?"

"Maybe. I don't know. I mean, I know I'm turning thirty, but honestly, it seems like something for someone else. I barely know how to have a boyfriend."

"You seem pretty capable."

I laughed and tried to change the subject. "You have no idea what goes on behind this facade."

"I think I do," he said. He still hadn't cracked a smile.

I felt a little uncomfortable, like when Diane was staring into my eyes telling me about her religious awakening. I really hoped Paul wasn't trying to convert me to motherhood.

"Please don't get me pregnant tonight. I just bought a new pair of pants." Still nothing, not even a little chuckle. I wasn't used to this kind of reaction. Paul's laugh and the sight of his smile were something I aimed for constantly.

"I guess I just want to know if you like kids."

"Well, if you have to know, I guess I don't really. I just don't see myself as one of those maternal types." I heard Jamie's voice in my head. She was telling me how hard it was to get a man to talk about commitment, and here I had one who was going beyond that. But I had never lied to Paul, and if he wanted my honest opinion, well, I was going to give it to him. He might as well know that Carol Brady I was not.

"Can I see the rest of your place?" I asked as he poured us two glasses of wine.

"Sure." He showed me the backyard. It was unthinkably big. Nowhere in Manhattan could you have found something like that. Maybe I should have looked in the outer boroughs. As I stood coveting his outdoor space, my stomach started churning and I prayed (thanks, Diane!) that I could get through dinner without any trouble. How was I expected to change diapers when I could barely take care of my own digestive track? He wandered back to his bedroom, which was big and sparse except for a queen-size bed and a weight bench. It was all super clean.

"Do you have a maid?"

"No, I just tidied up before you got here."

"Thanks. I hope I prove worthy of your efforts."

He smiled at me and rubbed my cheek. Something was on his mind. Would my lack of maternal instinct make him break up with me? For the first time ever, I felt really awkward around him. There was something between us. I had to keep things light. Maybe if I kept talking, he wouldn't have a chance to dump me.

"What's down that hall?"

"Another bedroom."

"Show me." I raised my recently sculpted eyebrows. I felt dumb. What was I implying? That I wanted to have sex with him in his second bedroom? Did I think I needed to so I could change the subject?

"Uh, actually, it's kind of a mess."

"Oh, I get it," I said, trying to sound as flirtatious as possible.

"You do?"

"Yeah, you tossed all your clutter in there."

"You caught me," he said, and smiled. He looked past me into the kitchen. "I think dinner's ready."

"Great, let's eat."

Throughout dinner it was more of the same. We were talking, but something was off. Who knows what I was saying. I was following the conversation, but in my head I was going through what it would be like when he ended it. I couldn't believe I had made such a disaster of this. Why couldn't I have lied and said I love kids? I could have pointed to my big hips and said they were ideal for popping out little ones. I was already hearing myself telling Jamie the story of every little thing he said. Was seven weeks my freshness date on relationships? I imagined Kelly poking her head into my room to see if I wanted to go on a double date with her and her new man, and having to tell her I had effed it all up.

The worst part: my stomach was killing me. My mouth told me the meal was delicious, but I couldn't really enjoy it. I was shoveling it in, though, because I didn't want him to add "ungrateful" to the list of reasons he was breaking up with me. Oh, Jamie was going to blame me for all this. I just knew it.

"Everything tastes wonderful," I said when we were diving into our second bottle of wine.

"I'm glad you like it. There's cannoli for dessert. It's from a bakery my nonna worked for when she was a kid."

So I would be staying for dessert.

When we finished our meal he stared across the little table at me. He was formulating his speech in his head. I could tell. Keep moving, I had to keep moving. If I didn't stand still long enough the shot would never hit me. I got up and started to clear the table.

"Voula, just leave it." He got up and took the plate out of my hand. He kept holding my hand and walked me over to the fire. We sat on pillows. He pulled me into him and we watched the fire for a while. I was so preoccupied with what was going to happen that I didn't feel scared of the flames.

A fire is hypnotic (especially when enclosed); you could watch it for hours before you realized you are crying. I really cared about Paul and now I was never going to get to that stage where I felt comfortable in his space. I was never going to be able to walk around this place in one of his T-shirts. I was going to get cannoli and then I was going to get the talk. It was cruel, really, when you thought about it. What kind of man could feed a girl authentic Italian pastry and then dump her? *The kind that wants babies, like all normal people should,* I heard Jamie saying in my head. Then I heard her *"don't you realize the whole world wants kids but you?"* laugh. Ugh. Why did I have to be "me cool"? Why hadn't I cherished all the moments with Paul more?

"Voula," I heard Paul saying next to me. There was something big coming after that. He wasn't even going to wait to satisfy my sweet tooth.

"Yes."

"I've been wanting to, uh, tell you—" he stumbled.

In that stumble, I kissed him. Shameless, I know, but if this was going to be it, I wanted it to be on my terms. Maybe it would be the last time. So I kept on kissing him and he didn't stop me. We moved into the bedroom and I kissed his leg, the one he hurt on the soccer field, the one I had wanted to kiss since that time in the park. This was my last chance. I kissed it and kissed it until he pulled me to him.

We fell asleep eventually. As I was drifting off, I realized we never ate the cannoli, but it didn't matter because I was still there.

I woke up to the smell of coffee and I stretched out in Paul's empty bed. It was after ten. That was the beautiful thing about being a writer and Paul's wacky schedule. We didn't have to rush off the way other people did, though maybe that morning that would have been better.

If this was to be it, I had to live the fantasy. I had to for once have a real boyfriend. I put Paul's T-shirt on and walked out into the kitchen. He had cleaned up and done the dishes and was standing in his pajama bottoms staring out into his garden. Was he contemplating what to say to me?

"Hey," I said.

He turned and smiled at me. His eyes looked especially green that morning. Man, I was going to miss this. I thought about ceremoniously burning his pack of condoms, offering to give birth to a baseball team if that's what he wanted. I think

I would have said anything to prevent the end, but instead I asked for coffee and he poured me a cup.

"You know all I have for breakfast is Lucky Charms," he said apologetically.

So maybe he hadn't intended for me to spend the night. Tricks were, after all, for kids.

"Or we could have that cannoli from last night."

"I love Lucky Charms," I lied. Perhaps if we blew up the bakery he would stay with me. Maybe if we avoided all pastry we could celebrate our silver anniversary.

Things seemed pretty normal as we ate our cereal. Immediately afterward he cleared the table. Keep moving I thought, just keep moving.

I had an idea.

"Sure, you're acting like the perfect housewife," I said. "But I know where to find out what you're keeping in the closet."

"Voula," I heard him shouting as I ran through the hall, but I was quick. I pushed the door to his other bedroom open. I was expecting to find a mess, but instead there was one of those little beds shaped like a teepee. There was also a PlayStation, a desk and a child's dresser. I was confused. He was behind me. I turned to get an explanation.

"Voula, I was trying to tell you last night. I should have told you sooner." He stepped into the room. "I have a son." He went to the desk and picked up a picture of a father (him) and son (his) with baseball caps and mitts. "His name is Joseph."

It all happened so fast. One minute he was my kind-of boyfriend and the next he was someone's dad.

And then the next I was on the subway back to Manhattan.

16

Anger makes me extremely productive. That day was probably one of my most productive days ever. I called Jamie and
left her a cryptic message saying that I needed to see her. When
she called, I didn't answer the phone. I wasn't ready to get into
it only to have her interrupt me to take some meeting on how
to market lip gloss. I sent her an e-mail saying I would be at
her place at seven-thirty.

In a way, I wasn't surprised that everything had gone bad.
This was to be expected when you got involved with someone, right? I don't know why I didn't just stick with my Warren Tucker fantasies. They never disappointed. Kids didn't pop
in those.

I decided now was as good a time as any to watch Warren's
audition tape. I felt like I needed to see him, to satisfy a craving. The sight of Warren would be something familiar. My
dreams about him something I could count on.

I rewired the TV from the DVD to the VCR and popped
the tape in. I fast-forwarded through the color bars until I got
to Warren holding a white piece of paper with his name written in thick black ink in front of him.

"Say your name, age and profession," a voice off-camera said.

"My name is Warren Tucker. I'm thirty-one. I work as a financial advisor for a major Manhattan firm."

"Okay, uh, Warren, tell us about what you look for in a woman."

"I like a sense of humor. I guess I like a girl who is adventurous—"

"Sexually?" the interviewer prodded.

Jeez, this show was ridiculous. I was never going to watch it.

"Um." Warren looked flustered, but then he seemed to realize what they were looking for. He grinned straight at the camera. "Yeah, I guess."

"What are you looking for physically?"

"I like someone who is in shape, maybe a little shorter than me, blond hair, blue eyes."

He was describing the farthest thing from me. He was describing Jamie.

"Would you say you are a butt, breast or leg man?"

"I like a nice rack."

I had never heard him say the word *rack*. I thought about when he saw my rack. Maybe watching this was going to rid me of my feelings for him forever.

"Why do you want to be on this show?"

Good question.

"I'm ready to prove to America that I am Mr. Right, not just Mr. Right...Now."

I had no idea what that meant, but it was awful. He said his buddies had dared him—what would be worth the dare? Then I heard Raj's voice.

"What is your idea of romance?"

"Romance?"

Duh! This was great. I needed this.

"Yes, what was the most romantic thing that ever happened to you?"

"Um." Warren Tucker was stumped.

I wondered if he saw his chance at proving to America who he was slipping away. He rubbed his chin, and my stomach dropped. I was reminded of his mannerisms the summer that I knew him. Suddenly he seemed to think of something.

"I used to work as a bartender in the summers while I was going to school. My senior year I did it on Block Island at this pub. There was this girl I had a crush on. She was a waitress at the pub."

Oh boy, I couldn't believe that he was talking about that summer. Now, on top of everything, I was going to find out that he had had a crush on Jamie.

I stopped that tape. I couldn't do it. My Warren idealization was something dear to me. I wasn't ready to let go of it. I had been disappointed enough for one day.

At exactly 7:05, I marched over to 8th Avenue and down to Jamie's apartment.

Since she hadn't e-mailed me back, I didn't really expect her to be home when I got there—these days she was lucky if she got home before ten—but I was hoping she would, that she'd heard the urgency in my voice and would come through for me. And she did: when I rang the bell, she buzzed me in. I climbed the stairs as Sparky barked and a pregnant woman held him back.

"Wow!" I shouted. There was a bump, a definite bump. My girl was not only pregnant, she had a baby in there.

"Tell me about it. I just popped. Crazy, huh?"

The last time I had seen her her skin had been full of acne; now she was kind of…glowing.

I kissed her hello. She studied me carefully.

"So what happened?"

I took a deep breath. "You know, I'm starving. I just realized I haven't eaten since breakfast."

"Do you want to go to Two Boots?"

"Yes!" I shouted. Pizza might be just what the doctor ordered.

I filled her in on everything as we walked to the pizzeria at the end of her block. I told her what I knew about Joseph.

What I'd learned from the many messages Paul had left on my voice mail. He's five years old. Paul had partial custody of him. It seems that some of the times Paul had told me he was work-ing, he wasn't really working, he was parenting. Now, he wanted me to come with him to take Joseph trick-or-treating.

I stopped my story long enough to order one regular slice and one slice of my favorite pizza, the Night Tripper, sun-dried tomatoes, roasted garlic and jalapeño pesto on a white pie with a spinach crust. If that couldn't make things better, nothing could.

I tried not to roll my eyes when Jamie got a slice of cheese-less Sicilian and the Earth Mother. Was she drawn to every-thing mother related? It was just boring old veggies.

"To go?" our favorite bearded counterman asked.

I knew he was going to give us a free slice as usual. That lit-tle thing cheered me up immensely. At least some things could be counted on.

"It's nice out, let's sit on the stoop. I could use some air," Jamie said.

I thought it was a little cold, but sitting on her stoop might be more private than this small place and calmer than listen-ing to Sparky bark.

I tried not to cry as I ate my pizza and told her everything about Paul. I explained how wonderful it had been for a little while and how much it sucked that he hadn't told me about the kid.

"I just can't believe he lied to me."

"Well, he didn't technically lie."

I shook my head. "Jamie, it's not something you don't mention."

She took a deep breath. "Voul, I'm not saying that he shouldn't have told you, but I mean, you just started dating him. You don't really date as much as I used to, but people play games when they date. It doesn't seem like he played games. He just didn't show his full hand. And that's kind of what you have to do when you're out there. How did he even know you guys were going to wind up together?"

"He should have told me as soon as we did it. As soon as he thought there was something, which I think he thought that night. I have to believe he thought it when I did. I don't think I made that up. But he didn't tell me then. I don't think that was very honorable. It lacks integrity."

"Voula, he's not a character in your favorite movie. You're not going to find Daniel Auteuil," she said. "And even if you did, he would be nothing like the roles he plays. Those perfect men, they just don't exist."

"I know, I know, but part of me was thinking he could just be mine, you know. Now I think I'll always come second to the kid. This is my fault. I waited too long. I mean, if I was twenty-two I might have found someone free and clear. Now there's another woman—the mom—in the mix."

"He didn't say he was still with her. I mean, it's just baggage."

"But why can't I find someone without baggage?"

"Voul, everyone has baggage."

"I don't."

"Voula," she practically yelled. Then she paused and shifted her awkward mass to let someone else up the stairs to the building. "Honey, you've got more baggage than just about anyone I know."

"Ugh," I said. I bounced my wrist against my forehead.

"It's okay," she said. She put her arm around me. "It's who you are. It's okay."

I took another deep breath. I felt a big weight on me. I hated the way I was acting. I hated that I'd let this happen. "You know, I just can't believe I fell so hard. I never do. I mean, you know me. I *never* do. All of a sudden all that mattered was keeping him as my boyfriend. You know, he tried to tell me sooner, well, last night, but I didn't want to hear it so I distracted him. I just wanted to be someone's girlfriend."

"I don't see it that way at all. I think if you really just wanted to be someone's girlfriend you could have done it long ago. You're not a hunchback. You've had your chances. It's just not your thing. But I think you wanted to be *his* girlfriend. That's not anyone's, that's his. There's nothing wrong with wanting someone, with wanting love or being vulnerable. There is nothing wrong with trusting. You are so hard on yourself sometimes, Voula. No one expects you to live up to this code. I know you spend a lot of time with yourself and you think about things, maybe too much. Sometimes—" She stopped to let another of her neighbors go up the stairs. "Sometimes you need to reboot. You know, turn it all off and start again. It's all just a bunch of moments. Sure, you wish you could take the moment when he told you away, but then you might not have all the other, wonderful moments. Does that make any sense?"

"Yes," I said. I felt my nose filling and my eyes getting teary. "Then there are moments when you sit on a stoop with your oldest friend and realize that you aren't as alone as you thought."

I heard her sniffle. I knew then why I loved Jamie. I hadn't thought about it in a while. And loving *her* didn't really hurt too much, so maybe I could love Paul, too.

At that moment she stopped being someone's mom and went back to being my friend. She hadn't really ever stopped.

That night I slept over at Jamie's in her bed, like we used to when we had sleepovers in high school. Raj was pulling an all-night edit. In the middle of the night, I felt Jamie fling her leg over me, thinking I was him, and it made me smile in my sleep.

In the morning I woke up to the smell of something delicious. I found Jamie sitting in the kitchen wrapped in her puffy down robe, as Raj made pancakes. Raj was a great cook. It would have been perfect—if their dog hadn't been jumping all over me.

"Sparky!" Jamie and Raj screamed at once.

Raj smiled and leaned to kiss me. "I'm glad you and my wife were able to get your lesbian on last night."

"Yeah, I needed my fix," I said.

"Poor Raj," Jamie said. "He has his dreams."

"Are you staying for breakfast?" Raj asked. "I'm making chocolate chip pancakes."

"Then yes."

"Hey, did anything ever happen with that fireman?"

I was surprised that Jamie hadn't briefed him.

"Jesus, Raj, I told you all about it last month. Do you ever listen?" she scolded.

"No, never," Raj said, smiling. He had heard it all before. "It goes in one ear and out the other. You might as well be talking to the dog."

Jamie shook her head but she was grinning. Her second trimester seemed to be sitting well with her. This morning, she was once again radiant.

"You look pretty," I whispered.

Raj heard me and smiled. "I missed spooning with the belly last night," he said.

"Too much information," I yelled.

Raj served us our pancakes, then pulled up a stool to the table in their kitchen. "So, can you believe we're having a baby?"

"Not really," I said. I loaded my pancakes up with butter and maple syrup and took my first delicious bites. "These are so yummy."

"You should have invited the man over," Raj said. "Is this The One?"

"Raj," Jamie said. "Not now. She's mad at him."

"He's an asshole," Raj said immediately. He had been trained.

Jamie patted his arm and then tipped her head to the side, studying me. "We're not sure if he's any more of an asshole than anyone else. The jury's still out on that one."

"Voula's the hanging judge, isn't she?" Raj asked. "Aren't you?"

"Yes, but—" I stopped myself. I wasn't sure what I wanted. I was softening in my old age. I decided to change the subject. "Have you guys picked out names yet?"

"Voula if it's a girl," Raj said, grinning.

"Voulo if it's a boy," I countered.

Raj and I high-fived.

"I hope it's not a boy," Jamie said.

I thought she was kidding, but she didn't look like she was. "Why?" I asked. I remembered how one of the mothers at

Alice's house had gleefully recounted being sprayed in the face with pee every time she changed his diapers for the first three months.

Jamie and Raj looked at each other. "Well, we haven't exactly agreed on what to do about the foreskin," Jamie said.

"That doesn't mean we won't be happy if it's a boy," Raj said. I felt that I was treading on thin ice.

"Of course, we just want a *healthy* baby," Jamie added.

"Right," I said cautiously. "What are you disagreeing about?"

"I don't see why he has to be cut," Raj said.

"Most American boys are cut, Raj, I don't want him to feel weird."

"It's unnecessary. I'm not cut. You like my penis."

Even though I already knew from Jamie that Raj had never been circumcised, I was going to remind them that this too was too much information, but they were already knee-deep in their argument. I knew that Jamie preferred circumcised to uncircumcised, but this hardly seemed the place to bring that up. Raj launched into a whole argument about not circumcising the kid. He had worked on some makeover show before this. One of the episodes featured a really expensive cream made of foreskins.

"I don't want some rich asshole rubbing my baby's foreskin on his skin to look younger. I think this whole thing is ridiculous."

"I don't know that anyone is going to get our baby's foreskin, Raj," Jamie said.

I could see she was getting angry. She looked over at me. "I don't know that we need to discuss this right now, either."

"Yeah, I prefer not to think about the baby's penis until I have to. Thanks. Please, Mom and Dad, don't fight."

"We're not fighting," they said in unison.

We all laughed. The circumcision debate was tabled for the time being. Everyone had seconds on pancakes. I felt like I could have stayed with them in their eat-in kitchen forever.

During the walk home, I checked my cell phone. Paul had left three more messages. All of a sudden I felt silly and I just wanted to talk to him. His having a son was more than I had bargained for, but who was I to talk? I had a seriously screwed-up family. If we were going to stay together (if that was still an option), Paul might eventually meet my mother, which would be harder to handle than any five-year-old.

It was Halloween. I knew that Paul was going to pick up Joseph from kindergarten and take him out in his authentic fireman costume. There was no way I could make it, I had too much work. I called Paul anyway.

"Hey, I'm so glad it's you." He didn't even say hello. "I should be, right? This isn't a breakup call?"

"No," I said. "I'm sorry I bolted yesterday. I was just kind of surprised. I guess I wish you had told me before."

"I know I should have told you before our first date when we were on the phone. The thing is, people get freaked out. Obviously, I was right. I guess I just wanted to see you and see how the first date went."

"It went really well," I said.

"Yeah, and then I didn't know how to tell you. Just that I had to."

"Well, you did."

"So," he said. "What do you think?"

"Well." I sighed. Maybe this was a longer conversation than I had time for. "I don't know how I feel about kids. I mean, I'm not ready to be someone's stepmom."

"I'm not asking that."

"Yeah, well, I guess I'm just worried. Things were going so well. I managed to fool you into liking me. Now, I have to impress a kid."

"Joseph's pretty easy."

"Yeah, well." I didn't know what to say about Joseph. "Do you ever think about getting back together with his mother?"

"No, she's remarried. Angela and I never should have got together in the first place. We barely were together. We were just foolish. I'm not going to say Joseph was a mistake, but he definitely wasn't planned."

"Well, I'm not really a kid person. Can I just date the dad for a while before I meet the kid?"

"But you will meet him?"

I took a deep breath. What was the big deal? "Yes."

"When?"

Oh *panayia mou*. "By the end of the year."

"You need two months?" He sounded horrified.

I thought of cannoli, of being dumped.

"Before Christmas. This way I can wow him with gifts."

"You're kind of a crackpot," he said. But he laughed.

I guess that meant we were staying together. I had until Christmas to figure it out.

17

As usual the holidays crept up on me. Suddenly I realized I had less than three days until I met the kid. Less than three days to find the perfect presents that would buy his love while at the same time not make me seem desperate to Paul.

It was the Sunday before Christmas, the last real weekend shopping day. I knew that I probably should have waited until the next day when people would be back at work, but I started feeling severe anxiety. Paul wasn't being much help.

"What do you want? What does Joseph really want?"

"Well, you know what I want," he said.

I had made the mistake of asking him in the morning in bed.

"I'm being serious," I shrieked. "I need to know."

"Oh, okay, serious." He sat up in bed. "Really, you don't have to get us anything."

"But, I do, I will. So just tell me. Didn't he make a list?"

"No, he's not so materialistic. Why don't you get him a Yankees jersey? He likes Jeter. Or get him a game for PlayStation."

"Those are so average. So impersonal. I want a gift that sets me apart. I don't want him to think I'm some stinky girl that takes his father's attention away."

"Don't worry about it." He started to kiss me. "Do you think maybe you want to go ice skating in Prospect Park today after a little morning fun?"

"Skating? Paul, I have to go shopping."

"Okay, we'll walk up Smith Street." He continued kissing me, trying to get the pair of his boxers that I was wearing off.

I giggled. "You know, you are very persistent."

"Tell Santa what you want for Christmas."

"I want him to be quick so I can go shopping."

"You really want that? Santa can give you whatever you want, because you've been such a naughty girl."

"I'm not sure I should be enjoying this. Fine. Have your way with me, Santa, but I plan on leaving at noon to go back into the city. Smith Street does not have what I need."

"Santa does," Paul said, and he pulled the covers over our heads.

I was way behind schedule when I got to Macy's at two-thirty. It was a madhouse. There were people everywhere. The floors were covered with merchandise and everywhere I went there was some kind of percentage off everything. I didn't even know where to begin.

First I found my mother's perfume. It came in a nice gift set. I was pretty sure that she would like that, and I got her a robe and some slippers to go with it.

Luckily, I had already bought Jamie's gift. I had gone nuts in a little boutique on Smith Street a few weekends earlier and bought her all kinds of mommy-to-be products, like milk baths and massage oils. I'd also gotten some of her favorite hot chocolate at City Bakery. For Raj, I got a book of bathroom humor. It was kind of a theme for me to get him a funny book that he would leave in the can.

My mother and I had a standing invitation to go to the Jacobses' house, but she usually bagged it, saying she was tired from being at mass on Christmas Eve. I bought them some nice ornaments for their Christmas tree. I also saw a little stork ornament that I bought for Jamie and Raj. The thing that sucked about Macy's was that I had to pay for everything in the department I got it in. I waited in three separate lines to get what I needed.

Then I went to the men's department. I found a nice button-down shirt for Paul. At least I thought it was nice. The line was huge and it seemed that the people at the cashier were moving at a snail's pace. Paul told me that Joseph liked some kind of snail. What was it? Secret Snail? No, Sonic Snail. I had to go up to Toys "R" Us to get some other sonic game he wanted. Already I was feeling hot. There were strollers and screaming kids everywhere I turned. The parents seemed to have no control. How was Jamie ever going to deal with this when she had her baby?

"How long have you been in line?" I asked the person in front of me. She had a double stroller of sleeping kids and another one on the way.

"At least a half hour. I hate Christmas."

As I was nodding, my phone rang. It was Jamie.

"What should I get Paul? What are you getting Raj?" I asked frantically.

"A rim job for both," she answered.

I laughed really loud, and the exhausted mother in front of me glared. Laughing wasn't allowed during the holiday season.

"Seriously, I need help."

"Where are you right now?"

"Macy's."

"Ugh. I'm over my all-day morning sickness, but that makes me want to vomit. When will you learn to shop early? You are so organized otherwise."

"I know. If it makes you feel better, I got your gift weeks ago."

"Well, at least you have your priorities straight."

"How are you feeling?"

"Big. I don't know if I can take much more of this."

"Two more months, right?" I counted on my fingers.

"More like three. Pregnancy is longer than they let on. It's more like forty weeks."

"Shit, that sucks." I waited a respectable two seconds before saying, "I need you to help me get Paul a gift."

"The first Christmas I had with Raj, I got him a watch. He still wears it. Does Paul have a watch?"

"He has a sporty one."

"Well, have you gotten him anything else?"

"I'm about to buy him a shirt. Is that boring?"

"Kind of."

"Well, what does a watch say?"

"It says what time it is?" She made a little comedy drum noise.

"Please don't quit your day job. Does it imply that I'm too serious?"

"No, but you are, by the way."

"I know. What if he isn't getting me anything?"

"What if he's getting you an engagement ring?"

I felt my eyes opening wide. "I don't even want to entertain that thought."

"What if?"

I knew she was just having fun with me. "Well, I got Raj a Fossil, but that seems a little too young. Try Skagen."

"They have Fossil at Macy's but where can I get this Skagen?"

"Keep looking. They have it too. It's like no other store in the world," she teased.

"I think that's Bloomingdale's." I moved up about an inch in the line. "How can you be in such a good mood?"

"I'm done with my shopping and sipping hot cocoa with giant chocolate marshmallows."

"You bitch," I said dramatically.

The mother in front of me turned around glaring. "Sorry," I whispered.

"That's okay. I've been called worse," Jamie said, thinking I was talking to her.

"You are worse," I said quietly into the phone.

Finally, I got to the front of the line. I had been in Macy's for almost three hours by the time I finally paid for the shirt. Then I went down to where the watches were on the first floor.

It was so packed with people, I could barely breathe. I didn't see any watches I really loved and I got impatient crouching by the glass cases. I knew it was going to be next to impossible to get anyone to help me. Then I went by some Swiss Army watches that caught my eye. They seemed more like Paul's style. Nice, but not too fancy. I was sold on the idea of getting him a watch, but I decided to come back the next day.

I was determined to get up to Toys "R" Us. One thing I could not skimp on was Joseph's gift. I had asked Paul to pick up the Yankees jersey and make it from both of us. I still wanted to get Joseph something great, but I took one look at the lines at Toys "R" Us and decided to just get him the sonic game Paul had said the boy wanted. I also picked up some slimy stuff that was at the counter, an electric drum set, *Lord of the Rings* action figures and a stuffed dinosaur. He was just a kid, but I wanted to have all my bases covered.

Times Square was swarming with people. There were moments where I was just standing and couldn't move at all. Around me, everyone seemed to be pushing and giving attitude. So much for the holiday spirit. It took me forty-five minutes to get home. It was so cold and dark outside that I just wanted to crawl into my bed when I walked in the door.

Armando was at the restaurant. The holidays were his busiest season. I knew he was especially homesick during this time of year. At times, I wished I could take him with me for Christmas, but usually he spent all morning on the phone to Italy with his crying mother, and had dinner at the chef's house.

Kelly was spending the week with her mom in Long Island. I knew she wasn't exactly looking forward to it. It was odd to me that nobody had the perfect situation. I would have loved it if my mom was in Cyprus. My dad and I probably talked more wishing each other a merry Christmas during a long-distance call than we ever would if he lived here.

I got into bed, exhausted. I had never been a sound sleeper; it always seemed like the worst things happened when I was getting some decent shut-eye. Since starting to date Paul, I felt like I was always awake. I just couldn't sleep. I don't think I wanted to miss anything with him.

I thought about what Jamie had said about the engagement ring. Being almost thirty seemed to speed things up. Paul was thirty-two. I was pretty certain that, believe it or not, he was as into me as I was into him. We hadn't said the L-word or gotten our names tattooed on each other's butts, but I just felt secure. When he looked at me, he focused. When I said something, he listened. I hadn't thought it could be this easy. Could he possibly be thinking of taking the next step?

Of course, it wasn't that easy. I still had to meet Joseph. I wondered how much Paul's feelings for me were riding on what Joseph thought.

What if he was holding back saying he loved me or really committing until I met Joseph? I had been afraid that this was some kind of test, but I hadn't really stopped to think about what would happen if I failed. I had had the breakup scare at his apartment, but since then I hadn't really considered that anything could get between us.

I worked myself into a frenzy thinking about it. By the time I finally fell asleep, I was completely petrified.

On Christmas Day, I transferred from the N to the F train at 4th Avenue in Park Slope. I had spent Christmas Eve at my mother's apartment. I was heading to the Jacobses' house for dinner. Paul was going to join us for dessert. It seemed easier to introduce him to Jamie's family than to my own.

On the outside train platform, I checked my cell and found a message from my sister, Helen. She wanted to wish me a merry Christmas. I was touched by that and I decided to call her back while I waited for the train.

"Hello," a crackly male voice answered.

Was this Andre? He would be my brother-in-law. It was disorienting to think I even had a brother-in-law.

"Um, I was looking for—" what was Helen's married name? "—um, Helen Pavlopoulos—"

"Who? Oh, hold on."

I heard the voice yell, "Mommm." My nephew was already almost a man and I didn't know him.

I heard Helen's footsteps coming to the phone and Spiro whispering that he didn't know who it was.

"Hello," Helen answered.

"Hi, Helen. It's Voula."

"Hey." She sounded so glad to hear from me.

I felt guilty. Calling her hadn't occurred to me, but my returning her call seemed to make her so happy.

"Merry Christmas," I said. "I can't believe your son sounds so old."

"I know, neither can I. It's hard to believe I was that age once. I feel like I should know all his tricks, but he's got me fooled. He's a good kid though."

"Did you have a nice Christmas?"

"Yes. We went to Andre's parents' house last night. They live in Sunset Park. And today the kids opened their presents. Did you go to mass last night?"

"Of course. As if Mom would let me miss it."

"What are you up to today?"

"I'm actually going to visit my friend's family. Do you remember Jamie Jacobs? She went to school with me, lived in Park Slope."

"No."

Both my sister and I had whole aspects of our lives that hadn't intersected.

"Well, I'm going there."

"And Ma?"

"She was tired." It was strange to say that to my sister. I was used to making excuses for my mom, but could Helen tell that "tired" really meant "crabby"?

"So you are going to be in Brooklyn today. I didn't know that, but either way I was going to see if you wanted to come over to our house for dinner. Andre is a great cook."

"Well, I am sort of already on my way to the Jacobses'. I have a bunch of presents for them." Really it wasn't an excuse, but it felt like one.

"Oh, okay," Helen said.

She thought it was an excuse. I sighed. It was do-or-die time. A new year was on the way. I never made resolutions, but it seemed like it might be nice not to miss another year with my nephew and niece.

"How about dessert? Can I come over for dessert? Are you even having dessert?"

"Yes, probably around seven."

It was perfect. If the Jacobses ate at one and then had their dessert around five, I could get a cab to Boerum Hill by seven, if she would have me.

"Well, if I can't make dinner, how about that?"

"That would be perfect." My sister sounded so pleased.

Then I realized I would have Paul with me. "Um, can I bring someone?"

"Yeah, who?"

She might have thought I meant our mother.

"Just a boy," I said.

"Oh," Helen said coquettishly.

I was smiling into the phone and I felt that she was too. As the train was coming she gave me her address.

The Jacobses brownstone in Brooklyn was as close to heaven as a house could get. I always thought how nice it must have been to grow up here and not just go over as a friend. It was right near Prospect Park and public transportation. It didn't seem like it was in the city, yet it was still so close.

I kissed everyone hello. Mr. and Mrs. Jacobs, Mike, Raj and Jamie were all wrapped in giant lime-green awkward-shaped scarves.

"Ana and Crystal made them for us," Jamie whispered in my ear.

"Craft Christmas," Raj and Mike sang.

"Very nice," I said to Ana and Crystal, even though they weren't, really. "I didn't know you guys were knitting."

"It's very therapeutic," Crystal said, but before she could

launch into a long and embarrassing story, Ana handed me a wrapped box.

"For you," she said.

I opened it up. It was a scarf. It was ugly. It was uneven. It was my very own. I loved it. I put it on.

"Thanks, guys," I said. I loved feeling like part of the family. I handed them the box that I had for them. It was a vase I had bought at one of the Smith Street shops. "For your new place."

"When is the stud getting here, Voula?" Maura asked.

"Mom, I told you he's coming for dessert." Jamie sounded really exasperated.

"Okay, okay," Maura said, winking at me. She leaned closer. "That baby can't get out of her fast enough."

Jamie's third trimester wasn't treating her as well as the previous one. I didn't see how she could get any bigger. Her belly was a watermelon and the rest of her was trying to compensate. She seemed miserable and awkward. Thankfully, she was over her puking, but she said that no matter what position she sat or lay in, she just wasn't comfortable.

We sat down to dinner. Crystal looked embarrassed as Mr. Jacobs said the blessing and Mike was mortified when Maura said the fake blessing "Rub-a-dub-dub, thanks for the grub."

We slurped our soup and everyone but Mike managed to spill some on their new scarves. Mrs. Jacobs had made her Christmas goose. And like nearly every year before, she said lines from *How the Grinch Stole Christmas* throughout dinner. I adored the tradition of coming here. Everyone was stuffing their faces except Jamie, who kept insisting that she was full because the baby was balancing between her stomach and bladder.

After dinner, the Jacobses gave me some presents. I got Christmas socks and Maura's favorite Baci chocolates. They also bought me a book of *New Yorker* essays and a gift certificate to a record store. Jamie winked and said she would give me my gifts later.

"That means they're dirty," Maura said.

Mr. Jacobs blushed and Mike shifted in his seat.

In between dinner and dessert, I told Jamie that I was going to be ducking out to go to Helen's.

"Wow! I can't believe it. You're actually going to meet your niece and nephew."

"It is a big deal, right? Is it bad to bring Paul along to this? He doesn't know what's in store."

"They aren't going to kill him, Voula. But it is big in that you guys are totally meeting each other's families. You're seeing what's what. I have always said that holidays make or break relationships. You should do a story on it."

"Maybe next year," I said. I wanted to analyze this more, but I heard the doorbell ring and Maura rushing to let "the stud' in. Jamie gave me a big smile and kind of punched my shoulder like I was getting into the ring. She was right. This whole thing was a big deal—his meeting the Jacobs family, and meeting my sister; me meeting Joseph tomorrow. I hadn't slept all week. I went downstairs and saw Maura smiling, almost flirting with Paul. She turned and looked at me.

"What a guy, Voula. He brought cannoli."

Paul winked at me. I knew then that he wasn't going to mind coming with me to Helen's. In fact, it would be better because he was there. It almost seemed as though everything was going to be okay.

There was Spanish music playing behind the door to my sister's apartment. I sighed and felt Paul squeeze my hand.

"This is going to be fine," he said.

An older woman opened the door. She said something in Spanish, and Paul answered her, calling her *abuela*. He knew a little Spanish from working in the city for so long, but whatever he had said made her smile. She called Helen to the door.

Helen hugged me and even hugged Paul. She brought me into her home and introduced me to Andre's family, her family. The last time I had seen Andre, he was a kid with long hair and big pants. Now, he was a big name at the board of education. He smiled at me, a crooked little smile, and I wondered if he was remembering the last time we saw each other, on the stoop of my parents' apartment. I don't think he quite knew what to make of this reunion. I couldn't blame him.

Helen handed us glasses of *coquito,* a spiked coconut-flavored eggnog. It was pretty tasty, and like the rest of the family, I helped myself to more when I was done. It was helping me take the edge off.

Spiro looked just like Andre, and seemed quite serious. I had no idea what to say to a studious teenage boy. Paul asked him about his Christmas presents and then Spiro invited him to play his new XBox game.

Before following him, Paul turned to me. "You gonna be okay?"

"I hope so," I whispered.

"You will be," he said. He kissed my cheek and left me alone with my family.

"This is Aunt Voula, Cristina," Helen said to the little girl she was carrying.

My niece turned around and blew me a kiss. I cracked up, but when I looked at her, I saw the strong resemblance she bore to her namesake. I wondered how Helen could look at her every day without the child breaking her heart.

"Thank you for the kiss," I said.

"You're welcome," Cristina said. She opened up her arms to me.

"She's very affectionate, especially with women. She wants you to hold her."

"Okay." I took Cristina and she rested on my shoulder.

"She's exhausted," Helen said. "She didn't get a nap today. Be careful that she doesn't fall asleep on you."

I danced Cristina around to the music. I danced over to where Paul and Spiro were playing some war game.

"That's a good look for you," he said.

"I thought you would like it."

"Dessert" actually meant dinner. It seemed that Andre's family ate dinner later than Jamie's. I was full, but I couldn't resist trying some of the pork that Andre had made. Helen told us all about her Christmas morning. Andre's two sisters and his mother kept stealing glances at me. I would have been suspicious of me, too. Between them they had five kids, so the house was full of noise. It was a lot like our house had been.

I didn't want to eat any more dessert because I'd eaten so much at the Jacobs house, but I wanted to be polite. After eating a couple of slices of different pies, I had a good idea what Jamie must have felt like. I was about to deliver a food baby.

But then, Andre's sister Joanne started dancing with her daughter and everyone paired up. I had no idea how to dance to this Spanish music, but I watched my sister and Andre dance. They moved together purposefully. He spun her away from him and then spun her back smoothly.

"I don't know where she got her sense of rhythm," I announced. "But that gene skipped me."

The rest of the room laughed, even Andre's mother, and I felt that the ice had been broken a little. Paul seized the moment and pulled me up from the table to dance with everyone in the small kitchen. I didn't fight him; the *coquito* had loosened my inhibitions. I sucked and he wasn't all that good, but we laughed along with everyone else.

It was close to midnight when we left. Cristina was sleeping, but all the other kids were still up. Andre's sister Marisa started bringing out more food and I said I really had to go. The dancing had reduced me from bursting at the seams to just plain stuffed.

Helen gave me a big hug when I left. She kissed Paul goodbye.

"Maybe Joanne can baby-sit one of these nights and we could go on a double date."

"That would be nice," Paul said.

"I'll call you next week," I said. "Merry Christmas."

We walked over to Court Street and Paul showed me all the Christmas lights in the neighborhood. It was freezing cold, but the walk was helping me digest.

"It's nice that you can walk to your sister's from my place.

Maybe you'll see her more. What's the problem between you guys anyway? You never talk about her. Or your other sister."

I had told him that Cristina died, but that's about it.

"I know. I will, I just don't want to, tonight. I want to enjoy this."

He nodded.

"Thank you for being such a good sport. It was a lot easier than I thought it was going to be, but I'm glad it's over."

"Yeah," Paul said. "Now you just have to meet Joseph."

He smiled and squeezed my hand in that way he had, but I knew I wasn't going to sleep that night.

Someone was pulling my eyelid open. I couldn't have been asleep long. The last time I had looked at the clock it was almost six a.m. Was Paul trying to get some nooky? I couldn't possibly look very hot right now. I let my eye focus on the someone pulling it open. That someone was a mini version of Paul.

"Hello, Joseph," I said.

"Hello, doodoo head."

Okay.

"Excuse me," I said in my most rational (yet still friendly) voice. "I don't think that's nice."

"Joe, Joey," Paul yelled, rushing into his room. He looked at me and the little sewer-mouth sitting on top of my legs. "I told you not to come in here." He looked at me. "I'm sorry. I told him to wait in the living room. I got a bit of a late start and I needed to take a shower."

"That's okay," I said. Joseph began to bounce on my legs causing the bed to shake.

"I see you met Voula, Joe."

Joseph kind of grunted and sucked on his Star Wars figure. Perhaps he was confused that my name wasn't doodoo head. I didn't think I should rat him out.

Paul smiled apologetically. "Sorry."

"No problem," I said. Joseph was bouncing a little harder now. "What time is it?"

"It's almost noon. I was sleeping when Angela got here."

"Mom?" Joseph asked, pausing for a moment.

"Yes, your mom," Paul said.

Joseph started up again.

"Joey, I don't think Voula wants you to be jumping like that."

"It's no problem," I lied. I tried shifting my legs. "Maybe we could just…there. That's great."

Joseph decided that he was tired of merely jumping on the bed and decided to add a little more complexity to his routine by jumping from the bed to the chair. Paul got him midway through the third jump.

"Joey, enough," he said.

Please don't let Joey get in trouble when I'm here, I prayed. If he did, I was prepared to be the good cop. Joseph scrambled off the bed and started running around the apartment. He was making chimp noises and kept adding lines of a Beyonce song. It would have been funny if it hadn't been happening to me. Had Paul thought about ADD? How was it possible to have this much energy so early in the morning? Okay, it was almost noon.

"Is this normal?" I asked, getting out of bed.

"Sure, he's a kid. He'll calm down in a little bit," Paul said. He smiled at me nervously.

I hadn't really thought about it on his terms, only that it might make him break up with me. I could see he just wanted us both to like each other. I was willing to try.

"Hey, Joseph," I yelled into the other room. "Santa gave me some presents to give you."

Joseph bounded back into Paul's room. Before I could wow him with Sonic Whatever, he spotted something on the floor and picked it up.

"What's this?" he yelled happily.

I could see how he would be attracted to the shiny foil of the condom wrappers.

"I'll take those," Paul said, pulling it out of Joseph's hand.

It was too late, because Joseph had seen my expression. He knew this was something he shouldn't have.

"Whatisitwhatisitwhatisit?" he yelled, jumping up and down.

"Nothing, Joseph," Paul said.

He had a poker face. I would have been laughing by now.

"Do you want to open your presents?"

"Dad, what is it?" Then the cherub looked at me. "Is it something for your butt?"

It was all I could do not to laugh. I hurried into the other room to get my gifts and let Papa Paul field that one.

"It wasn't so bad, was it?" Paul asked after Joseph's mother came to get him.

I had waited inside when she beeped her horn. Now I was lying in bed. My whole body ached. I didn't think I had ever been so tired.

"He's certainly got a lot of energy." I hadn't been the one jumping around like Joseph was or screaming as I played video games, but just watching him had tired me out. I had watched the boy like a hawk, fearing he was going to poke his eye out or crack his skull. We had had a whirlwind day—video games, pizza, Prospect Park playground.

I had called Jamie for help during the Prospect Park part to see if she was still at her mom's.

"Can't you come back to Brooklyn? I'm sending smoke signals," I'd said into her cell phone voice mail. "I think you should really consider what you are about to do by having this kid. I think the foreskin is the least of your problems. I don't know if I'll survive the day, but know that my last words to you were 'think this through.'"

She still hadn't called me back.

Paul picked my leg up off the bed and massaged it.

"You do that three times a week?" I asked.

"He was kind of keyed up today, because you were here."

Keyed up, huh?

"So," he said. "What are we going to do for New Year's Eve?"

I sat up in bed. "Does that mean I passed?"

"What?"

"The test."

"It wasn't a test. Voula, I hope you haven't taken this the wrong way. How have you taken this?"

"I thought if Joseph didn't like me, which I'm not sure he does, we were over."

"Voula." Paul shook his head. "Don't get me wrong, I wanted Joseph to like you. I actually think he does, but if he didn't it wouldn't change how I feel. We'd just have to keep trying. Joseph is the most important thing in my life, but you rate way up there."

I sort of liked how this conversation was going.

"If you were mean to Joseph it would be a different story. I think I know you well enough to know that you wouldn't be. It wasn't a test, silly. Don't you think we're beyond tests?"

I hadn't, but I guess now I would. I nodded.

"Do you have any tests for me?" he said slowly, like he couldn't believe he was having this conversation.

I shook my head.

"Did you think I wanted you to be a mother to Joseph?"

I shrugged.

"Voula, he has a mother."

"But when we talked that time, when you told me—"

"I know, I didn't know how to bring it up. I'm not sure what impression I gave you. All I want is for you to know that he's in my life and be okay with it. I'm sure he'll love you before you know it."

"I hope so."

"I know so." Paul smiled at me.

Then, I watched his face change. His look reminded me of the one he had worn at the Great Blackout. "I've been meaning to tell you—"

"Yeeeees."

"I love you."

I took a deep breath. "Thanks," I said.

He laughed.

"I mean, I love you, too."

"Cool," he said.

I'm not sure if it was exhaustion from the day or happiness

at being in the arms of the man who loved me, but that night I slept better than I had in my entire life.

And when I woke up the next morning, nothing bad had happened.

18

The beginning of the year was freezing cold. Normally, I would have hated the frost, but I didn't care. When I wasn't busy making up stories about my stunted apartment search, I was bundled up in front of Paul's fire. With a competent fireman by my side, I was only a little afraid of the flames.

Being a part of a couple opened a whole new world for me. Couldn't get out the door because of too much snow? It didn't matter. We made tuna melts and got drunk on Coors Light in the afternoon. I liked hibernating with someone. I liked having an excuse to not get out of bed.

There were times I wished I was more skilled in the art of dating but I liked the newness of it all. I was constantly amazed that I could be so fascinated about finding out about the time Paul fell off his mountain bike and got a concussion, or how *Witness* was the first time he saw boobs.

This was the thing I had never known. Love. It was awesome.

I pretty much avoided hanging out with Joseph. I didn't realize that I was doing it until Paul called me on it one night when we were on the phone. We got into a wicked fight, and I called Jamie crying, convinced we were going to break up.

I talked for a good twenty minutes without even asking about the baby. She just let me. She said that I should apologize and say I would try to make more of an effort. It was all so simple, I would have done that with a friend, but with Paul the stakes seemed higher.

I did what Jamie said and he was totally cool with it. He was shocked when I said I worried he was going to break up with me. I realized we had staying power. And soon enough I understood why Jamie always raved about make-up sex.

What's more, even Valentine's Day didn't suck. For the first time ever I got flowers. I had made it clear to Paul that I was opposed to store-bought greeting cards one evening when the subject of Valentine's Day came up. I was touched when on Saturday morning I woke up to a sweet cut-out card with a handwritten "Be mine." It was almost too good to be true. If someone had told me some of the things we said to each other, I might have barfed, but I kept it our secret.

I couldn't deflect the apartment questions forever. Even my editor at *Financial Woman* was anxious for the fictional me to close and move in. I had been stalling with articles on approvals, co-ops and co-signing. It was time to take the next step.

I decided to call Maureen. I was hoping to get her answering machine, but she picked up on the second ring.

"Well, hello, stranger," she answered.

"Hi, Maureen." I had been planning to leave a breezy message, but now we actually had to talk. I felt so guilty. We had seen every apartment under the sun and I wasn't satisfied with any of them.

"Tell me you found an apartment with another broker," she demanded.

"No," I said, shaking my head into the phone. "I haven't even seen any since November."

"Well, that's a relief. You were actually on my mind. There's a place on West 20th Street. In a carriage house. I want you to see it before the open house this weekend. Can you meet me there on Friday? If we do this right, Voula, if we don't dilly-dally, this could be the one."

I had stopped thinking anything could be the one. Lightning didn't strike twice. I was pretty sure I had found the one as far as guys were concerned. I couldn't expect to find the perfect apartment, too.

"Come on, Voula. Trust me," she said. "You're going to love it."

I doubted that. But I felt like I owed Maureen something, so I wrote down the address and told her I would see her on Friday at the carriage house.

"So what's a carriage house?" I asked when I met her two days later.

She was sitting on the stoop of a nice-looking building. I liked that this was Chelsea west of 8th Avenue. The buildings had real charm. They seemed old school, like a lost piece of New York. I was put at ease immediately.

"Hello, Voula." She stood up. "Let me show you."

I followed her to a gate next to the building. She opened the gate door and we walked along the side of the building into a courtyard, and beyond the courtyard was another three-story building. We entered that building and went into an apartment.

Maureen started her usual spiel as I walked around. I tuned her out. The place was small, like most of the places I had seen, probably smaller. In some neighborhoods it might have been a walk-in closet. The kitchen was separated by a wall that opened up onto a bigger—bigger being a relative term—room. There was yellow linoleum and yellow-and-white tile in the kitchen. A small table was pushed up against the wall in the bigger room. The main room was shaped like an L. So the bedroom wasn't its own room—but you couldn't see the bed when you first came in. Instead you saw a large closet. There was only that one closet in the whole place, but it was big.

Sun was streaming in through the courtyard. Yes, we were south facing, but I didn't think that being on this floor it would make a difference. There was something sort of cheery about the whole place. I knew the seller would probably take the table with two chairs with him, but I could picture myself sitting there.

In an unusual tactical move (for her), Maureen had stopped talking. I noted how odd it was to be with her in silence. She hadn't used the phrase "you just have to have vision" once. She was letting me explore. She was letting the place sell itself.

I looked at her.

She raised her eyebrows and broke the silence. "Are you in love, Voula?"

I was taken aback. "With the place?"

"That…and in general. You look different."

"Well, yeah, I'm in love with a boy—a man. A fireman."

She laughed. "And here?"

"Well." This was strange. I could see it all. I would buy a smaller desk. It would fit perfectly. Honestly, I felt a little dizzy. I needed reality.

"What's the maintenance?" I asked. If nothing else, I'd learned the right questions to ask.

"623."

Good, not great.

"The owner occupancy?"

"80 percent."

The banks would go for that.

"The co-op? They've got to be tough, huh?"

"Two of my colleagues have sold places here and the buyers went through approval with no problem. In one instance the credit report of the buyer was nowhere near as good as yours is." She was smirking. "I must also say that there is storage and laundry in the front building."

I rarely bought anything spontaneously—not even shoes. I really liked the place, though.

"I need to think about it," I said.

"How long did you think about the boy, the man, the fireman?" She hadn't seen me in months but she was completely comfortable making fun of me. Maybe it was the bond we shared from the Great Blackout.

"A long time, at least three weeks." I felt a small victory.

"But really, how long did it take you to *know?*"

Touché.

"I know you aren't going to tell me right now, but there is an open house this weekend. You can see how well this place shows."

"I'll call you on Monday."

"That could be too late."

"I'm going to have to take that chance," I said.

The next day I was slathering baby oil on Jamie's naked torso. Jamie was superstitious. In lieu of a shower before the baby was born, Jamie requested a belly cast. I had no idea what that was until Jamie sent me a link. Apparently we could make a mold of Jamie's belly and then decorate it for posterity. Paul said that it sounded crunchy, but kept asking me if any of us were going to get naked. I had no idea what to expect.

Once again, I had eluded hanging out with Joseph. I still cringed when Paul pulled out condoms.

Jamie, Maura, Morgan, Crystal, Ana and I snacked on wine and cheese as we got down to business. Raj had the digital camera, and I wondered if these types of pictures were the kind you e-mailed around. As usual, Ana was directing traffic while Crystal regaled us with stories from her dysfunctional life. I was assigned the job of greasing up Jamie.

"Voula's probably most familiar with her breasts," Maura cackled.

Jamie stripped off her shirt and bra. She folded her sweatpants down low under her giant belly. There is no way I would have felt comfortable being naked in front of this many people, least of all my mother, but Jamie didn't care.

Her whole upper body was shiny from the Vaseline. Sparky tried to lick it and kept barking. Eventually, Raj banished him to the other room.

Jamie giggled. "I feel like I'm about to make a porno."

"I'll get the DV cam for that one," Raj said.

The look she gave him made me think it wouldn't be the first time.

Ana told Jamie what position to get into. She sat on the floor, leaning back against the couch at an angle. Morgan and Maura placed the strips of cast after Crystal and I had dipped them in warm water. Ana continued to direct traffic and refill wineglasses.

"Make sure you get it all the way down to the pubic line," Ana yelled. She had done extensive Internet research.

"What happens to this thing?"

"When it's dry we paint it and then decorate it," Morgan said.

"Basically, it's some sort of neo-hippie tribal ritual," Crystal added.

After the strips were laid, we sat around and chatted while the cast hardened around Jamie. We fed her bits of cheese because she couldn't move. I liked this idea. I was definitely going to write about it for *On the Verge* magazine. It was a great way to get your women friends involved.

"My boyfriend kept asking me about this," Morgan admitted.

"Mine too," I said, smiling. Finally, I had something to contribute on the boyfriend front.

Ana and Crystal shook their heads, happy they didn't have to deal with what they considered juvenile behavior.

"I'm just glad I didn't get kicked out," Raj said from behind the camera.

He was used to following people around for all his reality shows. He was good at it too. I kept forgetting he was there and feeling like there were only women. Jamie told us about the Lamaze course she was going to start and when she would schedule her tour of the hospital. We had a long talk about breastfeeding, and Jamie reiterated that she was more scared of that than the labor.

"What about the episiotomy?" Raj asked, reminding us once again that there was a boy present, though one who perhaps knew too much.

"Where's Alice?" I asked Morgan.

"She's being really insane about the baby," Jamie said.

"Yeah, her mother-in-law was supposed to baby-sit, but then let it slip that her father-in-law had a sore throat and Alice got totally paranoid," Morgan said. There was dissention in the Olsen Twins ranks.

I was about to tell them about the apartment I'd seen, but Ana said it was time to pull the cast off. That was a job she trusted to no one. I feared that she would break the cast and we would have to start again, but it came off quickly. Then we had a big cast of Jamie's belly. It was wacky.

"The Vaseline really did the trick. I'm so glad I did my research," Ana said.

"I think I'm going to put a sweater on," Jamie said.

"Crystal, are you going to paint it?" Ana asked. I think it was more of a demand.

"Yep. Hey, Jamie, you still want the sunflower?" Crystal yelled into the other room.

"Yeah," Jamie yelled, coming back into the room. "Can you put a sunflower over a light green background?" Jamie rubbed the glistening area below her neck. "I think I actually need a shower."

As Crystal painted, the rest chilled out—drinking wine, eating cheese and listening to Maura talk about how she felt about her body when her kids were born. I was surprisingly interested in what Maura had to say. She made pregnancy seem cool and powerful and female. My mother had been pregnant just as many times. Had she ever felt those things?

Crystal had to let the coat of green paint dry, so the big giant green belly was set aside. We moved on to pizza and Raj made himself scarce. I noticed again how Jamie was changing—it wasn't just her monstrous belly, it was something about her demeanor that I couldn't put my finger on. She was quieter. Maybe it was her fear of labor.

We were pretty buzzed by the time the paint dried. Crystal suggested that we write the stuff we wanted to write on the back before she started the sunflower. She worried that it was going to take even longer and be harder to correct if it dripped.

"What stuff?" I asked Jamie.

"I wanted you all to write messages to the baby. You know, so that she can read them when she gets older."

"Like what?" This really troubled me.

"I don't know. Tell her what I'm like, tell her what you hope," Jamie said.

She hadn't really answered my question.

"Tell him to respect women," Ana said.

"Tell her to love women," Crystal said.

"Tell her all she needs to know is how to give a good blow job," Maura whispered, pointing out once again the vast difference between my mother and everyone else's.

"You're the writer, so I gave you the left boob," Jamie said, squeezing my arm. "Don't tell me you need time to think about it."

"Maybe just a little." Maybe the wine had affected my writing. Would the child look back and wonder why its mother's friends were such lushes? I let everyone else go before me, and then luckily, when it was my turn, everyone was listening to one of Crystal's endless ex-lover stories.

I stared at the inside of the left boob. Someday an adult or at least a teen was going to look at what I was about to write. Jamie didn't just have a big ol' belly. There was a person growing inside there. Someday that person would have trouble believing its mother was ever this young. The life Jamie had had would kind of not exist. It was already changing. Jeez! It was nuts to imagine what was in store for this whole new life. We were traveling forward and soon the kid would be here. Why the hell had I drunk so much wine? I felt outside myself, aware of too many possibilities. I was afraid.

"And so that's when I decided never to date anyone with brain damage again," Crystal said.

If that wasn't the end of an ex-lover story, I didn't know what was. I picked up the Sharpie and wrote: "Hey, little baby. I hope everything goes your way. Let me know if you need anything. Aunt Voula."

Jamie said she wasn't going to read anything until the baby

was old enough. So maybe I would have some time to sneak in with some white-out.

But after I wrote it, I couldn't think of anything else I'd rather say.

On Monday I called Maureen to ask how the open house went. I had found myself thinking a lot over the weekend about how much I liked the idea of living in a carriage house. I liked that it was set back. I liked the courtyard.

"Well, Voula, as we know, it shows very well. There was a lot of interest."

"But no takers, right?"

"No, Voula, but—" I heard her sigh. I think I had worn out my welcome. "I wouldn't wait. I think you need to take the plunge. Are you really serious about buying a place or am I wasting my time?"

I hadn't expected her to lay it on the line like that. I thought again about all of us careening forward. I could put my head in the sand but it didn't mean I could stop anything. It was time to act.

"Bid the asking price."

"Voula…"

"Okay, okay, twist my arm. Go up ten thousand." Why not be proactive?

"Good job. I'll call you on Wednesday."

And because I was proactive (and also really nervous) I called her first thing Wednesday morning.

"Well, Voula, are you sure you know what you want to hear?"

"What do you *think* I want to hear?" What the hell was this?

"Well, I hope you want to hear that you got the place."

"I do," I said, though I have to admit my heart was beginning to race.

"Well, you did."

"I did."

"Yep. Now you just need to find a lawyer and…"

She started talking about the next steps, but I tuned her out. I was going to be a homeowner. This was commitment as I had never known it. This was *real*.

When I got off the phone I vowed to call a real estate lawyer.

First I left Paul a message on his cell. Whenever I didn't get him right away I worried that he was out for a fire. I tried really hard to ignore the voice in my head that said he had a dangerous job, because that voice would remind that like so many things he could be taken away.

I felt my cell phone vibrating, and I looked down to see Jamie's name come up. It struck me that I had wanted to let Paul know about the apartment even before I thought to call her.

I picked up. "Hey, J."

"Actually, Voula, it's Raj. I wanted to let you know that Jamie is in labor."

Push, Push, Breathe

19

I waited around all day for Raj's follow-up phone call, but it didn't come. I couldn't concentrate on any work. I didn't want to call the lawyer in case I had to rush to the emergency room. The baby wasn't supposed to be here yet. We were supposed to have a whole other month. I asked Paul to come over to my place after work. Instead of chaining myself to my laptop during the workday, I sat on the couch and waited.

Kelly came home and saw me looking anxious. She cocked her head. "Voula, are you all right?"

"Yes, I'm just waiting for Paul. Jamie went into labor."

"That's great. Are you going to the hospital?"

"I don't know. I want to, but I'm waiting for Raj to call again. I don't know what stage she's at or if I need to go down there or what. No one's told me anything."

"Well, I'm sure she's going to be fine." She squinted at me. "But will you?"

"I don't know. I feel kind of…helpless."

"Babies are born all the time."

"But early? A month earlier?"

"This set designer I know went two months early."

"Did the baby live?"

"Yeah, he had to go to the ICU, but now he's totally fine. Cries all the time. She's pregnant again."

I nodded, considering this. I knew she was right. I just didn't know what I should do. I wanted Raj to call me with a name and a weight. I wanted pictures of the thing in a crib.

"Does Armando got any wine in this hizzy?" I asked.

"I'll get you something stronger." She went into the kitchen. "I'm glad to see you home. We've missed double dating. I guess we're both kind of in the honeymoon phase, huh?"

"Yeah," I said. She handed me a vodka tonic and I took a big sip. Kelly made a great vodka tonic. It was just the tartness I needed.

"So, you heard Armando's news?"

"No."

"He met someone. A woman."

"What else is new?"

"No, she's not a girlfriend. She's a British restaurateur. She wants him to open a Southern Italian restaurant in London."

"Are you serious?"

"Yeah."

"Is he going to do it?"

"I don't know. He said he hates the hours he's been working. How can the economy be suffering when people are constantly ordering six-hundred-dollar bottles of wine?"

"A good question," I said. "Perhaps a good article."

"Always thinking. So do you think he'll take it?"

"I don't know. I mean, after all the work for his green card, I doubt it."

"Well, you might have to do the roommate search again. This time, I'll help."

I appreciated that she was trying to take my mind off it. Unfortunately all the while we were talking, half my head was on when Raj was going to call. The other half was on the carriage house. I decided to come clean with Kelly.

"Kelly, I put a bid on a place and it got accepted."

"An apartment? You bought an apartment? That's great," she

said, getting up. She stopped in front of the coffee table. "Wait! That means you're moving out too? When?"

"I don't know that I would say 'too'. I don't know that Armando will wind up leaving, but usually it takes about two months or so to close. Maybe by May first."

"Wow! May Day. Unbelievable. Well, I'm happy for you. I'll miss you, though." She continued over to give me a hug.

"Thanks. I mean it's not like I'm moving out tomorrow."

"I know, but I'll miss living with you. You know, it's not easy to find a man in this city, but it's even tougher to find new girlfriends."

"I know. I'll miss you, too, but I'm only like ten blocks away. You can come visit. You can make me vodka tonics. There's even a courtyard where we can drink them."

"Stop bragging," she said. "I might cry."

The moment was interrupted by the phone. I leaped to answer it. It was only Paul. "Hey."

"You don't sound too happy to hear my voice. Still haven't heard from Jamie, huh?"

"No, you've been through this. Is this normal?"

"Some labors take up to twenty-four hours."

"Is that how it was for Angela?" I asked defensively. No matter how much Paul told me there was no relationship, I couldn't help being jealous of the babymama.

"No, she had a C-section."

"Oh," I said, like it meant something, as if I had any right to make any kind of judgments. I heard him laughing over the phone. He found my jealousy hysterical.

"You need to take your mind off Jamie and relax."

"You're trying to get me into the sack, aren't you."

"Absolutely."

"How soon can you get here?"

It wasn't until the next morning that Raj finally called.

"Ananda Maura Jacobs-Sarakanti. Five pounds, three ounces. She's in the NICU."

"What is that?"

"Intensive Care for babies. I'm not sure they really know what they're doing."

"Is the baby okay?"

"Yeah, I think they're just observing because she was so early. The labor was awful. I think the doctors let it go too long. Assholes. They let her push for hours, because she really wanted to give birth vaginally." Raj sounded spent, almost whiny.

I wondered how he had held up in the delivery room. I knew he was used to taking control of all situations. I could imagine him getting arrogant with the doctors.

"We were up all night pushing and then they decided to do the C-section. I pretty much told them I wasn't pleased with the way they were treating my wife."

"Is Jamie all right?" I knew she really hadn't wanted a C-section.

"Yeah. She's tired, though, and she doesn't want to see anyone. Maura is going to come tonight. But other than that, I don't think Jamie's up for guests. We can't really even hold the baby right now. Maura is going to go ballistic when she finds out she can't hold her granddaughter."

"Yeah, well, I'm sure she's just glad they're okay. They are okay?"

"Yeah, and I think Jamie will be able to see family tomorrow."

"When can I come?"

"Tomorrow," Raj said matter-of-factly, and I had never liked him more.

The next day all the Jacobses, Crystal, Paul and I were crowded into Jamie's hospital room. I was searching her for signs of change, but she just looked exhausted. She had a roommate, even though she was supposed to have had a private room. The roommate, she whispered to us, had snored all night keeping her up. She also said in hushed tones, shushing Raj when he tried to add something, that Raj had thrown an embarrassing fit, apparently before we got there, but an effective one. Jamie was scheduled to move to her own room in an hour.

"You can go see Ananda through the partition if you want. I heard crying all night. I hope it wasn't her."

"She's beautiful," Maura said. "Just beautiful."

"Just like her mother and grandmother," Mr. Jacobs added.

"And aunt," Crystal chimed in awkwardly. She was trying to protect Ana's feelings. It was hard for them not to be the center of attention.

Mike stood in the corner of the room, uncomfortable with all the emotion. Mr. Jacobs had already reprimanded him for not turning off his cell phone.

"How are you feeling?" I asked Jamie.

"I'm okay." She looked shell-shocked.

"How are the hemorrhoids?" Ana asked.

I wanted to kick her. I felt Paul squeeze my hand. I squeezed back.

"Okay," Jamie said, looking embarrassed.

"Um, I'd like to see the baby." These were Mike's first words of the afternoon.

The Jacobses and Raj filed out of the room to check out the baby. I hesitated for a minute, and seeing that I wanted to stay behind, Paul dropped my hand and went with the others.

"So are you really okay?" I asked when we were finally alone.

"Well, I don't really think Paul needs to know about my hemorrhoids. I just can't believe my family." She looked at the partition. "Thanks for the flowers and the onesie. It's really cute."

"You're welcome."

"It was nice of Paul to come, even if he does have to know about my ass."

"I think he's been curious about it for a long time."

She smiled a little, then looked away.

"Do hemorrhoids hurt?" I asked after a few seconds of silence.

"Sort of. But I've had them for a while. It's nothing new. What really sucks is all the stuff that keeps coming out of me when I get up to pee."

I didn't want to, but I made a face. Jamie appeared to take pleasure in grossing me out.

She continued, "It's like chunks, bloody chunks."

"Well, what the hell is it?" I asked, truly concerned.

"I don't know, stuff from the C-section." She closed her eyes and pressed back into the stacked pillows. "I really didn't want a C-section."

"It sounds like you didn't have much choice."

"I don't know, it all happened so fast. Raj was freaking out because I was so early. I think he really just wanted me to do it that way so the baby would be out."

Raj freaking out? The guy who talked about spooning bumps and episiotomies?

"I'm sure he just wanted her to be okay," I said. I worried that she wouldn't think I was on her side.

"Yeah, I know."

"At least you didn't have to get an episiotomy or whatever that thing is. At least your hoo-hah is still in top form." I was waiting for a little *"if only you knew how much I would have preferred vaginal birth but how can you know as you aren't even sure you want kids?"* laugh.

She just nodded. "Instead I had my stomach and intestines moved around, pulled out. Luckily, I didn't see any of it."

Unfortunately, *I* could visualize it. And it made me gag a little. I started to sit down on the chair near all the flowers. That smell made my nausea worse. I decided to sit on the bed.

"I guess I wasn't crazy about being pinned to an operating table. You shake afterwards for some reason… Everyone says she is beautiful. She is, right?"

"I haven't seen her yet." I said. "But I'm sure she is. She does have a beautiful mother."

"Right. Thanks for coming to see me."

"Everyone's here to see you," I said.

She pursed her lips. "Tell me something normal. Tell me you had great sex last night. Tell me about something dumb Paul did. Tell me something you would tell me if I hadn't just given birth."

"Well, about the sex thing—I did." Then, I worried that the snorer behind the partition could hear me.

"Showoff," she said.

"And…"

"Oh, God, what have I started?" She snorted.

"I got an accepted bid on a place in Chelsea."

"You're going to move?"

"I think so." I nodded.

"Did you tell Armando?"

"No. Not yet. But he got offered a job in London."

"Is *everyone* moving?" Then Jamie started to cry. She cried like a baby who had missed its nap.

I handed her a tissue.

"I can't let them see me like this," she sniffled. "What are they going to think?"

"You can do whatever you want," I said. "You just had a baby. You're entitled."

"Jeez, Morgan and Alice are coming tomorrow. I don't know if I can take it. Alice said she was ready to have ten more after her labor." She began to cry again.

Really, Jamie had never cried this much. It was sort of scary. I was more comfortable with her being slightly condescending than self-pitying.

"I'm sorry, Voul," she said, suddenly composing herself. "I have to go pee before they come in. If they see that I've been crying they'll never leave me alone." She went into the bathroom.

I could tell by the way she walked that she was in pain.

When she came back she had put on some makeup. She had a deft hand and you would never know that there'd been tears.

"Your eyes look great," I said.

"Yeah, luckily I went to Diane right before this happened."

I stood up so she could get back into bed. She arranged herself on the plastic pillow and pulled up the covers. "You know, you really should see the baby."

"I will," I said. I sat down on the bed again. "I'll see her on the way out. Now I want to see you."

"Thank you," she said. She took my hand and blinked.

"Don't start again," I said. I tried to be tough like I meant business. If she wanted to cry, I was going to let her cry. But I just didn't like to watch her shuffle over to the bathroom or imagine the pain she was in.

"I know, I know." She picked up our clasped hands and bit her own hand to stop herself.

The family came back in.

"Well, she is just about the most beautiful baby I have ever seen," Ana said.

I couldn't tell if she was admiring or jealous.

"They certainly make a good baby," Mr. Jacobs said.

Jamie smiled, and I know that two people could tell she had been crying. Paul knew, because he could read people. He winked at me when I caught his eye. And Maura knew, because she knew Jamie. She patted Jamie's hair for a minute, like Jamie was the baby. Everyone watched them.

"Well, Voula has some news," Jamie said to take the focus off her.

Everyone turned to me expectantly.

"Oh, how wonderful," Maura said, hugging Paul.

I realized that she thought we had gotten engaged. I started to explain, but Jamie did.

"Mom, Mom," she yelled. "Calm down! She's buying a place."

"Oh, I thought…" Maura said.

"Yeah, we know what you thought," Ana said, annoyed.

Jamie laughed, and I knew she was pleased that the attention had been diverted from her.

So I told the Jacobses how I had a bid on a place. I described the apartment in great detail, saying the words "carriage house" over and over for emphasis. I don't like too much attention either. But I knew that not everyone was really listening to me. Mike was probably anxious to get back to work and nervous from just being around people. Mr. and Mrs. Jacobs probably wanted more info on their grandchild. Ana was just bitter because she never felt loved enough. Crystal didn't like sharing the spotlight. Paul would later tell me that he was imagining the sex we had had that morning.

Later, on the way out, we walked by the NICU. Paul pointed Ananda out to me. She looked like Jamie, but with Raj's coloring. She was sleeping peacefully. I pressed my face to the glass and gasped.

"I can't believe that yesterday that was inside Jamie."

"Now it's here on our planet."

"It's crazy," I said. At that moment, without opening her eyes, Ananda Maura Jacobs-Sarakanti opened her mouth and let out the biggest wail I had ever heard.

She was making her presence known. She was in our world and we'd better like it.

20

I called Jamie every day for the first week of her motherhood. She sounded beat, and sometimes Raj—who was on paternity leave—deflected my calls, saying she was asleep. I wanted her to know that at the drop of a hat I would be there, because my pregnancy book said that new moms were on an emotional roller coaster. I felt a little better knowing that her mom was coming every other day.

I scheduled myself for an appointment with Diane the day before my first home visit with the new family. I filled Diane in about Jamie's labor and my accepted bid. Diane had given me the name of her lawyer when I started my house hunt, so when Maureen asked me who I was going to use, I said him. Now Diane seemed to be a little less obsessed with religion, but she let it slip that she had seen *The Passion* four times. I decided not to go for a bikini wax.

Maureen phoned as I was coming out of the salon. I had long since stopped looking forward to her calls. Usually it meant bad news, or more money spent.

"What now?" I answered.

"I called Rob Agranoff. He hasn't heard from you."

Maureen was turning into my mother. Rob Agranoff was the lawyer. I had never needed a lawyer before, but everything I had read said that one was necessary.

"I haven't had a chance. Besides, they just accepted my offer."

"Until the contract is signed, Voula, something could go wrong. Call him and get the ball rolling, because I would hate for the sellers to get tired of waiting."

"Okay, I can't call today, but I will call tomorrow." I was starting the column in my head. *My real estate agent, having successfully hooked me on a place, has now revealed that she is only interested in getting me to seal the deal so she can collect her commission.* Though we had never overtly talked about it, I was pretty sure that Maureen read my column in *Financial Woman*. I tried not to think about what she would think of this one.

I called Rob Agranoff and made an appointment for the next day. I wasn't due at Jamie's until one, or as Jamie said, "when she should be down." I finished my column about having your apartment bid finally accepted and then dashed off the outline for my next column: "Getting Legal." It would cover the lawyer aspect of my purchase.

I was going to sign the contract and hand over the biggest check I had ever written.

I was adding three zeros to the number twenty-two when it hit me that I wasn't really sure I wanted to do this. I had only seen the place once. Okay, I knew the location pretty well, but I hadn't been back at different times of the day. What if there were large, loud warehouses I didn't know about that started making noise at two a.m.? What if the neighbors sucked? They had an unusual sublet policy: you had to be there for a year before you could sublet three out of every five years. What did that even mean? What was I getting myself into?

But I had an appointment at eleven. So I went downtown to Rob Agranoff's offices near City Hall.

Rob Agranoff was a tall, thin man with a bird's nose and a thick New York accent. He appeared competent and told me that he would charge me seven hundred upfront and seven hundred at the closing.

That, in addition to the fee I was going to have to pay the bank for giving me a jumbo mortgage to cover the rest of the twenty percent, was more money that I hadn't anticipated. When did it stop? The only plus was that I managed to lock in my rate for sixty days.

After Rob went over his fees, he began explaining the contract and I began zoning. It was as if he were speaking another language. I knew I should be following. He had gone through the trouble of making a copy for me.

"Now, you should probably get a closing in early May."

Finally, I was paying attention. "What?"

"Well, I think that's fairly average for getting everything together. You know, you have to get co-op approval."

"It's so soon," I said. *Walk away. Walk away.*

I hadn't told Armando that I planned on moving out by May. I had just continued to be swept along in all of this. Maybe it was a sign that I needed more time. Fuck it. I was spending money, I wanted a house.

"Usually, people are happy to have this go quicker."

"I guess I am."

"Okay, so all I need now is for you to sign this and give me the check. Then the sellers will sign and we'll be all set."

"And then it's done. I can't break the deal."

"Do you want to do this?" Rob asked, looking over the contract. "It seems like a pretty good deal for the size and the neighborhood. Do you have a concern?"

"No." I didn't really. I mean, sure there were things I didn't know, but how long could I dilly-dally about this? "No, I'll sign."

And I did. I signed my name on the contract. That was fine. It wasn't until I handed over the jumbo check that I really felt locked in. What was wrong with me? I wanted this. I had to grow up.

"Okay, so we're all set. I'll call you as we get closer to the closing and tell you what we need."

That was it. Then I was back out on the street. I felt like I had never spent money so fast—but it hadn't been fast. It had been coming. I was moving with life. I couldn't fight it. I had to go with it. It had been about a year since Jamie announced that she was trying. Things had moved along without me. Maybe for once I could make them move *with* me.

When I got to Jamie's, she answered the door looking fatigued. Her body still seemed top-heavy and she was wearing the same outfit she had been wearing at the hospital. My ringing the bell must have set off Sparky, who began barking, setting off the baby. Jamie looked like she needed a Calgon bath.

"Welcome to the madhouse," she said to me, then she screamed, "Shut up, Sparky!"

I thought about the mother at Alice's lunch who had said Sparky would play second fiddle, and wondered if that had already happened.

Raj came in carrying the crying baby. She was still so small. I reached out to touch her and Raj jerked her away. It was awkward, but I pretended not to notice and sat down on their couch, hoping to at least get some affection from Sparky. He jumped all over me but wouldn't settle down and be cuddled.

"How are you?" I asked Jamie, who was staring toward the kitchen where Raj was attending to Ananda.

"Fine," she said, distracted by whatever Raj was doing in there. There was a line between her eyebrows. She called into the kitchen. "Raj, don't give her the formula. I'm coming."

I didn't know if I was ready to witness the breasts I had always admired being suckled by a tiny person, but I had no choice. Raj brought Ananda back in to be nursed. He seemed more uptight than Jamie, but both of them were looking pretty nervous.

"I still don't know if I'm doing this right," Jamie said, almost apologizing to me. Ananda made such weird gaspy noises it seemed like she could stop breathing at any second and it didn't matter whether or not she was being fed. This whole thing was pretty scary. Raj and Jamie didn't seem like they should know how to take care of this itty-bitty creature, but there they were, cradling it, trying to figure it out. It was surreal.

"How is she?" Raj asked.

"I don't think she wants anything," Jamie said, sounding unsure.

"She was giving the cues," Raj said defensively.

The little blob didn't seem capable of giving anything. How could they expect to decipher anything about this riddle?

"When's the last time she ate?" Jamie focused on the clock.

They would do this throughout my visit: try to gauge the last time the baby ate, slept, shit. The baby was on some kind of clock with constantly changing hands.

After the attempt at feeding, Raj put Ananda back to bed. The crib was in their room, where it would stay for six weeks (or at least that was the current plan). I was happy that Raj made himself scarce. I wanted to get the lowdown from Jamie about what was really going on, but I told myself to tread carefully. I was getting this vibe from her that she could crack at any second.

"So, how are you?"

"I don't know," she said. "I don't know how I'm supposed to be."

"But how are you?" I asked again.

"I just don't really feel connected to myself. I feel like I have no control. Raj has been wonderful. He's got this thing, though, about germs and the baby. He's really paranoid, because she was so early."

That explained the pull-away.

"Are you worried?"

"Voul, I'm worried about so much other shit, germs are the least of my problems. Also, this breast thing. I think Raj doubts I can do it. Hell, I doubt I can do it."

"You can do it," I said. I had no idea what "doing it" entailed, but I wanted to rally the troops.

"I don't know that I can."

She grimaced, and for a moment she started to cry, but before I was able to try to comfort her, she stopped, glancing into the other room to make sure Raj couldn't see.

She continued. "It hurts, sometimes. And I'm not sure she's

getting what she needs. I don't know if I can give her what she needs."

"Of course you can, you're her mom."

Jamie shook her head. "Well, I don't think Raj believes she is going to get enough to eat. It was better when my mom was here. She kind of deflected him. Now he wants to buy a scale so we can calculate the number of ounces she gains."

I didn't really know what to say. I waited so she could continue.

"This isn't my body," she said, gesturing to her milk-stained shirt. "I don't know what this is. It's like a machine that gives birth and makes food, just not very well."

"You're doing great."

"Not really. I called Alice the first day I was by myself with her. Raj had to go in and approve the promos for the season premiere. Ananda had been crying the entire day. In twenty-four hours, she slept maybe, *maybe,* three."

"Wow!"

"Wow is right. But you know what? Alice had acted like the first few weeks were so great that I didn't want to say anything. I just prayed that she couldn't hear Ananda crying."

"You could have called me," I said. She looked at me and I know she was thinking the same thing I was—what did I know about kids? I was still avoiding my boyfriend's at all costs. "Okay, so I'm not Dr. Spock, but I did read that book."

"Yes, that book, I know about the book. Thank you for that. I appreciate that you read that book."

"What I mean is, you could just call me if you wanted to complain." The thing is, I meant it. I was so in awe of the fact that she had actually created that alien thing, I would have done almost anything to show my respect.

"Be careful what you wish for," she said.

"I'm serious."

Jamie looked at me and nodded. She nodded for a long time, and then I realized that she was actually going to let herself cry again. This time, I got to her and hugged her before she could stop herself. If the baby got to cry all the time, she should be able to too.

"I just don't know what she needs."

"Don't worry," I said. "You're doing just fine. And I'm here. I don't have advice on babies, but I'm here for times like this, or, say, if you need to shower or something." The book I kept reading said new moms had no time even to shower.

"Do I smell that bad?" Jamie said, pulling away. There were still tears running out of her eyes, but she was smiling.

"Well, you've certainly had fresher days." I let her cry for a while and then she made me tell her about this new Peruvian place that Paul and I had gone to on Smith Street.

"I like hearing this stuff," she said when I was done. "I like feeling normal and I like that you and Paul are doing so well. This is so unlike you. You're actually letting this work."

"It wasn't me, you know, with the problems. It was just that I never met anyone worth it."

"Except Warren Tucker."

"Except Warren Tucker, but he was unattainable. This is happening."

"Speaking of Warren Tucker…"

"Here we go, just when I am happy with Paul."

"You never watched the tape, did you?"

"I watched part of it. I don't think I want to watch the rest. I don't want to see him. I'm happy now with Paul. I don't want to think about Warren." It was sort of true. I was happy with Paul, but I still thought about Warren.

"Oh," Jamie said. She looked so bummed.

"What?"

"Well, I was going to ask you something."

"Anything," I said.

"It's about Raj's show."

"Anything except anything having to do with Raj's shows. I have no desire to be a reality-TV star."

"Not star. You know *Mr. Right…Now* is premiering this week. Raj is really stressed, not just about the baby but about the fact that it's going head to head with *The Apprentice.*"

"Are you serious?" There was no way that was a good idea.

"Yes, but the premiere party is this week at the W in Midtown East. It's supposed to be in the penthouse."

"Cool."

"Well, yeah. If you aren't leaking milk. He really wants me to go."

"Of course, I'll baby-sit."

"No, I think *you* should go."

"Will you be there?" Maybe I could do it if she was at my side. It was kind of a good idea, I guess. I could get Warren out of my head once and for all. Maybe.

"No. I'm just not up to it. I don't feel like leaking all over some nice outfit that doesn't fit me right anyway. I don't feel like being judged by the super-toned women that he works with. I know it's going to piss him off, but I don't want to go."

"They do know, these women and Raj, that you just gave birth."

"If Raj was married to Alice, she would be there. Even if she was in labor. He's married to me and I'd like him to go with my best friend. That's you, okay?"

"I don't know."

"C'mon. See Warren. You can do it. Plus, it's going to be a great party. It's for the whole cast. And you can't reveal to anyone that Warren's one of the top two to get the Golden Condom."

"Did he win?"

"I don't know. It's going to be a live finale, but you might be able to guess from how he acts at the party."

"Okay. I'll go." Suddenly my stomach was dropping. I couldn't believe I was going to see Warren Tucker...soon. "When?"

"Saturday night." Saturday was my cousin Georgia's shower. I was trying not to stress about the fact that Helen and I had talked about her coming. We had seen each other only a handful of times since Christmas, but Helen felt strongly that now that she and I were getting along, she had a right to be involved with the whole family. She did, I guess.

I updated Jamie on what was going on with my family. I had

the same feeling I'd had in the hospital room, that she needed me to take her hand and link her to the outside world. I feared that she was starting not to be able to see out of her apartment, with its barking dog and crying baby. I feared that she was becoming overwhelmed by dirty diapers.

When I got back to my place, it was early evening. Kelly was home and on the phone with her new boyfriend, Joel, and Armando was in the kitchen making some *cucina povera* that I had no doubt would taste fantastic, like nothing I had ever eaten. I had the perfect opportunity to break the news of my move to them, but instead, I went in my office and hid.

My mom and I showed up at The Crystal Palace in Astoria for the shower. I only came to this hall for events like these, and I dreaded it. Bridal showers for Greek women are set up to torment the single. They didn't show this in *My Big Fat Greek Wedding,* but women greet unmarried women at these showers by saying *"Kai sta dika sou,"* which means "and at yours," which is kind of implying that you should get on the stick and find a guy (Greek, of course) so they can come to *your* shower and then the Greek god can get you pregnant before your ovaries shrivel and die or you become an old spinster woman making *melomakarona* for no one but yourself.

This time when people said it to me, I thanked them and smiled as usual, unlike my cousin Toula who always says with her Greek accent, "fingers crossed," like some kind of desperate freak. But my smile hid a little secret. So I wasn't going to be having a shower anytime soon, but I did have my prospects. My *melomakarona* could be eaten by my boyfriend—if I ever got the recipe out of my mother's hands.

Helen was there when we arrived. My aunt Effie sat her with some of Georgia's friends from her graduate program. I waved over to her as soon as we got in, and felt my mother tense.

"What is she doing here?" she hissed at me.

"She came to see her cousin?"

"You knew she would be here?"

"Yes, Ma." I acted like it wasn't a big deal. "I'll go get you some wine." I took my time, making a sport out of thanking everyone who wanted to come to the shower I might never have. I even bent to kiss my sister Helen, which seemed to mean a lot to her.

"I thought you were going to bring Cristina. She would have had fun."

"I was scared of Ma. I didn't want Cristina to know that her grandmother could be so mean. Andre's sisters have her thinking her grandmother is a witch."

I looked over at my mother. I could tell that Aunt Effie was doing some kind of damage control. My mother's face was contorted.

"She might not be that far off."

Helen looked toward our mother. "I don't want there to be a scene."

I scanned the room, taking in all the other older females. There is no way my mother would make a scene in front of these women. Her brand of anger usually had one direction: me.

"Don't worry. You're not a teenager anymore."

"I know," my sister said, meeting my eyes. "Neither are you."

She had a point. As I headed back over toward my mother, my aunt Effie stopped me and kissed my cheeks. She said, "your mother," but that was it.

My mother ignored me throughout the luncheon and the present opening. There were lots of pictures of the furniture that people had bought the couple. And underwear, a lot of underwear. Normally, it would have been embarrassing for me to see this stuff with my mother, but since she was ignoring me, I decided not to care. I laughed and whooped it up with everyone. It was freeing actually, to just not care.

My mother wanted to leave as soon as I had taken my last bite of dessert. I got my coat and told her to hold on while I said goodbye to Helen.

"Make sure you hurry," she said coldly.

"I hope it was okay," I said to Helen, gesturing to the table of chattering professionals.

"I learned a lot about modern advancements in mental health."

Again, I looked over toward my mother's grimace. "Well, I wish I had been sitting here, Mom didn't talk to me at all. So, are you still coming to the wedding? I think babba is actually flying over for it."

"Well, Andre will be with me, so it shouldn't be as bad."

It was funny that she said that, because the idea of bringing Paul, an idea that had been crossing my mind a lot these days, seemed like it would only make things worse.

I called a car to come pick my mother and me up and take us back to her place. She didn't say anything the entire way. She sat folded up in the back of the sedan, implacable. I could have let it rest and gone home when we got out of the car, but I didn't. I climbed out and called to my mother as she made her way toward her stoop.

"Your daughter and her husband are coming to the wedding, like it or not."

She stopped, but didn't turn around.

"That's right, that guy you didn't think was good enough has been her husband for years. They have two kids. You've been warned. And you better tell babba."

She turned to me. "*You* tell him. You're so good at telling everyone everything."

I wasn't sure why she was speaking English, but she was. I was surprised that she was fighting back. It was more like her to just ignore it and hope it went away. On the one hand I wanted her to fight back, on the other I feared what would happen.

"I'm telling you so you'll tell your husband and he won't make a scene and I won't have to call the police again. Or have you forgotten that he almost killed her."

"You called? You called?" She walked closer to me, not caring that her downstairs neighbor was putting his garbage out. "You didn't call. I am the one."

With that my mother turned and walked up the stairs and into her apartment. And I began to see things differently once again.

21

The thing about March is that it sucks for clothes. I was wearing the black wool pants I had worn to the shower and had changed out of the cashmere twin set I had borrowed from Jamie ("you can have it, I'm never going to wear it again") into a silk kimono top that was also hers ("that I want back"). The top was sexy, but I just felt bulky and pale. Why did my winter weight have to stick around for spring?

I was going to see Warren Tucker. I hadn't even told Paul about it, just that I was doing Jamie a favor by going to this party. It's not like I thought we were going to run off together, but to me it was a big deal. I had spent so much time imagining meeting him again. In my fantasies he hadn't changed a bit, he looked like he had on the jetty, not the tape. He would look at me like he did on the jetty, the night we finally hooked up, and he would say something like "It's you, Voula, it's always been you." Okay, I know that Ross said that to Rachel, but whatever, I thought of this in 1995.

So in a way I didn't want to see him. I purposely avoided the channel that the show was premiering on because I didn't want to see any promos for it, and I didn't watch any talk shows the whole week before the premiere. I didn't even want to catch a glimpse before the moment we met.

I knew that Paul was the guy for me. Rationally, I knew it. But I thought that if Warren said that to me and looked at me a certain way—oh, who knew what I thought... It was stupid, knowing that he had liked Jamie, but I had held on so long. I still couldn't stop thinking about Warren. The trouble was, Paul kept popping back into my fantasy whenever I tried to imagine that first meeting with Warren. The only way I could have gotten any further in the fantasy was to imagine Paul dead, and I definitely couldn't do that.

"Are you all right?" Raj asked, handing me a drink. We were at the W. It was swanky. The big terrace was full of people sipping drinks and grooving to the sounds of DJ Stinky. "I know it's a bit of a scene."

"No, it's awesome," I said, taking a canapé. "Don't feel like you have to stay with me, I know this is a work thing."

"Thanks, Voula. I should have told you to bring Paul."

"That's okay," I said.

Raj kind of stared at me.

"Really, he's with his son tonight."

"Okay," he said. "Listen, how does Jamie seem to you?"

"I think she's doing okay. I think it's probably an adjustment. Why?"

But Raj didn't get to tell me why, because the head of the network was there commending Raj on all his hard work, and as soon as I got introduced, they were off to meet some other VIPs. I took a coconut shrimp as it went by.

Then I saw Warren Tucker on the other side of the terrace with the backdrop of the city behind him.

I swallowed. I think I'd stopped breathing. I forced the oxygen down into my lungs and walked over.

As I got closer to him, he looked at me. His eyes were scanning the room and went right over me, but then quickly darted back to my face. In my fantasy about this moment, he never recognized me right away. I looked so good in my fantasy (of course!) that I was almost a different woman. In reality, he did recognize me.

"Voula?" he asked.

I was right in front of him.

"Is that you?"

"Hi, Warren."

The last time I had seen Warren he was a boy. His face was narrow and covered by scruff. I don't think I ever saw him without a baseball cap and a T-shirt. Now, standing on the terrace, he wore an expensive suit, a receding hairline and rounder clean-shaven face.

"I can't believe you're here. How great." He kissed me on the cheek, like you might greet someone you knew on a city street, but I didn't know him. Not anymore.

I could tell as Warren started talking that he was different. He started telling me about his job like I should know the company he worked for. He was a man. His life had moved forward. Sure, it was about to completely change when he got recognized on the street, but Warren hadn't fantasized about me the way I had about him. To him, I was just another hook-up on a jetty.

This was proven when he said: "Yeah, every now and then I wonder what you guys are up to." By "you guys" he meant the girls who lived in the Jacobs house that summer. He really meant Jamie. I knew that if I let myself think about it I would feel hurt, so instead I asked Warren if he thought that he was going to win and be *Mr. Right…Now.*

He laughed. "You wonder what these things are going to make you look like—you know they say it's all about the editing."

"Well, you must have seen enough of these shows."

"Yeah. My buddies sort of dared me, and now, I'm not so sure."

"But I guess it's worth it if you win. You get the girl and a million dollars."

"Actually, we only get a half mil. I'm not sure about the girl. She's pretty hard to read."

I assumed he was talking about Belinda, the contestant on

the show. I still wasn't sure what the point of this (or any) reality show was, but I didn't want to ask.

He looked around. "I think she probably picked Rod."

"Rod?" I nodded, and for some reason we both laughed. It
was strange to be having a normal conversation with him, but
as with most conversations with people you don't know that
well, there was soon a lull.

"Well, listen, Warren. It was good to see you."

"Oh, you too, Voula. You look great."

"Thanks."

He bent to kiss my cheek again. "Say hi to Jamie."

I shouldn't have been surprised by that, but it stung. Was
Jamie so hard to forget and our night together impossible to
remember?

I looked around for Raj, who was over talking to a bunch of
men in suits. I wasn't sure I wanted to disturb him. I walked away
from where Warren was and looked out over the city. It was
such a beautiful view, but I felt sunk. There was so much I still
needed to learn about myself, about everything. I had pined for
Warren even though he had wanted Jamie all along. I might have
pined forever, even though I was with Paul, if I hadn't seen him.

"Don't jump," Raj said, coming up next to me.

"Okay."

"I'm sorry if this is boring for you. I told Jamie I would be
okay by myself."

"But you wanted her to come, huh?"

He nodded.

I looked back over the city. "It's breathtaking, it really is."

Raj turned and looked out at the view with me. "Yeah, but
I would rather be there right now."

I put my hand on his shoulder. He may have been a germa-
phobe, but I shouldn't judge. I was a many-things-phobe.

"She's gonna be fine."

"She is, right?"

"Yes, she is." I stared at his profile. I wasn't sure *I* was going
to be. "Now, do you mind if I get the hell out of here?"

"Not at all."

★ ★ ★

When I got home, I checked my messages. There was one from Paul, who was calling me while Joe watched *Finding Nemo* for the eightieth time. It sounded loud at his apartment. I didn't want to call him right back. I just wanted to have a moment to myself while no one was home.

I wasn't sure how to feel about meeting Warren Tucker. It was good, I guess, in a way. I hadn't felt an overwhelming passion for him and that was right because I was feeling a lot of passion for Paul. But I had missed him for so long, wondered about him and compared people to him. In my world there were millions of irrational fears. Maybe the only time in my life where I had ever had irrational hope was when it came to Warren Tucker. I guess whenever things got me down, I comforted myself, knowing that there was someone out there who could make it all better. It was a ridiculous idea, but I had clung to it. I knew in my brain that we wouldn't be together—I must have. But after seeing him, and knowing that there really was nothing between us, well, after all that time, I just felt let down.

I went into my room and found the tape. I was going to be moving soon anyway—I might as well watch the rest of it and see what he said about Jamie and if I even came up at all. I popped it into the VCR in the living room. If my roommates discovered me, I planned on telling them I was doing research. I rewound the tape a little and pressed Play.

"I used to work as a bartender in the summers when I was going to school. My senior year I did it on Block Island at this pub. There was this girl I had a crush on. She was a waitress at the pub."

Oh, boy, It couldn't be that he was talking about that summer. Now, on top of everything, I was going to find out that he had had a crush on Jamie.

"She had these eyes, these dark eyes, you know, they were almost black. She wasn't even my type, but the way she used to look at me…"

Oh *panayia mou!* I stood up. He was talking about *me,* not

Jamie. All of a sudden I was scared. But fuck it. I had to hear the rest. I sat down again.

"All summer I flirted with her. She just didn't seem to like me."

Was he crazy?

"I used to mess up drink orders so she would have to come back to the bar."

I guess I had always thought he was stoned.

"But this one night, everyone decided to climb on these rocks on the beach. She didn't want to. I think she was scared. So I stayed with her. There was a fire on the beach. She told me all about—"

I paused the VCR. I felt tears coming to my eyes. For some reason, that night I had told him all about my sister. I didn't want to hear what I had said. I didn't want him to use it, use me, use Cristina so he could prove something to the judges.

Then I had to see. I had delayed this enough. I pressed Pause again.

"She told me about…all kinds of things. It was just a perfect night. It was like we were just talking. And then, I finally worked up the nerve and kissed her. We—we spent the night together, but it was that kiss and the breeze. That was it."

The judges didn't say anything for a minute.

"Thank you, Warren," Raj said. "We'll let you know."

Thank you, Warren Tucker. Thanks for not forgetting and not selling me out. If anything, this should have made me want Warren again, but it didn't. I felt…happy. Somewhere in his head, he thought about me, too. It had been important to him, that night on the jetty. But that was in the past. I had Paul and Warren had the Golden Condom.

I went to bed and slept soundly.

On Sunday I was reading the Vows in the Sunday Styles section before heading over to Paul's, when Maureen called. I hadn't recognized her number, and when I heard babies crying in the background I knew she was calling me from her land line at home. It seems we were getting closer.

"Hi, Voula. I'm sorry to call you on the weekend. I wanted to call you on Friday, but all three of the kids are sick, and even with Leona helping out it's a challenge. I know you're supposed to close on May first, but the co-op board is not going to meet with you until they get more information on your finances."

"What?" I had been hoping that the board would meet with me right before my closing, which I had been hoping would be the week of May third.

"Yeah, they say you haven't given them complete financials."

"Are they out of their minds?" I had rushed my accountant so I could get them my 2003 tax return along with my 2002 tax return. I had also given them two letters of personal and professional reference and they knew more about my credit (which was excellent!) than I did.

"They're confused about your job. Co-op boards have a tendency to be wary of freelancers. You're depleting your savings to buy this place. I think they want to see that you are going to be employed for the rest of the year."

"Of course I'm going to be working this year. But I don't know on what yet."

"Look, your sellers have already relocated to London. It's not like they're still in the building to push the meeting through. You have to play by the rules if you want this place."

I *could* walk away, I thought. I was feeling especially lazy spread out on the couch at that moment.

"Well, how can I make them happy? Is it even possible?"

"What I would do is get them all your stubs for the past year. They want to see consistency."

"I don't have stubs. I invoice, but it's not like every week. It's kind of a mess depending on when I complete stories. It's not going to look like your average job."

Maureen sighed. "Well, can you get an employer to write a letter saying that you will be working for them?"

"I don't think anyone is going to do that. I can't ask unless I pitch something, and even then I don't feel comfortable."

"Well, I don't know what to tell you, Voula. They aren't going to meet with you until you get this stuff together. If they don't meet with you, you can't close. Maybe you could just try to get one letter saying you have some jobs lined up and explain it when you go in for your meeting."

I heard a loud wail behind her and Leona cursing.

"Look I have to go. Give me a call tomorrow and I'll walk you through this."

I hung up. I didn't know what I was going to do. I had two more pieces left on my real estate series. Incidentally they would be covering the co-op meeting and closing. The editor of *Financial Woman* had said we might want to think about doing one more. There was no way I was going to be able to coerce him into lying on paper about getting a job for the year. I didn't even want to work for *Financial Woman* for a year. I was screwed! Who knew what was going to come up writing-wise? It just didn't work that way. I did have a meeting with Eve Vitali, at *On the Verge,* coming up. I had finally tweaked my baby pitch enough to present it. If she went for it, I wasn't sure that she would tell me right away. I couldn't expect her to commit to a series and then commit on paper. Who the hell was this co-op board? And why did they have a right to judge me?

"They're the co-op board. They can do anything," Maureen had said ominously when she first told me about all the personal information I would have to provide them with. Wasn't there some kind of amendment to protect me from this kind of thing? I wrote down "the co-op board can do anything" in my notebook. It was a good title for my co-op board meeting piece. Hopefully, I would actually have a meeting to write about.

I called Paul to find out what time he wanted me to come over.

"Actually, I was thinking of coming into the city tonight."

"Why? Do you have to work?"

"No, I thought I could have an actual date with my lady."

"You mean, instead of just doing it on the living room floor by the fire?"

"Yeah, I thought maybe we'd go back to Esme's Eatery. What do you think?"

"Sounds fabulous," I said. "I'll try not to talk too much about how my co-op board is made up of a bunch of Orwellian assholes."

"Really?" he asked, sounding generally interested.

"Yeah."

"Well, you can tell me over dinner, but I want this to be a nice night."

"Okay, wait, am I forgetting something?"

"Yeah, it's our six-month anniversary."

"It is?"

"Yep."

"You mean I've been going out with someone for six months?"

"No. You've been going out with *me* for six months."

"Cool." I was really proud of myself.

"So. I'll pick you up at eight."

"Is it easier for me to just meet you there?"

"Voula, let's go on a nice date. Okay?"

"Sure. See you at eight." I hung up.

Would it be wrong to wear Jamie's kimono top again? No, and I had to. It was the nicest thing I had. I had barely worn it last night. And with smoking going on only outside, it didn't even smell worn. Even the smoking ban was working in my favor. The tyrannical co-op board no longer presented as big a problem. I was in a six-month relationship.

I sat back down. I had plenty of time to get ready *and* to read the paper.

I had no idea Paul was going to pop the question.

22

No! Not *that* question!

Paul wanted me to move in with him. To *Brooklyn*.

He waited until we were on dessert to ask me. Right before he said it, I had just tried a gooey, delicious bite of his molten chocolate cake and couldn't have been happier.

"So I was thinking you should scrap this whole co-op board thing and move in with me."

"What?" I almost barked.

"I want you to move in with me."

"To...Brooklyn."

"Yeah. I figured we spend enough time together. You seem to want out of your place. This way, we could hang out even when I get home late."

"We could still do that when I get the new place," I said. "You can still just come over after your shift."

"I know, but why have two places? Why wonder where my deodorant is because I left it at your place? Or what about when you left your new Tori Amos CD at my house and you said it was affecting your writing because you hadn't put it in your iPod yet?"

"That was once."

"Voula, I don't know about you, but this relationship seems serious."

"It is."

"So why not take it to the next level."

"The next level is Brooklyn?"

"Voula," he said. He was taking a tone. "You're from Queens. Don't start subscribing to this bridge and tunnel bullshit."

"I like living in Manhattan."

"I thought you liked my neighborhood. You told me you wanted to pitch an article about how Brooklyn beats Manhattan."

"I do. I actually did pitch it, but it had been done already."

"You see. It's just like the sign says."

"What sign?"

"Brooklyn. Believe the hype." He nodded, pleased that he had made a point.

This Brooklyn line of defense wasn't working. I decided to try something else.

"I already signed a contract."

"But you haven't closed. I think you can get out of it. Say we're getting engaged."

"Is that what's coming? Are we going to get married?" I asked before I could stop myself. Suddenly, *I* was popping the question.

"I don't think it's that far off," he said.

"We've only been together for six months."

"Voula, I know it's soon, but I love you. I think we love each other. I would like to live together for a little while before we get engaged. If you need a time frame, I would say six months."

He was getting ahead of himself. I could barely keep up. "I'm not giving you an ultimatum. I'm trying to slow you down."

He looked down at his chocolate cake. I could tell that I was upsetting him. I didn't really want to slow him down, I just didn't want him to go any faster. I was still getting my bearings, and I knew that Jamie never considered herself serious with a boy until they had been together for over six months.

"I have to say, Voula, that I feel like you're always pulling away from me."

"What do you mean? Just because I don't want to move in with you, I'm pulling away?"

"You never really want to come over when Joey's there."

"And that's why you want me to move in?"

"I want you to move in because it makes sense."

"To you. I just decided I wanted to buy this place."

"You've never been sure about it. Not one hundred percent."

"Look, there's nothing in life that you can be sure of one hundred percent."

He looked incredibly hurt. I stared down at my pumpkin crème brûlée.

"I'm not going to die," he said quietly. "I'm not your sister."

"You're a fucking fireman," I said, a little too loud for this dark restaurant. "Tell me what guarantee you have of that."

He shook his head. "Of course it's a dangerous job, but that doesn't mean we can't live."

"I just don't know if I can deal with it."

"So you keep me at arm's length."

I kind of laughed. "You really have no idea how close you are to me."

"So is this it? Is this as close as I can get?"

"No, but I just can't rush into things."

"Instead you can be pessimistic about everything?"

"This is just how I am." I stared at him. "I guess I do still feel a little awkward about Joey. I don't want to come between you. I know he comes first and I'm scared to be around him. If he doesn't like me, what if that means you won't either?"

"Look, I'm going to like you no matter what. It's not a question. I just want you to trust me."

"I do," I said.

"But if you trusted me, you would talk about your sister, talk about your family."

"I don't talk about that stuff to anyone."

"Maybe you should."

I shook my head. "You never talk about 9/11—does that mean you don't trust me?"

"I don't talk about it because…" He stopped.

I almost didn't want him to tell me. If he was showing his cards, I would have to show mine.

"I don't talk about it because it feels cheap to talk about it. Everyone talks about it, but they don't know. Everyone co-opts it. And I don't talk about it because it makes me feel like a coward."

"Why?"

"Because I wasn't there."

"What?"

"I was in Disney World with Joey. I could have taken him in the summer, but he wasn't in school yet and I found a cheaper deal for after Labor Day."

"You couldn't have—"

"Of course not. It's not my fault. Right? Not really. I mean, I drove straight back up—you know the airports were closed. I went there. I helped. But I wasn't there when it happened, you know, I wasn't with my guys."

"No one knew what was going to happen," I said. "How could you have known?"

He looked at me and I understood that it didn't matter. There was nothing rational about feeling this kind of guilt. There was nothing that could be said. I just had to listen.

"If it hadn't been for Joey, I'm not sure I could've made it. That whole way up 95, I made it a game, you know. We sang songs. And after, if he wasn't around, I don't know how I would have dealt with all of it. If it wasn't for him, I might have done something desperate. Have you ever felt like that?"

I nodded. "Yeah."

"Well, you see, I knew that. I could see it in your eyes, standing out there on the street. I recognized some fear in you, some pain. I want to know that, Voula. I want to understand."

"It's not that easy."

He gave me this sidelong glance, like he was sizing me up for something.

I took a deep breath. "It seems like there have been so many wrong turns. Like my family could never get it right. I tried not to blame anyone. I tried not to blame myself."

I was talking now, and I knew I wouldn't be able to stop. I told him I didn't feel attached to it anymore, that I couldn't let myself. "You know they were so strict with all of us. And Cristina, Cristina was so good and so pretty and it didn't matter because they were so strict. And then all of a sudden they decided not to be. It was the summer she went to Cyprus and the rest of us stayed home. She said she wanted to go before she started at NYU. She wanted to see some guy. I don't even know how long she had been writing this guy. My aunt in Cyprus ratted her out and Helen and I were scared for her, but for once my parents were cool. They talked to his parents, even. Suddenly they gave in. They should have made her come home when she asked to stay an extra week. At any other time they would have. This time, she could stay. Her flight home was supposed to be two days after it happened." It was all coming out. The story, my tears—everything. "They were on a moped. I saw pictures of him when I cleaned out her room. Helen and I did it because my parents were in no position to. We would have done it anyway, in case there was something to hide. She had one picture of him. She had hidden it in one of her schoolbooks, right on the shelf. In the picture, he was on the moped. A skinny kid looking proud of his death machine."

"And?"

"And what? He was cute. He wrote I love you on the back of the photo."

"It sounds like she wanted to be there."

I nodded.

"It sounds like she was happy when she died."

"I guess—"

I saw my sister then, with the kid on the moped. I saw her laughing with her hair blowing in the breeze as she crashed. Of course, she wouldn't have messed up her hair with a helmet. I had never thought about how she may have felt—not in all this time. I had only thought about how we felt, how *I* felt. I began to sob, and Paul came over to my side of the table. He hugged me and then he paid the check. We took a cab to Brooklyn and I continued to sob quietly into his shoulder, although I stopped for a minute when he pointed to the sign on the Brooklyn Bridge that said Welcome To Brooklyn How Sweet It Is.

Back at his place, he helped me undress and tucked me in. Then he got into bed and kept holding onto me.

"I feel so safe with you," I said. "It's scary to feel so safe."

In the morning I woke up well rested. Paul was looking at me.

"Hi," I said.

"Good morning," he said.

I sat up in bed. "Sorry I turned into such a freak last night."

He pulled me back down and close to him. "You weren't a freak. I'm glad you trusted me enough to talk about it."

"I'm glad we talked about 9/11."

"You know, I think your life is going to change if you let it. I mean, I can't promise that nothing else bad is ever going to happen. For a while, I kept waiting, you know, waiting for another attack, waiting for something else bad. It fucked me up. When we went out on calls, I wasn't focused. You need to be focused. I think we just have to accept that these things happened to us and keep on being good to each other and being there for each other. We're never going to get a guarantee, but we have to keep on keeping on."

"I love you," I said.

"How sweet it is," he said, and pulled the covers back over our heads.

My co-op board decided to reschedule without giving me much chance to get any of my financials together. That meant I definitely wasn't going to be able to close the week of May third. They weren't going to give me a new date until they saw what they wanted to see.

"They're assholes," I said to Maureen.

"I know, dear." She liked calling me that now. "Just get them what they want, so we can all be a lot happier."

And you can get your money, I thought. I was on my way over to Jamie's for a visit. The baby was almost a month old. Fewer people were coming over now, so Jamie had more time with the baby by herself. She said every day was a different story.

The story when I finally got over there was that the baby had thrown up all over her and she hadn't been able to eat all day. She was wearing an open robe and sweats.

"I'll make you something," I said. When I turned on the gas of the stovetop, I held my breath the way I had ever since the fire. I started to make us grilled cheese sandwiches. I looked up to ask her if she wanted Swiss, American or provolone and noticed that she was holding the baby and looking really upset.

"I just don't know if I can take this," she said.

I abandoned the grilled cheese task and took the baby out of her arms. Immediately, she left the room.

I looked down at the baby. "You are going to make your mother crazy."

The baby looked at me and cried. It was actually seeing me. It was starting to look less like an alien and more like a human. I found myself rocking it. *Her.* I found myself rocking her.

She was heavy, so I sat in the rocking chair and rocked us both. In a half hour, Jamie came back into the room. She had showered and put on a pair of yoga pants and a cashmere sweater.

"Thanks," she said.

"You know if you need me to come over so you can shower or whatever, I can."

"It was just a really rough day."

"It—she—looks more alert," I said. The baby was quite content for the moment.

"Yeah, she's starting to track things. Watch this. Ananda—" She snapped her fingers to get the baby's attention. The baby looked over at her and she walked back and forth. The baby followed with her eyes. "We're lucky. She seems to be advancing at a normal rate even though she was a month premature."

"Cool." Jamie started to finish my grilled cheeses. "I can do that."

"No, I'll do it, if you don't mind holding her. It's just nice when someone else is here to help."

"Have your mom and Ana been over a lot?"

"Yeah, and they're only a phone call away. I just hate asking all the time. I need to figure this stuff out."

"You'll get it."

She nodded, but didn't seem sure. "There's just no one I trust to reassure me."

In my arms Ananda fell asleep. "She's out."

"Oooh," Jamie said, springing into quiet action. "Okay, we have to try to get her into the crib without waking her up. We might actually get to eat in peace."

Jamie guided me into the nursery and I laid Ananda down in the crib as carefully as I possibly could. There was a moment when the floor creaked and Jamie and I held our breath, but Ananda slept right through it. We smiled at each other.

Later we were eating burned grilled cheese sandwiches and soup. Jamie's eyes darted to the baby monitor with every little noise.

"Is it going okay?" I asked.

"I just wish someone had told me how hard it would be. It's like no one wants to say that. I don't know if I'm abnormal. I mean, I wanted this. Sometimes I just feel so up and down. I know it wasn't like this for Alice."

"Alice likes appearances," I said. "You can't believe her about how perfect her baby was."

"I know," Jamie said. "But no one else says it either. Why? I can't believe I'm the only one to ever feel this way."

"I can't either. It's like a conspiracy of silence."

She laughed. "I sense an article coming on."

"I'm meeting with Eve Vitali next week to pitch this kind of thing for *On the Verge*." Usually, I hesitated telling Jamie about my pieces before they came out. I know she often believed she was the cleverly disguised source. Sometimes she was. This time she actually smiled.

"I think it would be great if you did an article about these crazy feelings. It would be like a public service."

"I try to do my part."

"You know—" she dropped her voice to a whisper "—sometimes I think I hate her."

I looked at her. Her expression was sheepish. "Do you?"

"No, I love her. I know I do. I'm just not getting anything from her at this point. I'm not sure I like her. Can you write about that?"

"Yes." I often yessed people when they suggested things for me to write about, but this time I knew I was going to.

Ananda made a couple of hiccupping sounds. Jamie paused mid-bite and looked at the monitor. The noises stopped, and I could have sworn Jamie sighed in relief. But then Ananda let out a real wail.

"I can go," I said.

"No, I have to or she won't calm down." Jamie got up and hurried into the other room, leaving her sandwich half eaten.

Easter and Greek Easter happened to fall on the same day. Usually, my mom and I went to Aunt Effie's house, but my mother hadn't talked to me since the shower. I tried to call her to find out what she wanted to do for the holiday. It was Georgia who told me that my mother was going to be at Aunt Effie's. I decided not to go. If my mother wouldn't return my phone calls, I wasn't going to sit under her icy glare with our relatives. Let her explain why I wasn't there. I planned on spending the day by myself and maybe ordering some Indian food. This way at least I could get lamb.

Paul insisted I go to his mother's house. I had met her briefly one day in Carroll Gardens and she was the type of woman who hugged and kissed you immediately. The prospect of his mother's baked ziti (which I had eaten cold out of Paul's fridge) sounded much better than curry heartburn, so I went over to Paul's.

Paul had Joey for this holiday and as usual he was hyperactive—this time hopped up on the Cadbury Cream Eggs he kept popping. It was clear that Paul's parents indulged Joey. Paul's dad, Gino, was a shorter, stockier version of Paul who still had an Italian accent that reminded me of Armando.

I met Paul's older brother, Frank, and his wife, Clara. They had three kids who ran around with Joey demanding to play "Fight," a game I'd never heard of. I deduced that it was just wrestling on Mrs. Torrisi's plastic-covered couches.

There was also Paul's aunt Sadie, who was visiting from Florida with her divorced daughter, Teresa, and Teresa's teenage son, Owen. Owen sulked for the entire time and rolled his eyes when his grandmother declared that everything we ate could not be procured in Florida.

"There's nothing like Brooklyn bread," she said. She said the same thing about the pastries, mozzarella and roasted peppers.

Each time she sang Brooklyn's praises, Paul agreed loudly and directed his comments at me. I shook my head. He still hadn't given up his campaign.

We had ham instead of lamb, but it was really good, as was the rest of the food. I pretended the delicious lasagna was the *pastitsio* my mother made every year. After dinner when we were having dessert, Paul brought out a bread topped with red dyed eggs and set it among the pastries.

"That's not from Brooklyn," Paul's aunt said.

"No, it's *sreki*."

I was shocked. "A *tsoureki*. Where did you get it?"

"A friend at the station told me all about it. He gave me his mom's recipe. I made it. Joey dyed the eggs."

"You made it."

"Yeah, it was hell trying to find the cherry stuff. Try it."

I ripped off a piece and tasted it. It was delicious. "Paul, this is great. Thank you."

"What else did my friend teach us, Joey? Remember the game?" Paul called into the living room where Joey was attached to his PlayStation.

"Oh, yeah." Joey ran in and ripped some of the eggs out of the bread and handed them to me.

I taught the family the game Greeks play where you take

turns hitting the top and bottom of your eggs. The person whose egg breaks last wins. Joey really got into it and the rest of the family enjoyed it as well. I was teaching them what to say, *"christos anesti"* and *"alithos anesti,"* when we realized that Joey had left the dining room and returned to the table with a carton of fresh eggs.

"I think that's enough of the game," Paul said, and the rest of the table laughed.

"That was so thoughtful. Thanks, everyone. Thanks, Paul."

"There's nothing like Brooklyn men," Aunt Sadie declared, chomping on a second cannoli.

This time it was my turn to agree wholeheartedly.

I waited in Eve Vitali's Chelsea office for twenty minutes before she was able to see me. She came out to get me herself and apologized a bunch of times.

"It's no problem," I said. I wondered when I could ask her about writing the letter for my co-op board. It was totally inappropriate to ask this of her. Maybe I shouldn't ask her. Maybe it was a sign that I should move to Brooklyn.

"The thing is," she said, smiling, "today is administrative professional's day. You know, secretary's day?"

I nodded.

"Well, my two partners and I like to go out to lunch to celebrate. It's a big day for us—we'll do even more celebrating tonight. Anyway, we went to Chanterelle for lunch and of course Tabitha had to get dessert *and* the cheese course. Then Roseanne had to find out exactly how they did the fish. I'm really sorry about keeping you waiting."

"It's quite all right."

We chatted for a little while. I had already sent her some ideas, but I wanted to prep her for my writing more about *after* the baby was born, not just pregnancy. I told her about Jamie and how she felt completely alone.

"So, I actually got a chance to look at your idea for 'pulling the goalie'—great name, by the way. I like it."

I couldn't blow this by asking her for the letter. "Thanks."

"I saw you were consistent with your column for *Financial Woman*. Sometimes we get writers who make all these promises and can't deliver, but you did in that series. You made me start thinking about moving out of my place and buying something. It's adult. We can talk more about that later."

That would have been the perfect segue into the letter request.

"*Financial Woman* should do more columns like that. They need to focus on a younger demographic."

"I agree."

She smirked at me. I sensed she was sizing me up.

"I know the editor and I'm sure it would have been easy to pull one over on him, but you wrote solid stuff each month."

"Well, it's his magazine, but it's my name."

"That's true." She looked down at my pitch. "How many columns could you get out of this?"

"Well, I notice that some of your freelancers seem to do pieces every other month. Originally I was going to say six months, but now that my friend has had the baby, it seems the fun has only just begun. I think a year would be better. We start with the trying and then go into the pregnancy each month through to the first couple of months after birth."

Eve nodded, thinking about it. She was agreeing with me. Who knew what else she might agree to?

"I think it's really interesting. My concern is that I don't want it to ever be telling the readers that they should be at a certain stage at a certain time. We vowed to never do that. *On the Verge,* as you know, is about beating your own drum. We like your wry voice, but this pitch is more detached. I like the scientific facts, but I want more you. I know you're interested in this because of a friend's pregnancy. Put me there. Be the friend who isn't so sure. We all move at different speeds. Give it to us through your eyes."

"I will."

"Cool."

"Does that mean I'm hired?"

"Yes, but I'm not as easy as the editor at *Financial Woman*.

Well, actually, I am. It's my two partners that are hard-asses. I'm kind of the good cop. The success of our magazine surprised all of us and now we're scared of doing anything to lose it."

"I can imagine. Thanks."

"Thank you. I really like your voice. I actually wanted to tell you that we're open to anything you want to pitch. It sounds super New-Agey and like we've been to one too many human resources conventions, but this summer is about challenging ourselves. For the first time the magazine is doing a fitness challenge, albeit one that is pro all body types and not obsessed with thin. We are also trying to challenge our writers. If there is something that you haven't written about that could challenge you in any way, we want that."

"I'm not sure what you mean."

"For example, you might be giving a lot of women a chance to see themselves through your struggling mother friend. It's something that isn't talked about. It invites controversy. Think about your own life. We are doing more personal essays about the problems we face. It's not Dr. Phil. It's just reflective personal voice we're looking for. And it pays well. So keep it in mind."

"I will."

"Terrific. I'll e-mail you with a calendar of deadlines for 'Pulling the Goalie.' Is there anything else you want to talk about?"

It was now or never. I needed the letter.

"Actually," I said. "There is one more thing."

23

The whole idea of a group of thirteen units judging me made me more than a little uneasy. Who were these people anyway? I had procured a letter from Eve Vitali, who had laughed at the request and told me a story about how she forged a letter to rent her first apartment in the city.

Then I did some fancy maneuvering. Jamie wrote another professional letter saying I would be doing some catalog work for her company. That left me in the lurch for the two personal letters of recommendation I needed. Jamie insisted I use Raj for one of them, because according to her, people would be impressed by his reality TV credentials. I wasn't so sure. I couldn't ask Paul. He would probably try to undermine my plans. He still hadn't given up on the idea that I should move to Brooklyn. Truth be told, I was kind of entertaining the idea as well. He had made some good points. I was trying to avoid making a decision by leaving it in the hands of the fates. For example, if the co-op board didn't approve me, there was nothing I could do about it, but the mind games I was playing with myself prevented me from sabotaging myself. I asked Georgia, who had a different last name than mine, to write the other personal recommendation.

The co-op board consisted of ten apartments in the main building and the three that were in the carriage house I would be moving into. A representative of each apartment was looking at me as I sat at the end of a large table that was almost bigger than the apartment I was buying. It was eight in the morning.

"So we invited you here to explain the co-op," the guy with the receding hairline said.

Invited? I was under the impression it had been mandatory. I listened as he explained some detailed rules about garbage and recycling chores.

A woman who identified herself as the co-op treasurer explained when the maintenance fee was due and when.

An older guy who was the co-op board president told me about the offices that were up for election.

The youngest person in the room was probably ten years older than me. I wondered if they had already made up their minds that I was too young. I hadn't smiled at all. I wanted to convey I was mature and serious. I had actually borrowed a suit from Jamie. I wondered if they were just going through the motions. Brooklyn wasn't so bad, it was, as Paul told me the sign said, not just a borough but an experience.

"So what happens if you don't get hired to do more articles?" asked the woman who told me that any pets would have to be approved by the board.

I could not imagine a future gerbil's interview being more uncomfortable than this one.

"Well, as you can see from my professional references, I have two jobs lined up already for the year." Even though one of the offers was technically a lie.

"Well, that's only two jobs, and the money you will make from those will barely cover the mortgage," the co-op board president said.

"Let alone the maintenance," the treasurer added.

"Well, I usually get different jobs throughout the year. As you can see from my past two tax returns, I've done quite well at this job." *Take that, oldies.*

"But the economy is down."

"It was for the past two years. I think it's only getting better." I could pretend I read the Business section of *The New York Times.*

The co-op board appeared to be fooled. A couple of them nodded their heads.

"I live in the carriage house with my two kids," said a man sitting at the end of the table. "We make sure the volume of the children remains respectful. We hope that if you are going to have any parties either in the courtyard or your apartment, you would do the same. That is, if you move in."

"I would," I said, meeting his eyes. Did I look like a party girl? The thought of having a summer party in the courtyard did appeal to me. Who was I kidding? They weren't letting me in.

"Well, I guess that's it," the co-op president said, looking around the table for agreement. "Do you have any more questions?"

Shit! I should have had a question. My lawyer, Rob, had given me the minutes from all the co-op meetings. Maureen had told me I should study them and ask a question to prove that I had. I hadn't. Now I had nothing to ask.

"No."

"Very well, we'll let you know," said the man with the receding hairline.

Then the woman who owned the apartment, who hadn't really said anything except her name which I had promptly forgotten, got up and opened the door to the apartment. I took this to mean that the meeting was done and I should go. And I did.

"I can't believe they just kind of opened the door, like that was your cue," Jamie said.

I had her on the phone the moment I left. I didn't just stop by anymore. I made plans well in advance.

"Believe me, I took it. I doubt they're going to approve me. Those fuckers."

"So are you going to move in with Paul? I don't see why you don't."

"I know it doesn't make a lot of sense. I might do it."

"Why are you so resistant? Things are going well."

"That's one reason not to move in. The other is that I have never in my life lived on my own."

"I did it for a year. It's not all it's cracked up to be. You work alone, isn't that enough?"

"I just sort of want my space. Completely. I don't want to have anyone on top of me. Just for a little while. Just to see if I can. If the oldies did approve me, this place is still a great investment. It has a flexible sublet policy."

"Okay, I guess Voula knows best."

I didn't say anything. I knew I didn't always make sense, not even to myself, but I needed support.

"My mom is hounding me to find out if you are bringing Paul to Block Island for Memorial Day."

"Is he invited?"

"Of course. I can't tell you how happy my mom is to hear that you are getting laid."

"Well, yeah, I guess I will bring him—though I was thinking I might move that day."

"And miss Memorial."

"Well, it was only if I got approved. It would be nice to be in soon. And if the co-op board approves, I now have a tentative closing for the week of May twenty-four. So much for being out by May first."

"But they're not going to approve you, right?"

"Please don't root for that."

"Have you even told Armando that you are thinking of leaving?"

"I haven't seen him in weeks. Kelly knows and I think she sort of let it slip. Of course, when I see him I'll tell him myself."

"It's too bad you never tapped that ass."

"I'm probably the only one in NYC who hasn't." Jamie didn't say anything to that and I wondered again if they had ever done it. I wasn't sure if it mattered at this point. Then I had a bright idea. "Do you think anyone would mind if I asked Paul to bring Joey?"

"No, not at all. I can't believe you're going to be domestic."

"I think it would be nice."

I knew that I had to step up to the plate about Joey. I was committed to Paul and I wanted to show him. He loved Joey and I would too.

When I got home, Armando was just leaving for the restaurant. He gave me a hug and kissed me on both cheeks the way he did when we hadn't seen each other in a while.

"Voula, Kelly told me you leaving. Why you no tell me?" He looked kind of crushed.

"I'm not sure if I am. I haven't told you because I'm still not sure. It won't be until June first. Kelly seems to be telling a lot of tales. She said that you might be moving to London."

"Is a good job, but I stay 'ere. Dis is my home now. I am New Yorker."

"You definitely are."

"Voula." He said my name so definitely. "You mus' tell me when you know."

"I know. Don't worry. I'll find my replacement. As soon as I hear if I got approved, I'll put an ad on craigslist."

"No, Voula," he said. "You tell because I miss you."

"Oh, Armando, thank you." It was so sweet. Armando gave me a big hug. I wondered if in spite of himself, he had met a woman that he was friends with.

"I mus' go to the restaurant. *Ciao, bella.*"

"*Ciao,*" I said, waving. I might always have had a mini crush on him. Which was okay. It was harmless.

I went into my office and turned on my laptop. I had hung Eve's deadlines on my bulletin board. What if they did approve me, and then what if they were right? What if I didn't make enough and then I foreclosed? It was possible. It was daunting.

The smart thing, the wise thing was to move in with Paul. Why was I being so stubborn?

The cursor was mocking me as usual. If I wanted to ensure I paid my bills, I had to beat the cursor. I had to show it who was boss. I put my iPod on all my Prince songs. I took a deep breath.

"Whatever comes, let it come," I said to myself. Then I knew what I was talking about—Cristina. This time, I said. "Just try."

My sister choreographed a dance for us to "Baby, I'm a Star" by Prince. She was vigilant as we practiced, but after we performed it perfectly, she collapsed on the bed laughing. My sister told us all her daydreams. We believed she was a princess and we were her ladies in waiting.

Once I started it kept coming. I wrote for two straight hours. Then I stopped because it was done for the day and I knew I could go back to it. I'd never written about my sister before, not even in my journal. I was completely drained. In two hours, I had given so much of me. I felt as if someone had used a cheese scraper on my chest, but in a good way. It was amazing.

But was I writing to challenge myself for *On the Verge* magazine? I think I was writing it for me and for Helen. I was writing it to feel better, and it was working.

I called Paul. "Can I see you tonight? It's nice out and I just feel like walking around."

"Of course," he said. "I'll come right over after my shift."

Four days later I got an e-mail from the co-op board. They were welcoming me to the building. I couldn't believe it. I had been approved. I felt a bit guilty, like I had pulled one over on them. And I felt a little scared.

Almost immediately after getting the e-mail, I received a phone call from Maureen. She was the person expediting the whole process, hoping to get to the closing so that she could get her six percent or whatever it was she was going to get.

"Congratulations, Voula, you really impressed them."

I wondered if they had said that or if those were her words. Before I could ask, she continued.

"Have you heard from Rob about the definite closing date?"

"It's supposed to be the week of the twenty-fourth."

"Well, you should make sure that you are still on schedule. Do you want me to call him?"

"No, I'll do it."

"Give me a call back as soon as you hear."

So when I got off the phone, instead of calling Paul or Jamie, I called Rob. He had some bad news.

"It looks like the seller's attorney is going to be on vacation all that week and then the co-op's attorney isn't around the week after. This holiday is really screwing things up."

"I'll say."

"I'll give you a call when I get a date. Congrats on the board approval."

The ferry ride to Block Island was calmer than it had been in previous years. Paul and Raj spent a lot of the ride chatting at the railing, while Jamie and I sat in the seats and she rocked and occasionally nursed Ananda. She was getting much better at nursing, although it still wasn't as easy as Alice had made it seem.

I tried to distract her with questions about pregnancy for my article. She was excited about it and I think she was enjoying the idea that she had been through this pregnancy ordeal and, though it was tough, had survived intact.

She was also feeling better about Ananda. She said that she had recently fallen in love with her and she was happy. This was the way she believed she was supposed to feel. She thought she was finally starting to get it. Ananda was giving too. She was smiling and laughing a little.

The person that was *not* feeling so loved was Raj. It had been three months since the baby was born and they'd only had sex twice. Both times Jamie did it to please him and didn't enjoy it at all.

"I feel awful about this, but I just don't want it," Jamie said, looking down at Ananda's sleeping face.

It was a shock to me that this was the woman who in college used to e-mail me after a short absence, apologizing because she had spent four days fucking the guy who lived down the hall. I was distressed, but Jamie was already back on Ananda.

"She's being such a good girl, isn't she?"

"Yeah," I said, wanting to not admire Ananda for once, but to get the lowdown. "How is Raj handling all this?"

"Well, he was really good about not pressuring me. I mean you are supposed to wait six weeks. He kindly waited ten. I felt awful about it, though. You know, Alice gave Peter a blow job as soon as she got back from the hospital, and she told me she just couldn't wait the whole six weeks and did it at five."

"I never want to hear another Alice story," I said. The last time I had heard about Alice she was showing her child flash cards every night trying to get the eleven-month-old to become a genius. "Scratch that! Please tell me all the Alice stories. I can't resist, but for God's sake don't compare yourself to her anymore. I think she's a liar."

"Oh, Voula, so do I sometimes." Jamie laughed. "Anyway, I want to get my sex drive back. I know it's important, but the idea of anyone touching my breasts revolts me."

"He doesn't have to touch them," I said.

"No, I know." She nodded and glanced down at Ananda.

Jamie was constantly looking at Ananda. I think the number of times she looked at Ananda indicated the amount of responsibility she had taken on and the amount she had changed.

"My body doesn't seem made for those kinds of things anymore."

"Do you feel like being a mom and being sexual are mutually exclusive?"

Jamie thought about it for a minute. "No, I mean, I know they aren't. My mind knows. I don't know. I just don't have the energy. I'm just really tired."

Joey ran over to us and climbed in my lap. Paul called after him, but I waved that it was okay. I didn't necessarily love having a fifty-pound child in my lap but I liked that Joey and I were getting along.

"Easy, Joey," Paul yelled over to us. In minutes Joey had

scrambled out of my lap and was running around the slippery deck. Paul yelled and chased after him.

"Someday you're going to have to deal with that," I said to Jamie.

"Someday sooner, you are," she said and smiled.

The rest of the Jacobs family were already on the island and we sat on the verandah drinking margaritas after Maura picked us up. She whispered to me that the neighbors' grandkids were coming to visit the following day and they were around Joey's age so he would be occupied.

He was pretty excited to be on the island, and ran around the periphery of the building until the sun started going down and he was exhausted. Then he came and sat on his dad's lap and Mr. Jacobs gave him a root beer.

Mike had marinated some Cornish game hens, which I knew he would be ridiculed for later. There were no jokes when he started the barbecue. We were all starving. Mr. Jacobs brought out some hot dogs and Maura got her potato salad. I was content being there again. For one thing, I had avoided a bike ride, and also it was nice to finally have a date. Joey was even behaving himself.

Joey didn't say much as the adults talked during dinner. Occasionally someone would address him and be delighted by whatever he said. It was just about time for him to go to bed when he looked at Crystal. She had actually been considerate about not bringing up anything inappropriate in front of Joey. For once we were spared tales of her digestive or mental health concerns. She even refrained from mentioning past lovers.

"Are you a boy or a girl?" Joey asked her out of the blue.

"Joey," Paul began to scold.

"That's okay, Joey," Crystal said. "I am a woman, Joey. And I am a lesbian."

Oh *panayia mou.*

"Crystal," Jamie said, shocked. She had just put Ananda down, and looked like she was ready to relax.

"Well, honey, I'm not going to be the first one he meets."

"It's okay," Paul said. "But, Joey, that isn't very nice to ask people."

"'I don't mind, Joey," Crystal said. "I think sometimes we need to find answers. I admire your courage in asking me."

We were all quiet after that statement. Mr. Jacobs and Mike busied themselves with the grill and Paul got up to join them.

"Do you know what a lesbian is?" Ana asked.

"Ana!" Jamie yelled. It was easier for her to reprimand her sister.

"Yes," Joey said proudly.

"You do?" Paul asked from the grill. He was paying attention after all.

"Uh-huh," Joey said, nodding emphatically.

"Where did you learn that?" Paul asked.

Joey shrugged.

"Did you learn it at school?" Crystal asked.

Joey looked confused and then shrugged.

"What *is* a lesbian?" Paul asked.

Joey thought about it for a minute and then said, "It's when you touch butts."

Children—so much to look forward to.

The next day, predictably, the Jacobses wanted to go on a bike ride. I thought I was going to be able to get out of it because Jamie wouldn't want to leave Ananda. She wasn't up to going, but she told me to go on ahead. She was just going to relax and keep an eye on Joey and the neighborhood grandkids who were swimming in the neighbor's pool.

"I think I should stay with her," I said to Paul.

"Come on, you're not going to make me go with people I barely know, are you?"

"You're getting along with them fine."

"Voula, I came here to hang out with you. C'mon. I want to see you in your helmet."

"I hate biking."

"Mrs. Jacobs told me that's all there is to do around here."

"That and drink and swim. I prefer those."

He cocked his head.

"Fine, I'll go."

So I was biking and I hated it. I hated huffing up the hill and I kept my brake on for most of the downhills. The Jacobses took off racing with one another. Paul would cycle in front of me, zigzagging and pop-a-wheelieing, and then wait for me by crossing back and forth across the road.

"I hope you're being careful of cars," I said when I finally caught up to him.

"I hope you're being careful and not going too fast," he teased.

"You're the one who wanted to go biking."

"Maybe I just wanted to get you alone."

I glanced quickly at him and he winked. I could see him staring at me. How could he not worry about the road in front of him?

"I'll tell you one thing—"

"What's that?" He was really enjoying watching me struggle.

"The only thing I can feel between my legs is this bike. And I'm probably going to be sore."

"Really. I might have just the thing for that."

I sort of understood Jamie at that moment. With all the dirt on my face and the sweat on my body, sex was the last thing on my mind. We began to go uphill again. He was in great shape. He kept circling me. I wanted to get off the bike and walk, but I wouldn't let myself do that in front of him.

"So the closing is this week, huh?"

"You know this already."

"I know. I guess you're gonna sign, huh?"

I looked over at him. "I hope you're being careful of the cars, and yes, I am going to sign."

We continued cycling up. I stood ungracefully. He raced up the hill and zipped back down to me and then resumed riding next to me.

"Is that okay?" I finally asked.

"It's what you want."

"Are you okay with it?"

"I guess so. I respect that you need your time. But tell me if I am wasting mine."

"You're not," I said. I wanted to be emphatic, but I was having trouble breathing. We got to where the ground plateaued a bit, so I was able to concentrate on talking. "A year."

"What about a year?"

"Give me a year to stand on my own. Then we can see."

"A lot can change in a year."

He was right, we both knew that. He was testing me, too.

"I'm willing to bet that my feelings won't." I could see him smiling, but I wasn't about to look at him because we were coming to a steep downhill. There was even a sign with a truck doing something menacing on a triangle. I needed to stay in control.

"You think you'll still love me in a year."

"I think in a year I will still love you and you will talk me into going on a ride with you and I will be on this godforsaken bike once again."

"Whoo-hoo," he said, racing down the hill at top speed.

"Be careful," I yelled.

He was way ahead of me. My heart was pounding and my upper lip was sweating. He turned into a dot. The Jacobses were even farther ahead. I was on my own. I kept squeezing the brake when I picked up speed. I tried not to, but I just couldn't bring myself to go too fast. I thought of Cristina. I thought of her laugh and what Paul had said. She had been holding on tight as her fiancé speeded into the sunlight. She had never been so happy. She had thought, *I could die right now and I wouldn't care.*

I didn't want to follow in her footsteps, but I was happy too. For the first time in a long time. It almost hurt. I knew Paul well enough to know he was patient and he would wait.

Many things, most things, I could not control. Sometimes I just had to go with everything. Just around the bend, there was a lemonade stand where in past summers we met up to get super-sweet lemonade. I was more than sure Paul would be there waiting for me. I wanted to get to him sooner.

I didn't speed. I didn't try any harder than usual to go fast. But I stopped squeezing the brake. And I coasted. All the way down the hill, around the bend, until I saw Paul smiling at me with two cups of lemonade, I coasted.

24

My closing was scheduled for the first Wednesday in June at three p.m. As soon as it was over, I would get the keys. Then I would slowly start moving in. I had two weeks before Armando's friend from the restaurant, Pasquale, moved in. Armando was also planning on giving my office to someone else from his *paese* who was coming to America. I was sort of pleased that I didn't have to find my replacement. In spite of my co-op board lies, I was really busy with all kinds of summer-themed articles and working hard to make my first "Pulling the Goalie" piece kick ass.

The closing was held at the co-op's attorney's office. I was the first one to arrive. At three-fifteen, Rob blew in full of apologies because his last closing had gone over the time he expected. Once he was there, they let us into the back conference room where the closing was going to be held. Maureen arrived shortly after and gave me a hug. I wondered if she could feel that I was shaking. This was all too adult.

As instructed, I had deposited all my bonds profit into my checking account and I knew that when I left, my savings was going to be depleted. Then Rob gave me a pep talk. I tried to follow what he was saying but it seemed overly complicated. He kept mentioning letters and numbers and I felt like he should have squirted water into my face and rubbed my shoulders. I knew that this closing could last up to two hours—if anyone ever showed up.

"So you know that you aren't getting the actual mortar and brick, right?" Rob said as if we had already reviewed this.

We probably had, but I didn't remember. I looked at him blankly.

"I'm not?"

"No. In a co-op, it's one of these weird New York City things. You're buying shares of stock in a company, the co-op. Even though you pay hundreds of thousands of dollars, you don't actually own the land."

"I don't?"

"No."

Oh.

Then a guy arrived and introduced himself as the Payoff. I had no idea what his function was, and Rob explained that he was the guy who brought the documents that weren't actually a title, something about personal property and not land. It was three-thirty. I had a sinking feeling.

"Who are we waiting for?" the co-op attorney asked when she came back in the room. I thought her name was Lena, but she said, "I'm the transfer agent."

"Payoff," the new guy said, and snapped his gum.

"We're waiting on the bank and the sellers' attorney," Rob said.

The sellers weren't coming as they had relocated to London. It was still baffling to me that two people had lived in that one small space.

"Oh, did I tell you she called and said she was going to be about forty-five minutes late?"

"She's already beyond that," Rob said, checking his watch. "Voula, can I run downstairs and get you a coffee?"

"Okay," I said, starting to worry. Why would my lawyer be buying me anything?

While Rob was out of the office, a woman arrived and announced that she was the lender. She was a young woman in tight pants and biggish hair. She smiled brightly at me, and I returned the smile though I had no idea what her role was in all this.

When Rob returned, he explained that she was the person who controlled my mortgage. I was going to be handing some of the checks over to her. I sipped my coffee and it burned my tongue a little. Rob looked again at his watch and shook his head. I began to feel that he was my only ally in this. Without him I would drown.

"Well, it's four-thirty, you can start signing some stuff, I guess. She can, right?" He looked at the lender, who nodded. Payoff was staring off into space.

"Okay," Rob said.

He got out a legal pad and started writing down numbers explaining what checks I had to write and for what. The only thing I was sure of was the check I was writing to him. The rest made no sense, but I would have signed or done anything he asked at that point.

And so began the constant flow of paper that had to be signed in various spots and dated. Rob kept track of everything. I think I was developing a crush on him. Perhaps I had a thing for men who I thought could rescue me. At 5:20, the seller's attorney walked in, apologizing. I looked up from the sheet about not caring about lead poisoning, to glare at her.

"Yeah," Rob said, dismissively. "We already got her started. She's about a third of the way done."

A third? My hand was already beginning to hurt.

Then everyone started talking about different forms. I just kept on signing. Finally the Payoff said something about a certain numbered form not being cleared. I was barely paying attention, but the number they were talking about sounded just like the lien search Rob had told me was somehow important.

"I don't know anything about that," the seller's attorney said.

"It's not in your folder," Rob said.

Something in his tone made me glance up, but no, he would handle it. I continued to get the papers.

"Well, it isn't cleared," Payoff said. Now that he was talking, he seemed to be throwing a wrench in the works.

"Let me see if I can get the sellers. It's later in London," the seller's attorney said, as if none of us had ever experienced different time zones. She got in touch with them and started talking about this form. It was clear that she should have known about it when she looked into her folder, pulled out a piece of paper and said, "Oh."

I stopped signing at that point and looked at Rob. Here was the moment for which I needed the life vest.

"Hold on a sec, Voula."

I glanced over at Maureen. She also looked upset. Her commission was fading fast, for reasons I wasn't sure of. They all started discussing making a phone call to some guy who seemed to be Payoff's boss. They tried calling this guy, but as they had guessed, he was already gone. It was, after all, after six.

"Well, Voula, it looks like we are going to have to adjourn."

I noticed that the Lender and Payoff were starting to pack up their bags.

"Oh," I said. "So does that mean I get the keys?"

"No, we can't continue."

"Well, I signed everything, right?" I felt like I had signed everything. "Are you just going to call me when it's worked out?"

"No, Voula, unfortunately we are going to have to come back and do this all again."

"You're kidding."

"I wish I was. But don't worry, I won't charge you any more."

"So I can't move in?"

"Unfortunately not."

"I really apologize about this," the seller's attorney said.

I glared at her. She didn't seem fazed and she left.

"I need to run, honey, for the nanny. I'll call you," Maureen said.

"Take care," said Payoff.

It wasn't his fault, but I hated him anyway.

"Best of luck to you," the Lender said, shaking my hand. She appeared genuine. "I hope this works out."

"Me, too."

"I'm sorry," Rob and the co-op attorney said repeatedly.

I guessed it was time for me to leave. Rob explained that there had been a lien placed on the sellers that wasn't cleared. It was due to a home equity loan. He called it a UCC-1, which was different from a UCC-3 in a way I couldn't understand, except to know that I had been knocked out.

It didn't matter how much my hand ached or my tongue hurt, I didn't have the key.

I called Paul as soon as I got out of there. It was after six-thirty. He answered his cell phone right away.

"Hey, I expected you an hour ago. How did it go?"

"It didn't." I felt like I had wasted so much time. "I sat there waiting for two hours and then started signing things and then it got adjourned because somebody didn't check some dumb file."

"Well, are you okay?"

"No, not really." I felt like I wanted to walk away from the whole thing, but I wasn't sure I could tell him that. "Do you want to get that drink? I think I really need it."

"Um." He sounded like he was hesitating. He had insisted that we hang out tonight and celebrate. "Sure, how about Tier Na Nog."

"You really want to go there?" I liked that bar, but I thought we would go somewhere a little more special.

"Yeah," he said.

"Well, I guess I'll stop at home first."

"No," he said loudly. Then he calmed down. "I'm really close to there. Let's just meet there. I have a feeling I'm going to be called in to work."

"I thought you took off."

"Yeah, but you never know."

I was looking forward to just chilling out tonight; having some drinks, maybe a little dinner. I wouldn't have minded a full body massage.

"Okay. I'll go right there."

Paul was waiting for me at the bar when I got there. He handed me a Bloody Mary and kissed my cheek. On the subway, I had been a bit annoyed with him for picking this place and perhaps having to work. When I saw him, I realized that I was really feeling defeated about the whole day.

"Hey," I said, as he pulled me into a big hug.

We got a table by the window and I told him the whole story, what I understood of it. I appreciated that he had never again brought up his original offer of moving to Brooklyn.

"The worst part is, I'm jeopardizing my interest rate. It was only locked in for sixty days and then they charge you. My lawyer said the sellers would have to pay if the mortgage broker agrees to extend it, but what if she doesn't?"

I felt like I was talking about things I didn't understand.

"I'm sure she will, if the lawyer thinks she will." He was talking to me, but once again, he was distracted.

"I'm starved," I said. "Do you want to get a burger or something?"

"No, I'm not too hungry." He was unusually matter-of-fact.

"Okay," I said. Did that mean I couldn't order anything?

Paul's phone beeped. He looked at it and immediately started text messaging.

My mood soured again.

When he finally looked up from his cell phone, I was done with my drink. He started to say something, but then his cell phone beeped again. He looked down at it and then said, "You don't want another drink, do you?"

"I kind of did," I said.

"Well." He glanced around. "Let's go somewhere else. Actually, do you mind if we stop at your place? I want to change my shirt. I'm feeling a little sweaty and I know I left a couple of T-shirts at your place."

"Fine," I said.

Not only was my boyfriend not being particularly considerate after my day, he was also telling me far too much about his physical hygiene. Maybe this was what Jamie meant about the honeymoon period ending.

We walked back to my apartment. He took my hand and I held it limply. He didn't seem to notice that I wasn't my usual self. What was going on between us? We walked up the stairs. He was doing this annoying tapping against the banisters. Normally, I wouldn't have noticed or cared about this. But after the adjourned closing, it got on my last nerve. He continued his drumming once we were on my floor. I shot him a look and he smiled. I opened the door and—

"Surprise!"

I almost jumped out of my skin. Crowded in my living room were not just Kelly and Armando with their significant others, but a few of my neighbors, Helen and her family, Diane, Joey, Georgia and Victor. Even Andrew Libman, the editor from *Financial Woman,* was there. For the first time ever he was dressed down in jeans. He looked younger than I had thought he was.

"What the hell is this?" I asked the group.

"Is a party," Armando said. He came over and kissed both my cheeks.

"We wanted to have a going-away party and celebrate your closing," Kelly said, giving me a hug.

"Well, that's so nice," I said. Never mind that I hadn't actually closed. No one had ever had a surprise party or really any party for me. My parents never sent cupcakes to my grade school on my birthday. The closest I had come was the monthly Krispy Kreme celebration we used to have when I worked at the nonprofit.

"You should have seen her face," Paul told the group. "She was getting so annoyed with me, I thought she was going to clock me."

"I almost did," I said, laughing. "I couldn't believe how insensitive you were being." I looked at everyone. "My closing was adjourned. It's not going to be for another couple of weeks."

"Well, we're still celebrating," Diane said. "Right?"

"Absolutely," I said, picking Joey up. Kelly turned the music up and I danced Joey over to where Helen was holding my niece, Cristina. I kissed them both and then Andre and Spiro. I gestured to Joey and Cristina who were close in age. "Did they meet?"

"Yeah," Helen said. "We had a hell of a time getting them quiet before you walked in. Jamie and Raj are on their way, I hear."

"Cool."

I made the rounds, to everyone. Then the bell rang and it was Jamie and Ananda. I ran over to give them a hug.

"Where's Raj?"

"He's bringing everything in from the cab."

"Everything?"

Before she could answer, I saw Raj making the first of several trips with his hands full. He gave me a quick kiss and told me he would be back. Four trips up and down the stairs later, he was ready for a drink. Paul helped him move all the stuff into my room.

It appeared that Raj and Jamie had brought the whole nursery. There was the portable playpen, the car seat, a small changing sheet, a booster seat, multiple diaper and toy bags, and even a tub "in case we think we can get her to bed." Wow!

Immediately food started emerging from the kitchen: breadsticks wrapped in prosciutto, bruschetta, scallops in bacon, shrimp and polenta topped with blue cheese. When I went into my kitchen for another beer, I found Armando directing two of the restaurant staff. They were cutting up thin-crust pizzas.

"Armando, thank you. I can't believe this."

"I miss you very much," he said. "You been a very good roommate."

"So have you." I gave him another hug. I knew that part of him was still upset about the fire. "You have been the best roommate."

"We still see each other, after?" he asked.

"Of course, Armando," I said. I was still holding on to his arms. "We're friends."

Jamie came into the kitchen, looking to refrigerate some bottles of breast milk. I told her and Armando about the adjourned closing. I suggested to Armando that I could move into my office if my closing wasn't rescheduled in time for his friend to move in. He said that if necessary he could have his friend stay in his room. But he had been so accommodating of my schedule that I didn't want to put him out. Then Jamie had her brilliant idea.

"I have to go back to work on the fourteenth. The nanny that I really wanted can't start until two weeks later. I was going to have my mother come, but she's been having some bad migraines lately. Maybe you could move in instead, and stay with Ananda for the week."

Now if I was going to move in with anyone for any length of time, I would prefer to be with Paul and not with a crying baby, but I was so happy about everyone just coming out and celebrating me that I think I would have agreed to anything.

"Yeah, that might work out well. Depending on when they get my closing scheduled for. It might just be for a week."

"That would be perfect."

She was so relieved. It was almost worth it. It might be easier for everyone.

My party went on into the evening. We ate well and even danced. I couldn't believe my social circle was this big. Sure, people like to party, but the nice thing is that they had come out for me. I hadn't thought I liked being the center of attention. But then I realized that I had never had the opportunity before. I was kind of enjoying it, at least for one night.

Before Helen left, I gave her the piece I had written about Cristina. All the Peroni I had drunk gave me some bizarre courage. I didn't plan to publish it anywhere, so it might never get edited, but I wanted Helen's take on it. I thought maybe we could talk more about Cristina, about our lives, about everything.

"Read it when you get a chance," I whispered as I hugged her goodbye. She was holding her exhausted daughter in her arms. "It's about Cristina."

"I'll read it tonight," she said. Then she smiled at me.

I kissed her again. "I'm glad you came back into my life," I said. And I meant it.

When all the guests were gone and Paul had helped Raj and Jamie get all their equipment out of the apartment, Kelly and Armando insisted that I couldn't clean up. I agreed, but asked that we all have one more drink.

"I'm going to put Joey to bed in your room, Voula. He's got his sleeping bag," Paul said. Joey was exhausted from chasing my niece around all night.

"Okay," I said. I watched him gather Joey in his arms. I called out to him. "Hey, thanks for tonight. I know I wasn't in the best mood."

"You're worth it," he said. He looked at Kelly and Armando. "I'm probably going to turn in, so enjoy yourselves."

My roommates and I smiled at each other. It wasn't going to be my last time in the house or anything, but the night felt special and we stayed awake, chatting until the sun came up. I was sad that I wouldn't be living with them anymore, that that chapter of my life was almost over, but I believed that we could still be in each other's lives even if we didn't share the same address. The things we now shared were stronger.

25

I thought I was going to get out of moving in with Jamie and family when my closing was scheduled for June fifteenth, but then it got rescheduled again. The sellers with whom I communicated via e-mail and whom I had really come to hate had considered getting new counsel, but in the end they stuck with the original, which my lawyer felt was the right thing to do to expedite things. At that point *expedite* was a foreign term to me, and because of all the confusion, the closing got rescheduled to Friday, June twenty-fifth. I hired the movers for the next day, which happened to be a Saturday. I was getting into that place if it killed me.

So I wound up in Jamie's place for ten days. I had my laptop and a backpack full of clothes, a pair of sandals and a pair of sneakers. The rest of my stuff had been moved to Paul's. The movers would be picking it up (again) from there.

Jamie and Raj hadn't really had a chance to clean up the room I was supposed to be staying in. It was the nursery, but for the duration of my stay they were going to put the crib back in their room. I had read up on this in my baby book and it seemed like it might be creating a setback, but I sensed Jamie was feeling guilty about returning to work and this was a way to stay close to Ananda.

I spent my first evening wading through baby paraphernalia and making dumb faces at Ananda while Jamie complained that none of her old work clothes looked right and the new ones she had bought weren't her style.

"You know, it's going to be fine," I said. I was beginning to think Jamie was regretting asking me to baby-sit for Ananda. She asked me a million times if I was "into it." She went over the schedule of what to do three times verbally and then gave me a typed sheet. There were Post-its containing emergency numbers all over the house.

"I just wish we had time to get you CPR training."

I was worried about that too, but I never would have thought about it if Jamie and Raj hadn't harped on it relentlessly. Raj had calmed down a little bit, but I noticed he watched to see if I washed my hands before handling the child.

The morning of Jamie's first day back to work, she fought off tears. Ananda was quite content with her bottle of breast milk. I knew that in spite of herself Jamie wished that Ananda would make a bigger scene.

Raj had already left to start pre-production on a new show, *The Next Mr. Right…Now.* Unfortunately, the jury was still out on whether Warren Tucker was the Original Mr. Right, but the first few episodes had been so highly rated that the network ordered another batch.

"Now, are you sure I should do this?" Jamie asked as she stood by the door.

"Are you?"

"No."

"Well, you better get sure, because you're going to be late."

"I know," she said, looking panicked. "I know."

"Don't worry," I said. "We'll be fine. And if not, you'll catch it on the nanny cam."

Jamie didn't really find that funny. She left, after reminding me several times to call her if I needed anything.

The first few hours went fine. Jamie called four times before noon, but I tried to indulge her. Later in the day, Ananda got fussy. She didn't want her bottle, no matter how much she opened her mouth. She didn't want to nap, no matter how much she rubbed her eyes. She spit out her pacifier. There was nothing in her diaper, for once. I wasn't sure it was normal, but suddenly Jamie wasn't calling. I didn't really want to disturb her during her first day back. Ananda's fussiness turned to crankiness and the next thing I knew I had a screaming child on my hands.

I was going to kill the baby. I didn't think I was going to murder her, but the thought did occur to me that she might die in my care.

When she had been crying for almost an hour, the phone rang. I hesitated before picking it up. I didn't want Jamie to be alarmed by the wails coming out of her daughter. I could let the machine get it and say I had been at the park later. Maybe they did have a nanny cam and that's why she was calling. The caller ID box was in the other room, miles away.

"Hello," I answered. I must admit that my hand was lightly over the child's mouth.

"Are you having a *Three Men and a Baby* moment?" Paul asked.

"She won't stop crying. Where are you?"

"I'm at the station, but I can stop by."

God bless that man. He was always saving me.

Paul got to Jamie's apartment within twenty minutes. Ananda had just cried herself to sleep. She stirred a bit when she heard the bell, but remained sleeping. I was still holding her rigidly in my arms, afraid to change position, when Paul got to the door.

"This doesn't seem so bad," he said. "Why don't you put her down."

"I can't. I don't want to move."

"Voula, you can't hold her forever."

"You're wrong about that, Torrisi. I will hold her for as long as it takes to never hear that crying again."

He clucked his tongue and took her gently out of my arms.

I had held her stiffly, but Paul folded her into his arms. He whispered soothingly and brought her into Jamie and Raj's room.

"That's it, there you go. Work with me here, kid," I heard him whispering through the baby monitor. "We've got to get Auntie Voula to love kids."

I was laughing when he came back in. "Is she down?"

"Yes."

"Do you think it's safe? I mean, you think we can just leave her in there?"

Paul shook his head. "New mothers. You have the monitor."

"Okay."

"Have you done any writing today?"

"Is that a serious question?"

He smirked at me.

"It's only for a few days. I'll get the swing of it tomorrow."

The phone rang. I lunged for it so it wouldn't wake Ananda. "Hello."

"Voula, you sound so panicked. Is everything okay?" Jamie asked, sounding a little panicked herself.

"Yes, I just wanted to get to the phone before she woke up."

"She's sleeping?" Jamie sounded really surprised, and for a minute I thought I had done something wrong.

"Yes. And Paul's here."

"Paul? Is everything okay?"

"Yes, he just came for a visit."

"You are watching her, right?"

"No, we've been having sex with wild abandon. You'll catch it on the nanny cam." She didn't say anything and I saw Paul shaking his head. "Of course I'm kidding. He just got here. No worries."

"Did she eat?"

"I followed the schedule. She only ate twice, though."

"Okay, that's fine. I'll be leaving here at six. I'd hoped to get out earlier. Will you be okay?"

"Yes, stay as late as you want. I've totally got the hang of it." I winked at Paul.

"Okay, thanks for doing this, Voula, I really appreciate it."

I believed that.

When I hung up the phone, Paul was smiling. I knew that look all too well.

"How long will she be down?"

"Paul, I'm supposed to be watching her. Your intentions don't seem responsible."

"I just wanted to help you relax."

I glanced at the clock. She should sleep for at least another forty-five minutes, but more likely an hour according to my explicit schedule. If we stayed in the living room we weren't doing anything wrong, were we? I turned the baby monitor volume way up.

"Okay, let's just be quick about it."

Ananda was asleep in my arms and I was sleeping on the couch when Jamie came home. I was startled by the door. Jamie's face lit up when she saw Ananda. I'd always thought Jamie was pretty, but she had never looked more beautiful than when she smiled at her daughter.

"So how was it?" Jamie asked, scooping the sleeping baby up.

"She was good. I'm exhausted."

I got dinner ready while Jamie played with Ananda, then bathed her and put her to bed. Raj was going to be working late. At around eight o'clock we sat down for pasta with broccoli and garlic. Jamie opened a bottle of wine. Right before she took a bite, she sighed.

"Is it going to be okay?" I asked.

"I think so," she said. "It's just strange to only see her for a couple of hours after being home with her all the time for almost four months."

I nodded. "What do you think makes you more tired? Working or being here working."

"I don't know." She shook her head. "I don't know if it's just because it's the first day, but I don't know if I can ever be as focused on work as I used to be."

"Do you think you'll quit? I bet you could stay home on Raj's salary."

"You know, I've thought a lot about it. I like working too much. I want my daughter to have a happy mom. I love that my mom stayed with us, but I think sometimes she felt unsatisfied."

I had never thought of Maura as unhappy. It was funny how you saw people the way you wanted to see them.

"I think if anything, I might try to work from home one day a week."

"Do you think you'll get much done?"

"Eventually I will. What I've learned is that eventually it gets easier. You get the swing of things. Well, you'll see."

Jamie was right about that. I did find myself getting more accustomed to Ananda. I found after a couple of days that I was more comfortable holding her and I could anticipate what she needed. When we went to the park, the other nannies thought she was my daughter. Looking at her, I realized that we looked a lot alike because of our coloring. I think I was starting to like her more.

She got fussy at times, it wasn't all gravy, but sometimes I could actually put her in the Baby Bjorn and get some work done. I sort of liked the idea of her nestled up against my chest, sleeping peacefully. I wasn't getting soft—I still wasn't sure I wanted kids, despite Paul's constant polling—but it definitely seemed more doable. Like Jamie had said, I got into the swing.

It was exhausting, though. That didn't get easier. The few nights that I went over to Paul's I fell asleep on him. Most nights Jamie and I conked out on the couch, watching reality TV (she had lied to Raj about liking anything other than his productions) or a DVD. In some ways, it was like the days we used to hang out in high school.

Raj was back to working pretty late. He would usually go in and kiss Ananda before he went to bed, but he always made sure he washed his hands thoroughly and then used disinfectant gel. The one time he got home before Jamie, he insisted she change her entire outfit before he would hand the baby over to her.

Being with Jamie so much and taking care of Ananda made me think about my own mother. We hadn't spoken since Georgia's shower. She just wouldn't return the messages I kept leaving. She was going to see me soon at Georgia's wedding whether she liked it or not, but she wouldn't call me back.

I couldn't believe my mother would choose to be alone. I knew she was being spiteful, but I also knew that she was hurting.

When Georgia's invitation came, I called again. I wanted to gauge my mother's reaction before I decided to bring Paul. I knew that when she saw me with a strange non-Greek man she would be upset. I might make the situation irreparable. I wasn't willing to give up Paul for her, but if she called me I might not bring him.

She didn't call me. It bothered me that she could shut me out. Maybe it wasn't easy for her, but obviously it wasn't that hard. There was no way she could know whether I was okay, but she didn't care. We had been through these silences before but it had been three months, which is when she usually cracked. Rationally, I knew she would call me eventually, bitterly, but it still hurt.

I guess a part of me kept hoping that I was going to have this healing moment with her. It happened on *Oprah*. People seemed like they could change, but maybe they couldn't. Maybe the only thing I could do was accept it and change my attitude accordingly.

We weren't ever going to have one of those moments at the end of a movie where the parents come to their senses or the kids come to their senses. No one was coming anywhere. This was who we were. I had to continue moving forward with my life.

I RSVP'd for two people. I would bring Paul.

The night before the closing Jamie decided to come home early. I would be staying over at Paul's the following night to be there when my movers arrived. We didn't really spend a lot of time together with Ananda. Usually when Jamie got home, I prepared dinner and let her have time alone with her daughter. That afternoon, we took her over to the grassy area along the pier on the Hudson River. There was a cool breeze and the buzz of people talking as they enjoyed a summer night.

Jamie had packed some cold white wine in the diaper bag, and she poured us two plastic cups. We spread out a blanket and we let Ananda lie on her stomach. She looked adorable in a pink and yellow sundress. Jamie took tons of pictures of us. We asked a couple next to us to get a picture of the three of us.

"So are you sure you're going to be all right at that closing tomorrow? Do you want me to meet you there? I am going to have a summer Friday."

"No, Paul asked me the same thing. He was going to take off work. If it doesn't take, I don't know what I'm going to do. Maybe it's a sign I should walk away."

"Do you think so?"

"No. I'm tired of believing in signs. I do think things happen for a reason, but I think that maybe you can have more control over your own life than you actually think."

Jamie smiled. "You know, I took a pregnancy test this morning."

"What? Already?" More trying?

"Believe me, it wasn't intentional. And I'm not pregnant. Thank goodness. I guess we weren't being careful and it was nice to sort of get caught up in the moment."

"So I guess you're back in the saddle again, huh?"

"Well, we were that night." She glanced at Ananda. "It got me thinking—I definitely want another one. It seems to me that no matter how tough things can be, they get better, you just have to be patient."

"You're right," I said. "I can't believe you're ready to get knocked up again."

"Not just yet," Jamie said. "But soon."

Ananda was being so good. It was past her bedtime, but she

was still in a cheerful mood. It was as if she wanted her mom to have a lovely night. We propped her against the diaper bag and she giggled. Jamie gave her the last bottle for the evening, and then we watched the sun sink in the sky. I held on to one of Ananda's soft fat kicking legs and made a promise to myself to be there to help Ananda grow up the way her mom had helped me.

At the closing, the seller's attorney was on time and kissing my ass. Rob made it clear that she and her clients would be paying the adjournment fee and the cost to extend my mortgage rate. She tried to protest, but he quickly explained that it was not up for discussion. Maureen gave me an impressive nod as if to say that our side had scored. I wasn't confident about that much at that moment.

It was the bank that we sat waiting for in the conference room of the co-op attorney's office. Maureen tried to ease my tension by showing me pictures of the triplets on their first trip to her lake house. I appreciated her efforts, but felt my body tense. I didn't want to waste more time.

Finally the bank representative arrived with apologies. His previous closing had run over by an hour because of the sellers' lateness. I was amazed at the domino effect of all of it. No matter how self-sufficient you tried to be, the actions of others affected you.

Once again, Rob wrote out a bunch of figures on a yellow legal pad. I tried to follow along to get a true sense of how much more money I would be spending than I had anticipated. In the end, it made no sense and I wrote out whatever checks I was told to.

Then I began the process of signing form upon form. Again. My hand hurt when I looked up for another form and there was none. The seller's attorney was also cleaned out. I looked at Rob.

"That's it," he said, smiling.

"You own an apartment," Maureen said, handing me the key. "Now you can celebrate."

★ ★ ★

I called Paul as soon as I got out of the subway. "I'm one block away from my new home."

"Congratulations, you're a homeowner."

"I know, I'm going there now. I think I'm gonna lick the floor. I can't believe it's true. I've finally won the real estate game."

He laughed. "So, you are cool doing this on your own."

"I am fantastic." I was at the gate. "I'm here."

"Take it easy, Ms. Mogul."

"I'll see you tonight."

I walked through the courtyard, where someone had set up a picnic table and a grill. I got my keys out. I unlocked the hall door and then took a deep breath before opening mine.

Okay, it was still tiny. It had somehow grown in my memory. I had paid way too much, but it was mine. All mine. And it was sunny and cheery. This is where I would live. I couldn't get over it. I walked to the center of the room and twirled in the sunlight. It was unreal.

I couldn't wait to have my boxes unpacked and start my life here. It was all going to be okay. I felt for the first time in my life something I couldn't identify. I was a writer who just didn't know the words. It was beyond hope. It surpassed happiness.

In the center of a small room in a carriage house in Chelsea, I felt something foreign and wonderful.

For the first time ever, I felt joy.

Next month get an inside look at the
world of cool-hunting in

Mim Warner's
Lost Her Cool

MIM WARNER'S LOST HER COOL is the story
of one fashion know-all who suddenly loses
her ability to predict the next hot trends.
The first sign…Mim has just gone on public
television and announced that T-shirts with
"Slut" emblazoned across the chest are the
next trend in the tween girl's market.

**Available wherever
trade paperbacks
are sold.**

RED
DRESS
INK
™

Don't miss the book that *People* magazine
called "Spring's Best Chick Lit 2004."

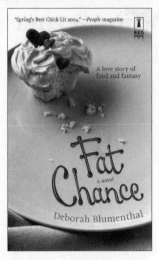

Fat Chance

Deborah Blumenthal

Plus-size Maggie O'Leary is America's Anti-Diet Sweetheart.
Her informed column about the pitfalls of dieting is the
one sane voice crying out against the dietocracy. She is
perfectly happy with who she is and the life she leads.
That is, until she gets the chance to spend quality time
with Hollywood's hottest star and she vows to be the
skinniest fat advocate ever. But is it possible for Maggie to
have her cake and eat it, too?

**Available wherever
trade paperbacks
are sold.**

On sale in March—a novel about a
woman who's knocked up, but not out!

A New Lu

by Laura Castoro

Lu Nichols has led a pretty normal life. Marriage. Career.
Two kids. But now she's turning fifty, and life for Lu is
about to change. Lu's much younger boss wants to do
an extreme makeover feature starring Lu, the magazine's
lifestyle columnist. And just as the ink dries on the divorce
papers Lu discovers that she is pregnant by her just-recent
ex-husband. Looks as if it is time for a new Lu...
and she is more than ready.

**Available wherever
trade paperbacks
are sold.**

RED DRESS INK

Another fabulous read by Ariella Papa

On the Verge

Twenty-three-year-old Jersey girl Eve Vitali is
on the verge of something…whether it be a
relationship, the fabulous life that she reads about
in the Styles section of the *New York Times,* or
a nervous breakdown. Despite her Jackie O suit,
Eve works as an unappreciated assistant for—of all
things—a *bicycle* magazine. Everyone keeps telling
her that she's got her foot in the door, but the rest of
her is surfing the Net and schlepping around with
Tabitha, an Amazonian sex goddess. Between glam
parties, obligatory visits home and myriad men,
Eve is realizing that it takes a lot of work to get
beyond the verge and on to the next big thing….

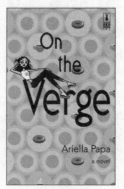

Up and Out

Ariella Papa

Life on the up and up was great for Rebecca Cole, creator of the new cartoon sensation Esme—fancy nights out and a trendy new wardrobe. But thanks to a corporate takeover, Rebecca soon finds herself on the up and out. Can this food snob find a way to afford her rent and her penchant for fine dining?